Quilt
the Town
Christmas

Quilt
THE TOWN
CHRISTMAS

Ann Hazelwood

C&T PUBLISHING

Editor: Elaine Brelsford
Proofreader: Chrystal Abhalter
Book and Cover Designer: Chris Gilbert

Published by C&T Publishing, Inc., P.O. Box 1456, Lafayette, CA 94549

FEATHERED STAR

INTRODUCTION

By now, everyone knows how much I love Christmas. Going back to my childhood, it's where I capture my fondest memories. I feel quilts can represent the holiday like no other medium.

I hope *Quilt the Town Christmas* will engage your imagination and appreciation for this festive occasion and provide you a very Merry Christmas!

Ann Hazelwood

CHAPTER 1

We were soaked! It was the kind of soaking that makes every fiber of clothing cling to your body. Had anyone been looking, Ellie and I could have been winners in a wet T-shirt contest! We shivered, shoulder to shoulder, underneath the pavilion at the Saxon Village Fall Festival. The sudden downpour caught us totally off guard while we were sampling some of the home-canned pickles, neatly lined up in a row, ready for purchase. We screamed and giggled as we made a running dash for cover at the other end of the village.

It was my first visit to the festival, but Ellie had come religiously every year and bragged about its authenticity when it came to food and crafts. We had only been there an hour, enjoying the best-of-the-best homemade German food in the area. Ellie knew who made the tastiest cheese, platz-kuchen, sausage, bread, pickles, and coffee cake. Anna's bread, fresh out of the outdoor oven, was my favorite of the day. I wanted to take as much as I could home with me. However, as we kept eating, I knew that wouldn't happen!

The continuous downpour had folks scrambling for their cars which were parked in nearby fields. Booths of crafts and food were quickly shutting down while vendors protected what they could from the drenching rain.

"We can't stay here looking like this!" Ellie exclaimed, shivering. "We're already soaked, so what are we waiting for? Just look at me!"

I erupted into laughter. We were truly a sight to behold. "I've never seen you without makeup," I teased. "Okay, I'm sorry. Let's make a run for it. We can have a nice dry and warm visit at my place with a glass of wine."

"Not until I go home and get into some dry clothes," she said, attempting to wipe the blowing rain from her face. "I'll drop you off."

"Good plan," I nodded. "Get out your car keys and you go first!"

She looked at me like I was crazy. With that, she gave me a shove into the pouring rain and off we went, running like two schoolgirls escaping trouble. What a sight we must have been! We easily managed to get water everywhere in Ellie's SUV, but now our goal was to get me to my home at 6229 Main Street, in the heart of Borna, Missouri. That accomplished, Ellie sped to her home next door to dry off and change clothes.

Ellie Meers was the first person to greet me when I first traveled to Borna to sell my house and acreage. I had no place to stay, so she graciously offered her small, adorable house. When I eventually made the decision to live permanently in Borna, we became best friends. Ellie owned the Red Creek Winery near Borna. She was single, independent, and kind, causing me to admire her immediately.

When I met Ellie, I had recently lost my husband, Clay, in a tragic car accident. Adding insult to injury, the crash was due to his excessive drinking. It left me devastated, as it also did my grown son, Jack, who lives in Manhattan. In his will, Clay left me a house and property in Borna. Having spent my entire life in South Haven, Michigan, I had never been to Borna until I came to list the home for sale. Quickly, however, the beauty of East Perry County drew me in, as well as the large, intriguing house. I came to realize I had little reason to stay in South Haven, so I put my Michigan house up for sale to rid myself of bad memories and moved to a house that was begging for my attention. Restoring the house was challenging, to say the least. Some folks were eager to see me fail, but they misjudged me. I fell in love with Borna and soon became part of that wonderful community. I am here to stay.

CHAPTER 2

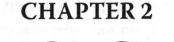

As the hot water from the shower slowly warmed me, I chuckled once again about running in the rain with Ellie. It brought back a feeling of childhood. I had always loved to play in the rain, much to my mother's disapproval.

As I prepared a fire a few minutes later, Ellie walked in the back door wearing a large raincoat. Shrugging it off, she placed it by the door on the sunporch. "What am I doing here, for heaven's sake?" she joked.

I laughed, wondering the same thing, considering the weather conditions.

Ellie said, "I called Trout and the winery is dead. I told him to close early if he wanted."

"Well, the whole day doesn't have to be ruined," I said, going into the kitchen. "Will your pleasure be coffee, tea, or your favorite wine?"

"You have to ask?" Ellie peered at me smiling, knowing full well I already knew the answer.

"If you're hungry, I have leftover lasagna," I offered as I poured.

"Oh, no, not after that big brat I had!" Ellie said, lazily patting her stomach.

"I don't know how people can eat meat like that," I said, making a sour face. "It doesn't even look good. I do enjoy a ballpark hot dog once in a while, though. I filled up too much on Anna's bread. Darn, I wish I could have brought some home."

Anna, the Saxon Village director, lived on the Saxon Village grounds with her family and was known for her good breads and pastries. She was a member of our Friendship Circle group, so we were privy to many of her goodies at those gatherings.

"Did you get Ruth Ann's fancy invitation to her open house?" asked Ellie as she refreshed her glass of wine.

"Very nice, wasn't it?" I nodded. "I hope everyone responds and gets to see it. She has spent a fortune restoring that monstrous place and we need a banquet center with meeting rooms here in town. She was pleased to already have a booking for the East Perry Lumber's Christmas party."

"Thanks to Ellen," Ellie mentioned. "It doesn't hurt to have Ellen in our Friendship Circle to help promote the things we come up with."

I nodded and chuckled. "That party alone will give her amazing exposure. She said she has some bookings for the meeting room. She thinks that will be her bread and butter until dates fill up with weddings and other events."

"Say, Kate, I have been pretty good about not asking about Clark, but have you heard from him or do you have any idea what is going on with him?" Ellie's gaze fell on me, waiting for a response.

I didn't want to pursue this particular turn in the conversation. "I would have told you if I had heard from him," I said, shaking my head. "He has a lot going on and travels quite a bit, as you know. He is so private. I found that out pretty quickly when he was doing that cabinetry work here at the house."

"I thought his communication would have gotten better after you approached him about it. For all we know, he may have left Borna for good."

"I doubt that," I responded. "He's quite fond of everyone in this community. We all know how this town talks, and he just chooses not to disclose too much about his personal life."

"Well, I'm glad he returned his tree carving to you and that all that mess got straightened out." Ellie stood to get her coat.

Clark had given me a carving of a tree behind my house, a piece he had personally handcrafted. A guest of mine had stolen it awhile back and posted it for sale on eBay. Clark was made aware of it and purchased it back. Despite his frustration with me, he decided it should stay with me in this house, for which I was grateful.

"You don't have to go so soon, Ellie."

"Oh, I need to take advantage of some time at home before I go back to work tomorrow." Ellie slipped an arm into her raincoat. "When is your next guest arriving?"

I paused to think. "Not anytime real soon, which is great." A suppressed giggle escaped from me.

"You are something, Kate," Ellie stated firmly. "I think you like the idea of having a guest house but not the duties it entails."

I nodded, grinning, knowing she may be right as I walked my friend to the door and closed it behind her. I was glad to see Ellie leave before she pressed me more about Clark. Clark had come to see me before he left town to go to St. Louis, Missouri, to be treated for prostate cancer. He was concerned because it was a fast growing cancer and his father had died from the same diagnosis years ago. Clark and I were very close friends, but the relationship had really never developed in a romantic way. It was obvious that we were attracted to one other, but we both wanted our lives to stay the same. He lived happily in a remote, artistic cabin near Indian Creek, and I was not anxious to feel tied to another man after a confining and disappointing marriage. I respected Clark's wishes that I not share his health information with others and was pleased that he felt comfortable enough to share his personal concerns with me. I had to believe he would contact me soon as he had promised and that the treatments would go well.

CHAPTER 3

My cell phone was ringing and I was pleased to see it was Maggie, my best friend from South Haven. "Hey girlfriend, what's up?"

"Well, not much, but I wondered if you knew Jack was in town this weekend."

Since Jack was now dating Maggie and Mark's daughter, Jill, Maggie would be aware of Jack's presence in South Haven. "No, but I'm glad to hear he's making some use of our condo."

"Well, he certainly is making use of it! Jill has spent the last two nights there, and Mark is none too happy about it."

I wanted to chuckle, but thought better of it. "They are both adults now and this was our dream, remember?" I teased her, recalling how we had often talked about the possibility of our children dating one another.

"I know, I know," Maggie conceded. "By the way, Max said to tell you hello."

"That's nice," I said, smiling to myself. "Please tell him the same. I'm sorry your little fix-up date didn't work out as planned. Even though he was much older than me, he certainly was energetic and handsome."

"So, have you heard from John, your young neighbor friend at the condo?"

I knew she was really curious about where my friendship with John was heading. "Not recently, but I think he still plans to visit here around Thanksgiving," I reported. I began to smile just thinking about John.

"Now, what do you suppose his intentions are, Kate?" Maggie asked, making no effort to hide her sarcasm.

"His intention in coming to my guest house in Borna is to write a story about East Perry County, which is fabulous! He's a travel writer, for heaven's sake, and I find him fascinating."

"That's what worries me," Maggie moaned. "You'd better watch out, my friend. It sounds like he's one that could take advantage of you."

Although I was entertained at the thought, I wanted to bring the conversation about John to a quick end. "I'm not worried and I don't want to hear any more talk like that from you. You know me well enough, Maggie."

There was a pause. "So, when are you coming home again?" asked Maggie, changing the subject.

"I am home, Maggie," I reminded her softly. "I probably won't visit South Haven until early spring. I missed Christmas in Borna last year and don't want to do that again. I think Aunt Mandy is going to visit at Thanksgiving or Christmas. I'm hoping Jack will keep his promise to come for Christmas as well. I'd be thrilled if he brought Jill. What would you think of that?" I knew I was asking for trouble.

"I don't want to hear that nonsense," she responded curtly.

"Well then, I would suggest you and Mark come as well," I said, invoking a humorous tone. "Okay, let me ask you about Carla. Have you seen her lately?"

"Yes, I saw her at the bakery a week or so ago," Maggie reported. "She said she had picked up a small cleaning job at a dentist's office. Does she still do things for you at the condo?"

"I sure hope so. I send her a check every month to clean the place and sort through any mail." Carla was our cleaning lady and my close friend when I was married to Clay. "With Jack visiting, I'm glad I have her stopping by there once in a while. I really miss her. I will try to call her soon and ask about Rocky." Rocky had been Clay's dog, and Carla had reluctantly taken ownership of Rocky when I moved to Borna.

I tried cheering Maggie up before I said good-bye. I think she was missing me, and even though she was pleased to see me happy, things would never be the same with me living here. Maggie and I had been joined at the hip since grade school. At this point in my life, she wanted me to have a man in my life, but one that met with her approval.

After our conversation, I realized that Maggie asking about John, the downstairs neighbor at my condo, made me think about him and what he might be up to. John had purchased his condo around the same time that I had purchased mine. He is much younger than me, but seems to be fascinated about my life. He played wonderful soft jazz most evenings, which wafted up to my floor when the deck doors were open. He fixed me a fabulous dinner one night. Another time, he helped me with a heavy box that needed to be brought from my car. Okay, it's also true that I couldn't forget the innocent kiss that occurred when he left that night. I embraced it for the innocence it was, which made me think I was making progress with my new life.

CHAPTER 4

T he next morning, I was greeted by bright sunshine and the promise of a beautiful day. I set out to bake, which was my favorite pastime. In South Haven, I was known for my blueberry muffins and I had won awards for them at the National Blueberry Festival there, one of the longest running blueberry festivals in the United States. My guests loved these muffins, and I featured them on my website for the guest house. There I promised that all my guests would go home with my special recipe.

As I was entering the kitchen, Cotton, my handyman and yard guy, was walking up the back steps. He loved stopping by in the morning to see what was baking at Josephine's Guest House. He knew I would often send home leftovers from breakfast with him.

"Good morning," I said, opening the door.

"A good morning to you as well, Miss Kate." He greeted me with his usual simile. "I had planned to mow today, but it looks like the ground is too wet from that terrible downpour we had yesterday. What a shame for the festival to be rained out like that. Luckily, Susie, Amy Sue, and I went in the morning before the rain began."

"Yes, Ellie and I got soaked through and through! Come on in and have a cup of coffee. I just started to bake some muffins if you want to stick around."

He happily came on in as usual.

"So, how is little Amy Sue?"

He laughed before answering. "You should have seen her dance to the music yesterday. Everyone around us enjoyed it. I don't know where she gets her desire to entertain. Anna gave her one of her home baked cookies, so Amy Sue had a great time. Oh, Susie said to ask if you need her to clean for you tomorrow."

"Yes, I think I do," I answered, thinking about the various chores she did for me. I was truly grateful to be able to find Cotton and Susie when I first moved here. They helped me with so many things as I restored my place on Main Street.

"Looks like you're getting company, Miss Kate," Cotton said, looking out the window. "I'll be on my way and I'll bring Susie back tomorrow."

I followed Cotton out to his truck and greeted a woman getting out of a green Volkswagen.

"Good morning. Can I help you?"

"I was wondering if you have a room available for tonight," she asked, using her hand to shield the sun from her eyes.

"Why, I suppose I do. Come on in and we'll get you registered. Would you like to see the place first?"

"I'm sure it's fine," she said, following me into the house.

"Would you like a cup of coffee while we get started?"

"Oh, that would be great, thank you." She watched as I poured coffee into a mug.

"My name is Kate Meyr," I said, reaching for her hand. "I'm the owner."

"Hi, I'm Susan," she said quickly. Something about this exchange gave me the feeling Susan was going to be an odd acquaintance.

"Come on into my office, Susan," I said, leading the way.

"Are you here for just one night?"

"Yes, I think so. My, your house is really beautiful!" Her eyes seemed to want to take everything in at once.

"Thank you," I answered proudly. "It's a labor of love, I'm afraid. How did you hear about the guest house?"

She looked bewildered and then answered. "I think it must have been your website." She had nearly mumbled the response. "I want your cheapest room and I'd like to pay with cash, if that works for you."

Now I knew her visit would be unusual. "That's just fine," I nodded. "I have a room on the first floor that I have named The Study. I think you'll like it."

"I'm sure it'll be fine," she said, getting up from her chair as if she suddenly found herself in a big hurry.

"We have a guest book over there that I'd like you to sign." I pointed it out as we went into the entry hall. "This quilt on the wall is where guests can sign their name as well. It's known as Josephine's Guest House Quilt. This house was named after the wife of Dr. Paulson, the man who built this house."

She nodded, but I don't think she cared.

"I hope you can sign it before you leave."

She smiled and nodded once again.

"Where are you from, Susan?" I asked as we walked toward her room.

"Up north a ways," she replied flatly.

I knew not to ask any more questions. I had to learn that some folks just wanted to be left alone.

"I'll be baking some muffins shortly," I informed her. "You are welcome to have some when they're done."

"How kind. Thank you," she said as she went into the room and pulled the door closed.

It was very odd for someone not to respond in one way or another when shown to their room. I had a lot to learn about dealing with the public in this business!

I spent the rest of the morning baking muffins and then made a custard pie for later in the day. I answered emails in between. One of them was from John, my condo neighbor. It read: *Good morning! I had a short chat with your son and his girlfriend yesterday. What a cute couple. Wish you could have been here as well. How was the festival? John.*

It made me smile. He was always so polite and easy to talk to. Clark could be like that at times, but he had to be in the right mood. Men!

CHAPTER 5

The house was filling up with wonderful breakfast aromas and it didn't take long for Susan to appear in the kitchen. She looked well rested and had a smile on her face.

"You look as if you had a good rest. The coffee is ready. Do you need help with your luggage or anything?"

She looked at me strangely. "Oh no, I just have a few things with me," she said, taking her coffee to the sunporch.

Admittedly, I never knew how much conversation to encourage with guests.

After Susan finished eating a muffin, she walked out to her car and got inside to move it. She pulled to the side of the garage, which was strange. I sometimes parked there when I had to make room for more cars. She then returned, carrying only a plastic bag.

"Susan, I don't know if you'll be going out to dinner tonight, but I'm happy to share some leftover lasagna with you. There isn't much nearby in terms of places to eat, unless you go next door to Marv's."

"Why, that's very generous of you and I will accept since I don't plan to go out," she said, walking toward her room. "I'll be happy to pay you. I thought I'd just stay in and read tonight."

"Great. The meal's on me and I'd enjoy your company," I responded freely. What had I just done? Do guest house owners typically do this?

Throughout the day, I could hear Susan's cell phone ringing and she did not respond. *She really did want to be left alone,* I thought. I checked the quilt and the guest book, and she had not yet signed either of them. Her simple registration did not show a last name or where she was from. This, too, was quite odd. Should I be concerned?

I was tempted to call Ellie for advice. Was it risky to have someone stay here without more information? She seemed so nice and innocent. Surely she couldn't be a criminal on the run! I supposed I was just being too nosey. I determined to just wait until dinner to learn more about her. She had paid me in cash, so why should I care how much she tells me about herself?

The crisp fall air was delightful today, so I went outdoors to cut mint from my kitchen garden and pick some red and yellow mums for the table. Some of them were here many years before me and I liked to think they were planted by Josephine. Before I went in, I looked to see Susan's license plates, which surprisingly said Missouri on them. I almost felt disappointed. Why was she staying here? I went in the house and started arranging the vivid colored mums.

"Are you going to all that trouble for me?" Susan asked, taking me by surprise.

"Oh, Susan, you scared me!" I gasped. "It's no trouble. I like having fresh flowers around. Would you like a glass of wine before I start preparing our dinner?"

She smiled and nodded. "That sounds good," she said with a big smile.

"I have wine glasses on the table, if you'd like to fill them." When she reached to take the wine bottle, it was then that I saw the horrible bruises covering her arms. I tried to pretend I didn't see them. As she walked toward the table, she limped a bit and she was holding her back. She was definitely in pain.

Making conversation the rest of the evening wasn't going to be easy. I said one of my quick, personal prayers to God, asking for some help.

CHAPTER 6

"Well, Susan, I think I have everything ready," I announced as she flipped through a magazine on the sunporch. "I didn't make a salad, but I have some delicious bread that I just pulled out of the oven, so I hope that's okay."

"This is plenty," she said, sizing up the food I had placed on the dinner table. I could hear her cell phone ringing from her room.

"Is that your cell phone?" I asked, sitting down.

"I'll call them later," she said with disinterest.

"Well then, shall we make a toast?"

Susan smiled and nodded.

Not knowing quite what to say, I offered, "Welcome to Borna!" We tipped our glasses. "I hope you like red wine. I neglected to ask," I said, taking a sip.

"It's perfect. Thank you," she said, taking a rather large swallow.

"Susan, I don't want to pry, but is your back hurting?"

She stiffened. "Oh, it's nothing. It does act up once in a while."

I nodded. "The wine will help." I paused and then queried, "Do you have children, Susan?"

She put her fork down like I had asked about something terrible that she didn't know how to answer. Slowly, she nodded but didn't speak.

"Are you okay?" As my glance fell to her bruised arms, she pulled them away from the table and crossed them so they would be sheltered by the tablecloth. I watched her take a slow, deep breath.

"I would like to ask a favor," she responded quietly. "Please don't tell anyone I'm here." She swallowed and continued, "If I can ask, who was the man that was here when I arrived?"

I had to think. Then I remembered. "That was just Cotton. He mows my lawn and his wife cleans my house."

She seemed to relax.

"No one knows you're here."

"If anyone calls here looking for me," she blinked and looked away, "I hope you'll say that I'm not here."

"Susan, are you in trouble?" I felt I had to ask. "Have you done something wrong?"

She shook her head, her sadness apparent.

"You see, I just had to get away," she said, her voice trembling. "If you're uncomfortable with that, I can leave. I don't want to cause trouble."

"Get away? Tell me a little more about that." I could see her hands beginning to shake.

Moments passed. "My husband," she said in a whisper.

Now things were starting to add up. "Did he hurt you?" I asked, concerned. "Is that why you are bruised and walking with a limp?"

She nodded as tears streamed down her face. "He'd kill me if he found me," she said with certainty. Her voice escalated. "He has our little boy. I hated to leave but I had to. I couldn't take it anymore. I can only hope he'll take him to his mother's house, because he'll never want to take care of him! He's not a good father. I need to get as far away as I can."

As I took in her story, I began to feel sick inside. For her to leave her child, this had to be bad. "Have you called the police?"

She nodded as a new flood of tears made its way down her cheeks. "I did and took another beating something terrible," she confessed. "That cannot happen again."

"Why does he feel justified doing this to you?" I asked angrily.

"He's hated me since I got pregnant with Casey, our son," she explained, sniffing. "I told him I was going to the grocery store, but I knew once I got in the car I was never going to go back. I just kept driving! I don't think he could ever imagine me leaving Casey."

"There are people who can help you, Susan," I advised. "It doesn't have to be like this. He should go to jail for what he's doing to you. In South Haven, we had a shelter for women and children. Perhaps there is something like that in a bigger town near here. You can't keep running, plus you need your son and he needs you!"

Susan broke into sobs.

Why couldn't this have waited until after dinner?

"I won't go back, I won't go back!" she repeated between sobs. "You don't understand!"

"Okay, maybe I don't, but I want to help you," I reassured her. "No one will know you're here. Take a sip of wine. What are your plans?"

"I'll leave right after breakfast," she said, taking a deep breath. "You've already given me food and have been very kind. All I ask is that you keep my visit a secret. I cannot underestimate his determination to find me. He is plain mean, Miss Meyr. He isn't about to let me outsmart him."

"I can't keep people from coming around here, Susan, but I will do my best to help you in any way I can. You have no idea how angry this makes me!"

CHAPTER 7

I calmed Susan down long enough to have a bite to eat with her. I picked at my food, but it was obvious that Susan was hungry and enjoyed this good meal. "You are welcome to stay here as long as you like. I have no guests booked for a while."

"No, no, you have a business to run and I can't afford to stay at such nice places like this for very long," she explained as she sipped more wine. "Staying in one spot will only make it easier for him to find me."

"Well, I'm certainly going to refund your money," I stated. "You will need that for other things. If you're so determined to go, I'll send some food with you."

"I can't let you do that. I don't know what I would have done if I hadn't seen your sign. Something made me pull in the driveway and get out of the car."

"Well, many years ago, this was a doctor's house and a medical practice," I explained. "People pulled in here for help many times, and I want to offer help as well."

She smiled.

"Where are you actually from?"

She hesitated. I knew she didn't want to tell me. I went to get the custard pie from the kitchen. I returned, cut two slices, and set one in front of her.

"I'd rather not say," she said, eyeing the beautiful pie placed in front of her.

"Do you need some medication for your pain?" I offered. "How did you hurt your back?"

Her face tensed. "I fell down our stairs when he hit me. I thought I broke every bone in my body. It hurt so badly. I would appreciate some aspirin if you have it."

"Of course." I rose, got some aspirin from the cabinet, and placed the bottle near her. "Keep it, but don't take any more than the recommended dose because of the wine."

We ate our pie and did not continue to talk about her situation. Before long, it was time to turn in for the evening. As I went upstairs to bed, I realized that my husband had been nothing compared to what Susan was experiencing. I hoped God would give her guidance that would lead to a happy ending.

As I got undressed, I thought about how I was keeping two secrets. This was not my strong suit. I stayed awake thinking about what she may be up against in her travels. Where would she end up? How she must miss her sweet son! I finally turned on the light and made a list of things to send with her. More clothing, a quilt, a pillow. The bedding would be a good idea in case she had to sleep in her car for a night or two. I wasn't going to judge whether she was doing the right thing. I'm sure Kate Meyr would have given her husband a good fight before running away!

I jumped when a text caused my phone to buzz. I couldn't believe it was from Clark, of all people. It read:

> Late night here. Just finished working on a piece. Sorry I haven't contacted you sooner. This treatment wipes me out sometimes. Hope you're behaving yourself! C.

That's it? Just a C? I quickly responded,

Finally! When are you coming home?

I watched and waited for an answer and finally gave up. It was just like Clark to leave me hanging. I comforted myself by believing he must be okay if he actually felt like doing some work. Would he ever be honest with me about his health again? Would these treatments even help him? I decided that after Susan left tomorrow, I would drive out to his cabin and check on things. Then, I could at least leave another reply telling him how things were back at his cabin.

I continued to find myself wide awake. I knew I had to get Susan out of the house tomorrow morning early and before Cotton and Susie arrived. I hated to have to explain anything to them as they saw me packing things in her car. I did not want to put Susan in an awkward position.

Now, back to fluffing my pillow!

CHAPTER 8

I was dead tired when the noise of the trash truck awakened me. I sat up quickly as I realized I had much to do this morning. I peeked out my bathroom window to make sure Susan's car was still parked behind the house. I was pleased to see it was, so I put on my bathrobe to greet the automatically-brewed coffee waiting for me in the kitchen.

Susan's bedroom door was closed, so I quietly started a spinach and ham quiche for breakfast. I also pulled out a small coffee cake made by Mrs. Grebing. That done, I started filling a grocery bag with food and drink items that Susan may need as she traveled. I worked quickly. I wanted her to be ready to leave before Cotton and Susie arrived.

While I waited for the quiche to bake, I ran upstairs to find a quilt for her. I had more quilts than I needed and my hall closet was filled with them. I chose one I had purchased with Maggie one day at the local flea market in South Haven. It was scrappy with a heavy influence of cheddar gold which I thought at the time would be an interesting addition to my collection. I had never used it and it was in pretty good condition. I put it in a plastic bag and then went to one of the guest room closets to find a pillow.

When I arrived downstairs, there was Susan, dressed and ready to go.

"Good morning! Did you get some sleep?" I asked cheerfully.

"I have never slept better," she admitted. "I guess for some time now I really haven't felt safe enough to fall into a deep sleep."

"That's all good, Susan, but you're not leaving until you've had breakfast," I insisted. "I also put some food together, along with a quilt, in case you need it."

"Really? That is so nice of you. You know I may not be able to repay you."

I nodded and smiled.

Susan ate as if it were her last meal. It made me happy to see her enjoy every bite. "I hope you'll keep in touch, Susan. I'm going to worry about you. At some point, this is going to come to a head. You should try to be back with your son as soon as you feel safe."

"I can't promise anything, Kate," she said sadly. "I have to be so careful. I really appreciate all you have done. It's been such a blessing to find you. This little town is so charming. I can see why you decided to stay here."

"Well, if you need a welcoming place yourself one day, you can always move here," I suggested.

She just smiled without saying anything.

With a coffee to go and a big hug, I sent Susan on her way. As I waved good-bye, I said another prayer and asked God to keep her safe. I walked back into the house with a heavy heart. As I cleaned up the breakfast dishes, Susie and Cotton came in the door.

"Good morning, you two," I greeted them. "I thought you'd be bringing Amy Sue this morning."

"She spent the night at my mom's last night," Susie explained as she eyed the leftover breakfast food.

"I saved some breakfast in case the two of you were hungry," I said, pouring them coffee.

"Miss Kate, you truly spoil us," Susie said, accepting her coffee. "Did your guests leave already?"

"Yes, I just had one, but she had to leave early," I explained.

"Oh, was it that woman that arrived when I was here yesterday?" asked Cotton, sipping his coffee.

"Uh, no," I said, knowing it was a lie. I had to cover for Susan in any way I could.

They both had breakfast before starting their chores. I gave Susie a list and told her I would be leaving as soon as I got dressed. Still having thoughts of Susan, I got in my car and headed to Clark's cabin to check on things. I thought that a text from me saying I checked on his place would be comforting to him. It was a beautiful day to head that direction with color already showing in some of the trees.

When I turned into his gravel driveway, so many memories popped into my head. The last time I was here, it was raining cats and dogs. I was delivering blueberry scones to make peace when he was ignoring me. Clark had pulled up in his SUV to find me on his porch. The visit didn't go well, but it did open the door for better communication.

My footsteps crunched in the sticks and leaves as I walked around the back of the cabin which aligned itself along Indian Creek. This was where Clark had once shown me a family of deer that appeared each night as Clark fed them. I'm sure they miss him.

Nothing seemed to be out of place as I admired the secluded spot. His curtains were pulled so I couldn't see inside the cabin. It was truly the perfect spot for an artist to live and work. As I got in my car, I had a smile on my face and I realized I missed my good friend. I could only hope he would be well and back home soon.

CHAPTER 9

O n the way home, I thought I needed a pick-me-up, so I stopped at Imy's Antique Shop. Two cars were parked out front. I was pleased to see she had some business. It was a very handy spot, being just a quarter mile down the road from my house.

I briefly waved to Imy as I entered. She was helping a lady who was interested in a feather tree that Imy had for sale. I had never seen it in here before today.

"Oh, it can't possibly be that much!" the lady complained. "It's in terrible condition!"

"Well, it's over two hundred years old," Imy explained. "This was the first rendition of an artificial Christmas tree and they came from Germany. It's made from goose feathers. That's why they call it a feather tree."

"Goose feathers!" the lady repeated, clearly astonished. "That's hard to believe!"

"Yes, they dyed the goose feathers green before they wrapped them around the wires." Imy demonstrated. "It makes it look like pine."

"Well, if that don't beat all!" the lady said, shaking her head. "I think I'll just take the pitcher and bowl."

"Very well," Imy responded with her usual smile. Imy carefully wrapped the pitcher and bowl. As she did, the other customer in the shop left empty-handed. "Have a good day!" Imy said as the lady departed with her package.

I smiled at both of them. At least Imy made one sale. "Goodness, Imy, when did you get this in?" I moved closer to the tree. "I've never seen a feather tree this tall."

"It's over four feet. Despite how brittle these wire branches are, it's really in pretty good condition."

"My friend Maggie in South Haven has a smaller white one," I shared. "I remember when she bought it at our local antique mall and it was very expensive."

"Yes, they can be very expensive," Imy added. "I almost decided to keep this, but I have to start clearing out some of the Christmas items from my back shed. I have a weakness for antique Christmas things, I'm afraid. So much of it reminds me of my childhood. Folks buy Christmas items early, so I thought I'd bring some of them into the shop."

"I can believe that," I said, looking at the tree more closely. "So, that little building behind you has more of your stuff?"

She laughed and nodded. "I'm afraid so," she blushed. "Look at this little village that was probably sold in the 1920s. People would put cotton under their trees so it would look like snow and then place these little buildings here and there. There is even a little fence that goes with this. They don't make detailing like this anymore. Now, people expect everything to light up and come already assembled."

"Oh, Imy, this is adorable," I said, leaning in. "Look at this tiny church with the pews inside. "You should place all of this under your feather tree!"

"I plan to, but I just haven't had a chance," she said, shrugging her shoulders. "So, what can I do for you today?"

"Oh, I just came to look," I said as I held up a linen tablecloth. "It's hard to pass you by. I never want to miss anything. You'll be bringing out more Christmas things?

This is my first Christmas in Borna, so I'm getting pretty excited."

She smiled at my excitement. "I will be," she said as she continued to arrange her display. "Are you looking for anything in particular? Are you going to be here for Thanksgiving?"

"No and yes," I answered, laughing. "I have guests registered, so I'd better not go anywhere. Michigan is frightfully cold along the lake, so I'll be here for both holidays."

"Well, that's good news," Imy expressed as she moved the tree to another spot.

"I need to get home, Imy. I can't believe I am leaving empty-handed for the first time."

Imy laughed. "I'll let you know when I put out more Christmas things. Christmas is just around the corner!"

I got in my car and felt envious of Imy and her little shop. She was so knowledgeable and honest. I liked that she knew she had to display new things for regular customers like me!

CHAPTER 10

When I got home, I reminded Cotton that I wanted the barn cleaned out before winter. Seeing the fall colored leaves reminded me that winter would soon be here.

Susie was still cleaning, so I went upstairs to pull out my unfinished Lighthouse blocks. If I wanted to have this quilt completed for Jack before Christmas, I needed to stay focused. The pattern I had purchased from Cornelia's Quilt Shop had six lighthouse designs that needed to be appliquéd. I hated to appliqué, but the challenge was good for me. Ruth Ann had agreed to quilt it for me when I had the top ready. Like any handwork, once I got started, the process was calming for me. My mind was sending positive thoughts to Susan on her journey.

"Cotton and I are leaving now," Susie called from downstairs.

I jumped out of my seat to reply from the hallway. "Give Amy Sue a kiss from me!"

"Will do, and thank you for breakfast!" Susie yelled back.

Returning to my handwork, my thoughts roamed to my plans for the evening. It was such a beautiful day and I knew these days were numbered. Joining Ellie at the winery for dinner might be a good idea. I then thought about calling Ruth Ann to join me, so I picked up the phone before I changed my mind. She was totally on board with the idea of getting out of the house because she was trying to sort out her parents' medical bills. I agreed to pick her up.

Disappointed with my progress on the blocks, I was happy to see Ruth Ann as she got in my car.

"I am so glad you called, Kate," she said, out of breath. "I may have to hire some help with the mess I have. Having parents with two different medical plans isn't helping."

"I feel your pain," I sympathized. "I hear it's a nightmare. I must remind you, however, that you are very lucky to still have them with you."

She smiled and nodded in agreement.

"They know I'm making a lot of changes to the building and they are concerned about that," voiced Ruth Ann. "I occasionally show them pictures, but I know they will never be able to return to see it."

"Speaking of our elderly family members, have I told you my Aunt Mandy is coming for a visit from Florida?"

"When? That's wonderful," Ruth Ann said with a chuckle. "I wonder where she'll stay?"

We laughed.

"I think she is aiming for Thanksgiving," I surmised. "If not then, she'll come at Christmas."

We arrived at the winery and Ellie was thrilled to see us.

"Hey, Kate!" Trout, Ellie's young, handsome bartender always greeted me warmly. "How are you?" He flashed a warm smile.

"I'm great, and you know Ruth Ann, I'm sure."

Trout smiled at Ruth Ann and nodded. "Kudos on that big project of yours, Ruth Ann," Trout said.

"Thanks," Ruth Ann replied with excitement in her voice.

"I hope you can make it to the open house."

"I doubt if my slave driver here will let me leave this place," he teased. "I'm sure she'll be there with bells on!"

"I sure will," Ellie chimed in. "This has been the most exciting thing in decades for Borna. Oh, well, I mean besides Josephine's Guest House!"

Everyone laughed.

Ellie showed us to a table on the deck that had an awesome view of the countryside. Trout brought the three of us a glass of wine as we glanced at the menu.

"Kelly made his gumbo today and we have a pulled pork sandwich special," Trout announced.

"Are you sure you're not too busy to join us, Ellie?" Ruth Ann asked as she looked at all the full tables.

"I've eaten, but I'll join you for a drink until I am called to duty," Ellie replied.

"Okay, now that I have the two of you here together, I want to put you on the spot," Ellie began. "Have either of you heard from Clark?"

Ruth Ann and I looked at one another.

"I have," I said with some hesitation. "Don't get too excited. He just sent a text saying that he had completed a piece. He didn't say where he was or when he'd be back."

"Well, that's strange, don't you think?" Ellie responded. "Did you tell him we were all concerned about him?"

"Of course, but I didn't get any response," I said, shaking my head. "This is just like him. He isn't crazy about everyone knowing his business. You know that."

"Well, if he isn't telling you anything, he isn't telling anyone anything," Ruth Ann said sarcastically.

"You don't think he would just move away without telling

anyone, do you?" asked Ellie as she filled our glasses from the wine bottle on the table.

"I would be surprised if Clark moved away from Borna," I said with certainty. "He loves it here and his cabin is perfect for his work. He knows that everyone respects his privacy."

We placed our dinner order as Ruth Ann described her preparations for the big open house.

"Asking folks to bring a friend is very generous and smart, but how do you prepare refreshments for an unknown number?" I asked, curious.

"Hey, if she runs out of something, so be it," Ellie answered on her behalf, ending that subject.

"I'm sorry I had to skip my turn to host the Friendship Circle meeting," Ruth Ann apologized. "I will try to make it, but to have it here this time was just too much."

"Esther said it was no big deal for her," Ellie noted. "So what else is new with the two of you?"

"Well, I just had a frustrating afternoon trying to get Jack's appliqué lighthouses done," I complained. "I want to give him the quilt for Christmas. He may actually make it here to Borna this year. This is my first Christmas here, and I plan to make the most of it!"

"I'm glad you brought up Christmas, Kate," Ruth Ann said with a grin on her face. "I was thinking of hanging Christmas quilts all over the banquet hall for the season. I have so many blank walls right now. My students are all willing to loan me what they have."

Sadly, I immediately thought of Tina, the burglar who stole my tree carving.

Ruth Ann continued on the merits of hanging the quilts.

"It would absorb some of the sound, too."

Pushing Tina out of my mind, I exclaimed, "I love the idea! I especially like that they will be hung for a definite period of time. Quilts can easily absorb all sorts of aromas. Thank goodness your hall will be a non-smoking venue."

"Good points, Kate," Ellie said, agreeing. "I think it will be fabulous."

"I want a real Christmas tree in every guest room this year." I announced. I was eager to get their reactions.

"That would be so awesome, especially if you chose cedar trees," praised Ellie. "I loved the big tree you had right in front of your living room window last year. It looked so pretty whenever I drove by."

"It makes it extra cool that they come from my property," I stated. "Thank goodness I have Cotton to do all those lovely chores."

"Here's to Cotton!" Ruth Ann toasted as she raised her glass.

CHAPTER 11

Ruth Ann and I left the winery in good spirits. Our conversation about Christmas plans had gotten me excited. Christmas quilts are a perfect way to celebrate family traditions. I love the combination of red and green. As the saying goes, quilts are a way of keeping the peace and doing away with the scraps! Why couldn't we just quilt the whole town Christmas? Who could object to that? I knew I was getting ahead of myself. After all, we had to celebrate Thanksgiving first. Thanksgiving meant I might be seeing John again. And, if all went well, Clark would be back in Borna by then.

The next morning, I got up to bake chocolate and blueberry cupcakes to take to Esther's house for our Friendship Circle meeting. I could only think of Jack and how much he loved these. Just as I was busy filling the cupcake papers, my phone rang.

"Hey, Kate, how are you?"

It took a moment for me to place the voice. It was Carson. For a short time, Carson and Ellie had been involved in a relationship. It was further complicated by Carson being married.

"Just fine, how are you?" I responded, maintaining a professional tone to my voice. "What can I do for you?"

"Well, I'll need a room next week on the night of Ruth Ann's open house," he announced. "Do you have The Study available where I stayed the last time?"

"I do," I answered. "How did you hear about her open house, if I may ask?"

"Ruth Ann is buying wine from our company and she said everyone is welcome," he bragged, as if he knew I would be bothered by him coming. "I'm going straight to the event, so I won't be checking in until later that evening. Look forward to seeing you!"

"See you then." This would be interesting. Ruth Ann was an innocent party in this case. She had no idea about Carson's affair with Ellie. Ellie was the one who broke it off and she would be shocked to see him at the open house. Should I warn her or say nothing? I certainly couldn't keep him from booking a room.

I was putting the dishes in the dishwasher when I noticed Cotton raking the first of our fall leaves in the backyard. I wiped my hands and went outside to tell him I would have some cupcakes for him to take home to Susan and Amy Sue today.

"I was telling the girls last night that I want small cedar trees in all the guest bedrooms this year," I said, my excitement of Christmas returning. "They could be two to three feet high. Then, of course, I want a big one for the living room, like last year. I thought you could start keeping an eye out for them when you are out working on the property."

He grinned and nodded. "No problem. I'll be glad to. I can tag them for cutting ahead of time. You have some great woods back yonder. I thought I might start on the barn when I get done raking."

"You can pitch a lot, but if you're in doubt about anything, put it aside for me to look at, okay?" I could feel the chill of colder air coming in.

"Absolutely. Better get a jacket on or go in, Miss Kate. It looks like you're getting cold."

I went inside, realizing how lucky I was to have a trusted friend and helper like Cotton. I knew he and Susie were grateful for employment. As I packaged up the cupcakes, I knew they would be appreciated.

CHAPTER 12

I was glad it was still daylight when I made my way to Esther's house. I was on the lookout for her yellow mailbox.

"Welcome! Come on in," she greeted Peggy and me as we arrived. "It's getting colder lately, so I made us a little fire."

"Lovely!" I said with a shiver. "I brought cupcakes."

"Thanks so much, Kate," she said, taking my container. "I know whatever you bake is going to be delicious."

"Hi, Emma." I joined her on the couch. "How have you been?"

"Oh, as good as I can be with old age creeping up on me," she divulged, patting her knee. "I think I'll have to address getting my other knee repaired. I'm not looking forward to that!"

"Sorry to hear that, but you'll do fine, I'm sure," I encouraged her.

Esther made sure everyone had something to drink before she started the meeting.

"If you recall, we were going to decide on a charity that will benefit from our raffle quilt," she began. "Having that chosen ahead of time will help sell the tickets. We need to get that quilt done as soon as we can. Ruth Ann will machine quilt it for us and Charlene has arranged to have the Dresden Bank print out tickets for us. So, does anyone have their block done?"

Everyone laughed when no hands were raised. Since the quilt was my idea, I knew I'd better get going on mine.

"I have plenty of fabric to set it together," Ruth Ann announced. "Kate has given me some of her extra batting, so we're all set. By the way, are all of you planning to come to my open house?"

The group seemed to perk up with excitement.

"I just want to say, on behalf of our Friendship Circle, that we congratulate you on this huge accomplishment," Ellen announced. We clapped.

"If I may have the floor for a second, I am curious. How many of you own a Christmas quilt of some kind?" I asked.

Everyone either raised a hand or nodded in the affirmative.

"Why do you ask?" Mary Catherine wondered.

"I think it would be fun to display Christmas quilts somewhere nearby during the time that Sharla Lee has her Christmas trees at the museum," I suggested. "If we ask for a donation, I think we could make a little money and it would really enhance the feeling of Christmas."

"Where on earth would we be able to do that, Kate?" asked Emma.

"Didn't that church hall next to the museum have a quilt show one time?" I noted.

"Oh, I think that is used for other things during the Christmas season," Ellen shared.

"Well, let's us just think about Kate's idea. But, you know, there isn't much time for planning," Esther warned. "Now, we need to get back to deciding on a charity."

"The only one that seems to have the most impact here in the county is the Lutheran Family and Children's Services," voiced Mary Catherine.

"She's right, of course," agreed Anna, "but there are other charities—like the NASV, you know, the Network Against Sexual Violence—that also need help."

My thoughts immediately went to Susan. "Is there a place in the county where women and children can go when they are subject to physical abuse?" I asked.

"I'm not aware of any," Ellen stated.

I figure if Ellen didn't know about such a place, there likely wasn't one.

"All good comments to think about, but I am going to make a motion to use the LFCS as our designated charity for the raffle quilt," said Ruth Ann. "Most folks know about that organization and they help with such a variety of needs."

Most of the group nodded their heads in agreement.

"I'll second that," voiced Anna.

"Any objections? If not, all those in favor, say aye. "

The vote was unanimous. That accomplished, we helped ourselves to a variety of goodies and delicious homemade ice cream Esther's husband had made for us.

Leaving the meeting, I realized that I needed to rethink my Christmas quilt show idea. I was learning that it did indeed take a village to accomplish something in Borna!

CHAPTER 13

Ruth Ann's open house was on everyone's schedule today. It was from two to six, so I wanted to go when I thought the most folks would be there. I could only imagine how nervous Ruth Ann must feel. It was a dark, chilly day so I wasn't sure what to wear. I finally settled on a plain black pantsuit with a cream turtleneck sweater. This was going to be a nice affair for the whole community.

Ellie and I had agreed that I would pick her up at four. When we arrived at the hall, it was filled with guests. Ruth Ann was at the door greeting everyone personally as they arrived.

"I can't believe this turnout," Ruth Ann said as she gave me a hug.

"I'm so happy for you!" Ellie exclaimed.

"I told you this would be a wonderful way to introduce your facility," I added. I took a moment to look around and see who was in attendance.

"I wish my mom and dad could see this," Ruth Ann lamented sadly. "But, Mary Catherine is going to do a story for the newspaper and take some photos for me. My folks will get such a kick out of that. Let me know what you think of my chef. Everything looks great, so I hope it tastes good as well."

Ellie and I left Ruth Ann to gaze at the long table of food delights. Although the foods looked delicious, the centerpiece of the table was a large ice sculpture of an L and an H, standing for Lueder's Hall. It was impressive! There certainly weren't too many events in East Perry that displayed ice sculptures at events. This would be a great inspiration for those wanting to do weddings and other events at this venue. Fall leaves were intermingled with trays of unique delicacies.

"This is all quite lovely, don't you think?" asked Ellen as she approached us. "I am so glad we decided to have the company Christmas party here this year."

"It means a lot to Ruth Ann," I said directly to Ellen. "She said she is going to put all Christmas quilts on the wall during the Christmas season, which will be stunning!"

"Kate, if we can't figure out something for your show idea, how would you feel about making sure all the local businesses have a Christmas quilt to display at their places of business?" Ellen suggested with a burst of energy.

"That's a great idea, Ellen," I said, picturing it in my mind.

"I'll make sure we hang one behind our bar area," said Ellie.

I could tell this variation of my idea could go over very well and would make it fairly easy for everyone to participate. "Well, I'll have some hanging in the guesthouse, too," I promised.

"Of course, we should have a special day when the businesses will offer some light refreshments so everyone will want to enter the stores and see their quilts," added Ellen. "I'll have to think of a catchy name for that."

"Awesome," I nodded, approving. "If you plan it, they will come, and it will be wonderful!"

Ellen blushed as she walked away.

"You are quite something yourself, Kate Meyr," Ellie teased. "You certainly can get the creative juices going around here."

We chuckled.

"Sometimes it helps to look at things with fresh eyes. Remember, I'm from Michigan!"

Ellie shook her head, snickering.

As we walked around chatting with folks we knew, I found myself wishing Clark were here to enjoy all the compliments about the gorgeous bar he designed and built for Ruth Ann. I decided to take a photo to text to him later. We were happy to spy an open table where we took our plates of food and glasses of wine. It felt good to settle into a table where we could enjoy the delicious food in front of us.

"Well hello, ladies." My heart sank. It was Carson. We were speechless.

It was Ellie who first found her voice. "Why are you here?" Ellie eyed him evenly.

Carson grinned and shook his head slightly as if surprised by her question. "Ruth Ann has to buy her wine from somewhere, so she purchased from me and invited me here, that's why," he said curtly.

Ellie's displeasure was clear by the look on her face.

"I'm spending the night at Josephine's Guest House," he continued. "I'm surprised Kate didn't tell you."

Ellie stared at me, astonished.

"How are things at the winery?" Carson seemed determined to continue the conversation.

Oh, this was not going well. Ellie did not respond to his question. After an awkward moment, Carson excused himself.

"Oh, Ellie, I was about to tell you that he asked for a room," I started. "I was hoping he wouldn't show up and was relieved when I didn't see him here. Please don't blame me. What was I supposed to do?"

Ellie shook her head. I could see that she was searching for something to say. "To think he has the nerve to show up here makes me sick!" Ellie finally said. "Ruth Ann must not have any idea what kind of man he is. He shouldn't even be selling here, knowing that I am right here as a competitor."

"I'm sure she didn't think," I said quickly. "She doesn't know about the two of you."

Ellie shook her head.

It was a disappointing way to end to the evening, and understandably, Ellie was ready to go home.

CHAPTER 14

I arrived home before Carson and turned on as many lights downstairs as I could. I hadn't wanted to leave the house unlocked for him, nor did I want to encourage any further conversation with him once he arrived. I was in my office when he entered the front door.

"That was quite a nice affair this evening!" Carson was clearly enthusiastic about the success of the open house. "I think she will do very well in that venue, don't you?"

I nodded. "Come on in and make yourself at home. Were people still there when you left?"

"About ten or so," he reported, taking off his jacket. "It was good to see a lot of the same faces that I was used to seeing at the winery. Say, I brought you a bottle of wine. Would you like to join me for a nightcap?"

"No thanks," I responded, surprising myself by suddenly feeling shy. "I think I've had enough wine for the evening. As soon as I get you checked in, I think I'll head upstairs."

"Am I the only guest tonight?" he asked, glancing around to see evidence of any other customers.

I wanted to lie but decided against it. "Yes, you are," I said, taking his charge card. My plan was to check him in and move the good-night niceties along as quickly as possible.

"So, has business been okay for you?" he inquired, sounding like he really cared.

"Yes, it's been good so far and has not tied me down."

"So, how's Mr. McFadden?" he asked, catching me by surprise. "I didn't see him there this evening. Ruth Ann sure was pleased with his work."

Why was he asking me? "I guess he's fine. I really don't know," I answered, hoping he did not pick up on the awkwardness I felt so keenly. I handed back his card and hoped he didn't go looking for his signature on the quilt. Josephine had decided to remove it after he had been here the last time. She had a way of deciding whose name would reside on the quilt and whose would not.

"What time would you like breakfast?" I said, walking toward the stairs.

"Oh, I'm not one for breakfast, so coffee and perhaps one of your muffins will do," he said, following me. "I have to stop at Ruth Ann's before I head out of town."

"Great. I'll see you in the morning then," I said, careful not to look his way.

I locked my bedroom and the hall bathroom door when I got upstairs. I wasn't really afraid, but he had previously shown some personal interest in me the last time he was here and I wasn't taking any chances. His room was underneath my bedroom and I could hear him moving around. Perhaps he went to the kitchen to get a glass for his wine. Then I heard him talking, so he must have called his wife, or for all I know, it could have been Ellie.

I told myself to mind my own business. Would I ever get used to having people in my home that I did not know well or at all? As I was getting undressed, I saw a text from John. This time of night seemed to be when he was most likely to text me.

It read:

> Please book the night before Thanksgiving for me. Visit will be short unless you beg me to stay. John.

He could certainly make me smile. I sent a text back which read:

> Reservation completed! I don't beg anyone for anything, just so you know. 😉

There was no response, so I went ahead and texted Clark a photo of his bar from the party this evening. I texted:

> You are missed, Ruth Ann had a great turnout and everyone admired your handiwork. Do you have any news on your return?

Just as I thought, there was no response. It was too late to call Maggie, so I sent her a text saying:

> I'm missing my bestie! I went to Ruth Ann's open house tonight. Please don't be angry that I'm not coming home for the holidays. Is there any news about Jill and Jack?

Maggie responded immediately with:

> I cannot sleep. Jill is worried that Jack may still have a relationship in New York. Is there any truth to that?

I texted back:

> Jack is a one-woman man. Do you know if he has asked her to come to Borna with him for Christmas?

Her response was:

> No mention of it. Are you still hearing from John?

My next response was:

> Yes, he has booked Thanksgiving. He seems excited about coming.

There was a pause before Maggie responded with:

> You're asking for trouble in Borna City.

I quickly sent her my usual smiley face. I loved keeping her guessing about my private life!

CHAPTER 15

I had just pulled the blueberry muffins out of the oven when Carson arrived in the kitchen the next morning. "Carson, would you like some coffee?" I offered. "The paper is on the dining room table."

"Thanks, but I already read the news on my phone. This town needs a coffee shop."

"That would be great," I agreed. "A lot of men hang out at Marv's in the mornings."

"You could do it!" Carson suggested. "There sure are a lot of empty buildings around here. You could open a coffee shop!"

"No thanks," I chuckled. "I have my hands full. I have a busy day today. I want to stop by the museum."

"Well, it's been a pleasure as always, Miss Meyr," Carson said, pulling on his coat. "I'll see you on my next visit."

I felt relief watching him go out the door holding a warm muffin in a napkin. Traveling salesmen were the ideal guests. They were low maintenance and mostly all business. I made a grocery list and put on a light jacket due to the cooler fall air. When I arrived at the museum, Sharla Lee was behind the desk and Gerard was giving a tour.

"Oh, honey, I just missed you last night at Ruth Ann's party," Sharla Lee complained. "It was fabulous, don't you think?"

"It was," I replied. "I'm so proud of her."

"We're proud of you too, Kate. What can I do for you?"

"I'm still poking around for any information on the Paulsons," I explained. "I wish we could at least find a photo of Josephine. I would frame it for the guesthouse."

"Splendid idea," Sharla Lee responded.

"You know, it's my first Christmas in Borna and I really want to contribute to the community in some way," I said, looking around, wondering if a possibility might hit me right then and there.

"Well, honey, as you know, we do a Christmas tree exhibit here every year. I think it would be cool to have a tree representing Josephine's Guest House."

Once she made the suggestion, I could picture it. "I had never thought about that," I said slowly, allowing the idea to sink in. "Sure. I'd be happy to!"

"I really wish there were more people like you in this world," Sharla Lee complimented.

"I told the Friendship Circle I liked the idea of a Christmas quilt show somewhere, but it's just too late," I shared. "Quilts are such an inspiring way to celebrate any season."

"I agree with you there. They are so Americana. How about a cup of tea and let's brainstorm a bit here. What do you say?"

What did I just get myself into?

CHAPTER 16

A nd brainstorming we did, with the help of Gerard who joined us after his tour left. He began telling us about various German traditions as he recalled his childhood memories. Ironically, my family shared many of the same traditions. I took notes as we talked. He described an authentic German dinner and I was all ears, thinking about how I could duplicate it sometime at the guesthouse. As our conversation turned toward plans for the holidays, I was also touched when he said there were many unfortunate families around the county that depended on charity to have any kind of Christmas.

"Is there a way to find out who those families are?" I asked, concerned.

"I can get a list that the schools hand out to nonprofit agencies," Sharla Lee suggested. "Most of the time, toys arrive for them, but I think it's sad how the moms and dads get ignored."

"The moms would probably like a nice quilt or something personal," I said, not thinking carefully about what I was saying.

"Who wouldn't love that?" Sharla Lee teased.

"Well, let's see. I can bake and I sure know a lot of quilters," I surmised. They both looked at me strangely and wondered where I was going with my line of thought.

"I think you're getting a little crazy here," Sharla Lee said with a chuckle. "I know your heart is gigantic, but I think you'd best start with a small project and work from there. First, decide what is doable for you and then figure out how others can help."

I nodded in agreement.

"I'll get a list of the needy families in the area," volunteered Sharla Lee. The list doesn't give their names, but it does give the genders and ages of the family members. Perhaps there's a way you can contribute, but in the meantime, I'm putting you down to decorate one of our trees."

"Oh, absolutely," I said, excited. "Let me know when you get that list. I think I'll stay here for just a little while to mosey around on your computer, if you don't mind."

"Have at it, Miss Kate," Gerard agreed.

When I entered the name Dr. Paulson, it didn't take long for a photo to pop up. It included him and his friend Dr. Schall, who had a practice in Cape County as well as East Perry County. When I reread the note, it confirmed that he married Josephine Lottes. It said that she was the daughter of Gabriel Lottes and his second wife, Ann Dornhoefer. Gabriel Lottes established a saloon in Altenburg in 1877, making him prominent in the community. Josephine had a brother named John, who was a banker in New Appleton. It went on to say that Dr. Paulson was one of the leading physicians in eastern Perry County for many years. He graduated in 1896 from the Homeopathic Medical College in St. Louis. He was a progressive and popular citizen of Borna and belonged to the American Institute of Homeopathy. This was a little more information than I previously had found, but time was getting away from me. I thanked Gerard and Sharla Lee and headed out the door.

I rushed to the grocery store where I ran into Milly, Harold's wife. She said Harold was doing well and would be going back to work tomorrow. I asked her to tell him hello for me and said I would be by to check on him.

For the remainder of the evening, my mind was spinning with ideas regarding Christmas. I was beginning to realize that helping and giving to someone in need through the holidays would be much more beneficial than adding a new activity for the fortunate. Why hadn't I done more of that in South Haven?

CHAPTER 17

After the excitement of Ruth Ann's open house, the days that followed were uneventful. Aunt Mandy's letter arriving this morning was just what I needed to get excited about Thanksgiving. Having my aunt and John here at the same time would prove interesting. She didn't say how long she would be staying. She indicated she'd be driving, which surprised me. I would still offer to have Cotton pick her up at the airport in St. Louis if she decided to fly. So, what does one do if a relative comes to stay in your home but it's also a place of business? I hadn't seen her for so long, but I was secretly hoping she was as sweet and gracious as I remembered.

It was time I gave serious thought to planning Thanksgiving dinner and any meals that would follow. Somehow, I couldn't see Aunt Mandy sharing a hamburger with me at Marv's. I hoped the stairs would not be a problem for her since I assigned her to the Wildflower Room across from my bedroom. John would be in The Study downstairs, which would be a comfortable room for him.

I started to write a letter to Aunt Mandy when Ellie's name showed up on my phone. "Having a busy day? I'm snowed under here. The beautiful foliage certainly is bringing in the tourists. If you're not doing anything, I can put you to work. This is probably the last good weekend before winter."

"Gee, thanks, my friend," I replied calmly. "I do want to get out today while it's nice. I need to see Sharla Lee about something, and I want to stop and say hello to Harold who is back at work now."

"Well, good for him! Give him my best. Say, the reason I'm calling is that we had a man stop by the winery asking some questions. I happened to be behind the bar because Trout was running an errand for me. The man asked if I had seen a single woman traveling alone in a Volkswagen. He said folks were looking for her. He may have been an undercover cop, for all I know. Have you ever heard the like?"

I took a deep breath. I had been hoping this would never come up. "No, I haven't," I lied. "He didn't say why they were looking for her, did he?"

"No, but he gave me the impression that she was on the run from something."

That was an understatement! "If he happened to be from the authorities, he would have told you, don't you think?" I asked, wanting to know more.

"I guess I should have asked his name, but I was a bit taken aback that he would be asking at a winery if we had seen anyone like that. If I were on the run, I wouldn't be coming to a place like this."

"Well, I'll be on the lookout for a bug with a female in it," I teased.

"Feel free to stop by for dinner if you're out," Ellie offered.

"Thanks, but you're busy and I have a list of things to do," I said before hanging up.

It sounded like this could have been Susan's husband looking for her rather than any detective. I'm sure getting the law involved was the last thing her husband would want. I could only wish that Susan remained safe somewhere out there. How bad does life have to get when you leave your child behind? What will I do if he stops here? I'm not sure I could hide my anger if I saw him face to face. Nothing makes me angrier than a dominating male taking advantage of a female. I couldn't help but again wonder where abused women and children went here in East Perry when they needed a safe place.

After a bite of lunch, I headed to the museum to see Sharla Lee. She was in a meeting, but a volunteer by the name of Carolyn said she would tell Sharla Lee I was here to see her. In just a few seconds, Sharla Lee came to greet me.

"Kate, you are such a dear to help out," Sharla Lee expressed as she gave me a hug. "I don't know what you have planned, but all these families on this list are at the bottom level of income. I know who some of these people are by the description, and I can tell you they would appreciate anything you could do for them. They want a Christmas like everyone else. You'll notice that many are mothers with young children."

"Thanks. I'll do what I can," I assured her. "Christmas should be joyous for everyone, not just the privileged."

"Let us know if we can help," Sharla Lee said before going back to her meeting.

"I ditto that, Miss Meyr," said Carolyn. She had overheard our conversation. "There is so much need out there."

I smiled and nodded. I tucked the list in my purse and headed to Harold's Hardware store.

CHAPTER 18

"Well, if it isn't Miss Kate," Harold greeted as I walked in the door.

"How are you, Harold? It's so good to see you!" I gave him a hug.

"I'm just dandy, just dandy," he reassured me. "How about you, young lady?"

"Staying busy and out of trouble," I teased. "You sure had everyone scared, you know."

"Well, it was a scary deal," he said, shaking his head. "It's heck to get old. I don't much like this new diet Milly's got me on, and I sure don't feel like exercising. I guess it's better than the alternative, like Milly tells me!" He gave out a hearty laugh. "I asked the folks here if anyone has seen Clark lately. He's just disappeared, unless you can shed some light on the subject." He winked at me.

"He's out of town working and that is truly all I can tell you. He'll come around when he's back in town. He thinks the world of you."

Harold smiled. "Well, I know you don't like it when I tease you about him, but I sure hope the two of you can end up together one day," he countered, wearing a sheepish smile.

"Now, Harold, you know I'm pretty darn happy right now," I said, returning the same smile.

"You can't fool me, Kate," Harold continued, his tone more serious. "I know a match when I see one."

"I just stopped by to say hello and to see how you were doing."
I gave him an even gaze and a friendly pat on the back in hopes of
moving the conversation to another subject.

"That's mighty nice of you," he said with a big grin. "I heard
Ruth Ann had a good turnout the other night. Milly didn't think
we should go, but I sure would have liked to. She's the boss
though, you know."

"You need to listen to your boss," I confirmed. "She knows
what's good for you. I have to run, but please don't work too hard.
I'll be back in to see you soon."

"You tell that Mr. McFadden to get back here soon."

I nodded as if I agreed that I could achieve that mission.
When I got in the car, I thought about how upset Harold would
be if he knew Clark had cancer. I slowed down when I got to
Imy's shop, but she had a sign on her door that indicated she was
closed. I needed to get something to eat, so I went to Marv's. I
could hardly find a parking place. The bar stools were filled, so
I went to the end of the bar where I knew someone would take
my order to go. I did not recognize the bartender, but was able to
get his attention and order a cobb salad to go. While I waited, I
made conversation with a young man who said he was working
in construction and had just stopped for a few beers.

I finally arrived home and perched myself on a stool at my
kitchen island. While I ate, I looked over Sharla Lee's list of
needy families. One single mom had five young children under
her roof. How could I best personalize their Christmas? Making
my muffins wasn't going to make their Christmas any brighter.
This was a bigger task than I realized. I would need others to
accomplish anything worthwhile. If I could get one person to
take one family, we could make a difference. How could I get
folks to sign on to this effort? I was pretty sure I could count on

the Friendship Circle, but I shouldn't just assume that. I could stress that their gifts didn't need to be expensive, just thoughtful and age appropriate for each family member. If I made it a fun Christmas event for the folks who donated, it just might be possible to pull this off. If I got Ellie's approval, that would be all I needed to proceed. Feeling excited and impatient, I decided to call her at the winery.

"Sorry, Ellie, I know you're busy," I began. "Can you talk?"

"Sure. I'm in the storeroom getting some things. What's up?"

I quickly shared my idea, talking as fast as I could. I wasn't quite sure she was absorbing everything. When she spoke, she agreed to be on board but didn't exude the excitement I had hoped to generate.

"You don't have time to wait until our next meeting date," Ellie explained. "You're going to have to call each person in the Friendship Circle. I don't think anyone will want to be left out."

"Well, if they all agree, I'll host a potluck before Christmas so they can bring their gifts to show. We can all help to wrap them." I could picture the joyous evening in my mind.

"So, who delivers all those gifts? You're going to have tons and tons of them. You'd better think every detail of this through."

"I don't have that answer, but I'll ask Sharla Lee how others do it," I suggested. "If it falls on me, so be it."

Ellie gave a loud chuckle of disbelief. "You really are crazy, you know it?"

"I know I'm getting ahead of myself, but in all of those years in South Haven, I served on lots and lots of charity committees and I never saw the results or was directly involved in the process. I want things to be different here."

"You go, girl," Ellie cheered. "You know I'll support you. I'll talk to you later."

CHAPTER 19

With Ellie's approval, I wrote down the names of people I would approach who might be interested in contributing gifts. Enjoying my quiet moment, I also planned Thanksgiving dinner which was now just weeks away. I was so sorry I let October 22 slip away. It was Josephine's birthday. I must make a special note on my calendar from now on and do something special at the guest house. She would have been 137 years old, had she lived. She would always still be alive here in this house if I had my way about it. The guest quilt in my entryway was a good reminder of her presence.

I hadn't counted how many weeks Clark had been gone, but it was starting to feel like a very, very long time. I couldn't help but wonder what he'd be like when he returned to Borna. Maybe if I texted him a picture of my blueberry muffins, it would make him smile and he'd have to return a message. I looked in my phone and found the perfect photo. It was a heaping basketful of muffins that had just come out of the oven. I wrote the following:

Yum, yum. Come get some! How much longer will it be? K.

I had to smile to myself as I pictured him reading the text. Please God, let him return soon and be healed.

It was getting dark outside much earlier now. I convinced myself to make a fire to take the chill out of the air. If I added a glass of wine and a good book, I would be set for the rest of the evening.

After I poured a glass of wine, I went to open the back door to retrieve some logs from my stack of wood on the deck. When I turned on the porch light, I discovered a pile of black coal placed right in front of my back door! I nearly stepped on the scattered blackness. I had to step back to determine what this was all about. Where on earth did this come from? I didn't have coal anywhere on my property. Would Cotton know about this? It had to be at least two bucketfuls of the hard, black rocks. What kind of prank was this and who would think it was funny?

I reached for a few logs as I stepped around the mess. I quickly shut the door, telling myself I would clean it up in the morning. I couldn't help but look out the windows to see if I could see anything unusual. I was surprised that I hadn't heard any of this happening. Usually, I know when a car comes and goes on my property. A bit rattled, I carried on with my evening plans. However, the coal had me wondering. Were there more of Blade's friends out there to make my life miserable? What if Blade had somehow gotten out of jail? My cell phone rang, causing me to jump. It was Ruth Ann.

"Hey, would you like company?" she asked, sounding like she was in a good mood. "I didn't see any cars at your place."

"Sure, come on over," I agreed, feeling a little hesitant.

"I baked an applesauce cake today and I can bring some over," she offered.

"Sounds delish," I responded. "It'll go with my wine or I can put a pot of coffee on."

"Hold that thought. I'll be there in five minutes."

"Oh, Ruth Ann, please come to the front door when you come, okay?" I asked, without offering an explanation.

"Sure," she complied.

CHAPTER 20

Before Ruth Ann rang the front doorbell, I had built a fire and put on a pot of coffee.

"When did you get so formal by asking folks to come to the front door?" Ruth Ann teased when she arrived.

"Well, most of my guests use the front door, so I'm getting used to using it," I explained. "Come on in and get warm by the fire."

"Oh, it is becoming the season, isn't it?" she commented as she handed me a plate of cake slices.

"This looks so good," I said, removing the cover. "All I had for lunch was a salad from Marv's today, so this will hit the spot! So, what shall it be, wine or coffee?"

"The wine looks pretty good right now," she decided.

"I don't suppose you've heard from Clark, have you?" she asked as I poured her wine. I shook my head. I wanted to avoid any conversation about Clark.

"I'm glad you called, Ruth Ann," I began. "I have a plan to help the needy here in the county for the holidays and I thought of the Friendship Circle as a possible group to help me. I was going to call everyone individually, so I'll begin with you."

She sat down, ready to hear my latest idea.

I started from the beginning about how my thoughts had changed from adding a new holiday event for the community into making the holidays better for the less fortunate. Her face lit up when I said it could turn into a wrapping party for those who participated.

"It's a wonderful idea, Kate," she responded enthusiastically, raising her wine glass in approval. "Who can't add a little something to their shopping list? Or, maybe they already have something they can give these families. Having the ages of each family member is going to be really helpful."

"That's what I thought," I said, feeling more secure about my idea.

"I have one improvement to your plan."

"Tell me, tell me."

"I really like the idea of the celebration at the end and wrapping the gifts together. There will be tons of gifts to wrap and we'll need a lot of space. So, why not do this at my hall? We can spread out and we can have food served out of the kitchen. There is no way you could have it here in this house. I just don't think there would be enough room."

She was right. "I guess I hadn't thought that far. Good point. I could certainly provide most of the food."

"I really prefer your idea of making it a potluck. That way, everyone gets to participate and bring a fun holiday dish. And, who doesn't love a potluck?"

"Well, it's decided. I think it's time for cake!"

We laughed and continued with some small talk about the holiday plans as we readied our slices of cake. When we settled back on the couch, I decided to tell Ruth Ann about the coal pile on my deck.

"You have got to be kidding!" she said, nearly choking on her cake. "So this is this why you had me come to the front door?"

I nodded.

We stood and walked to the door. I opened the back door to the cool air and looked down on the dangerous pile of coal that could have caused me to fall. She was speechless. After a moment she asked, "Are you going to report this? This is such a sick joke."

"This isn't my first rodeo with having something on my doorstep, Ruth Ann," I said, shaking my head in disgust. "Blade is in jail and his other buddy is dead, so it's hard for me to believe it's another buddy that is defending Blade. It may have nothing to do with Blade at all. I just don't know."

"I can help you clean this up," Ruth Ann offered as I closed the door.

"Thanks, but Cotton might be by in the morning, so he can do it for me," I assured her. "There's nothing damaged, so that's good. I have an alarm, so I'm good inside the house at least."

CHAPTER 21

Very early the next morning, I put on old jeans to tackle a very dirty job on my back deck, just in case Cotton was not able to stop by. I sipped a cup of coffee as I thought about how to best clean it up. Donning my jean jacket, I headed to the barn to get gardening gloves and garbage bags. I was about to start my task when Cotton's truck pulled into the driveway.

"What on earth happened here?"

"Well, someone left lumps of coal on my doorstep last night," I said, attempting to insert some wry humor. "I wonder if it was Santa Claus trying to tell me I've been bad."

Not appreciating my feeble attempt at humor, Cotton dug for more information. "Did you step into this?" he asked, taking the garbage bags from my hands. "You could have gotten hurt. I don't get this."

"I'm fine, but it could have been a disaster," I said, beginning the process of putting handfuls of black grit into the bag Cotton had situated for that purpose.

"Do you have any idea who might have done this?"

I shook my head. "Of course, my thoughts went back to Blade and his friends," I confessed. "I even find that hard to believe. I haven't done anything to anyone."

When we got down to black crumbs, I asked Cotton to hose off the deck.

"You get on inside. I've got this," Cotton said, heading for the hose. "Say, Kate, you never said anything about the barn since I cleaned it out. Did you see what I put aside for you to look at?"

"Yes, I did, and you made good choices, especially with those glass canning jars," I answered. "I wonder if Josephine used those. I'll look through the things more carefully later. It does look so much better. I'm sorry I didn't thank you sooner."

He grinned from ear to ear.

"I've got coffee on if you need it." I went inside to fix some toast for myself. I kept thinking about all the obstacles I had encountered since I arrived, going back to the family that barged into this place when I was getting ready to put it on the market. They were wild and rude and I boldly chased them off. Ellie thought they were likely squatters that try to take over vacant houses.

I sat down to make a list of potential people I could ask to help me with providing the needy families gifts for Christmas. I liked the way Ruth Ann thought it could be an annual event and that she was willing to offer her banquet hall. Suddenly, I was interrupted by a man ringing the doorbell.

"Can I help you?" I asked before opening the front door. He looked unshaven and was dressed in workman's attire.

"Sorry to bother you, but I'm looking for someone and wondered if you could help me." From his appearance and breathlessness, he appeared to be in distress. I knew immediately that this visit pertained to Susan. I didn't want him to come in the house, so I opened the door and stepped out onto the porch.

"Are you with the police?" I asked, knowing the answer.

"No," he said, shaking his head. "We are looking for a

woman that is driving a green Volkswagen and we think she may have driven in this direction."

We? I decided to ask some questions of my own. "Why are you looking for her?" I pressed. "Did she do something wrong?"

He shook his head again. "We think she's confused and we want to help her," he explained.

"I can't help you, I'm afraid. I hope she'll be okay. I'm so sorry."

"Here's my number if you see her, okay?"

I nodded and took the small piece of paper.

"Is there anyone else here I could ask? I see there's a pick-up truck out back. Is that yours?"

"Yes, my help uses it now and then," I lied, hoping he would not spot Cotton and decide to ask him questions. As I held my breath, the man drove off in his red SUV. I ran out the back door to locate Cotton. I called his name and he suddenly came from the other side of the house where he was raking leaves.

"You lookin' for me?"

"Never mind. I just didn't see you, so I thought you'd left," I muttered.

Cotton turned and went back to his work. That was a close call. Not knowing the circumstances, I'm sure Cotton would have told him about Susan arriving here that morning. I could only hope she had found a safe haven somewhere.

CHAPTER 22

Attempting to catch up in the journal that Maggie had given me before I left South Haven, I described my Christmas charity effort. I listed all of the Friendship Circle members who had been contacted and were on board with the project. I wrote that I sensed Maggie was unhappy about me staying in Borna for the holidays. Jack had agreed to come to Borna for Christmas, and that was important to me. I knew he wanted to see Jill as well, so I had extended an invitation to her. Everything was falling into place.

I couldn't imagine the holidays without Clark, who had been such a friend from the beginning of my life in Borna. I would be eternally grateful that he had saved my life when Blade attacked me. I had hoped to at least get a reply text when I sent him a photo of the blueberry muffins, but it didn't happen. I can only assume that he smiled at the gesture. Was he responding well to his treatments or was he experiencing a lot of pain? I may never know. I was writing a lot of unanswered questions in this journal entry. I heard from John every three days or so. I loved the attention and looked forward to his visit next week. This I would only admit to you, my journal confidant!

Aunt Mandy said she had all the time in the world to drive to Missouri, so she would be arriving in her ten-year-old Cadillac that I remembered well. She drove it as if she were queen of the highway! I was looking forward to catching up with her. She and my father had so many similarities in their mannerisms. I was also eager to introduce her to my Borna friends.

I still worry on the hour about poor Susan who is on the run. I pray that her husband never catches up to her. It must be a terrible thing to be so afraid that you are willing to leave your child behind. She must worry at every turn, wondering if she is followed. I just wish I knew how she was doing today.

My Thanksgiving weekend will be interesting. I wish Ellie could join us, but she always hosts a wonderful community event at her winery every year. It was just last year that I announced at her dinner that I was going to be a permanent resident of Borna. Has a full year actually passed since that announcement?

I moved on to plan my Thanksgiving dinner menu. I preferred it to be simple, but it has to include traditional dishes like creamed onions, German apple stuffing, sweet potato casserole, and cranberry relish. Of course, I'll need to add the usual dishes of green beans, mashed potatoes, and my homemade bread. For dessert, I'll make blueberry cobbler and also pumpkin pie for the diehard pie eaters. I can hardly wait; however, it will be a challenge for me. And yes, I'll bring out the champagne like my dad used to do. I think I'll text Clark a dinner invitation and see what happens. The dinner should take place about the time his treatments are completed.

It's a good thing I have Susie and Cotton to help me. Despite the beauty of fall leaving us, things still looked pretty great at 6229 Main Street. Until next time...

CHAPTER 23

O n the day before Thanksgiving John's text said:

I'm on my way! I'm happy to leave six inches of snow here in South Haven.

The text implied he would be arriving around cocktail hour if everything went according to plan. Aunt Mandy could arrive anytime, so I found myself straightening each and every nook and cranny. Another guest, Fred Mills, had arrived last night. He was a retired dentist and looked to be about sixty-eight or so. He was charming and had a great sense of humor that I discovered as I visited with him at breakfast.

"These are the best blueberry muffins I've ever had," he exclaimed. "I'll bet you spoil your guests into coming back again and again."

I smiled at the thought. "I'd like to think so, Mr. Mills, but I'm still new at this," I said as I refilled his coffee cup. "I think I told you on the phone that I'm expecting two more guests today. One is my Aunt Mandy, visiting from Florida, and the other is a neighbor of mine at a condo I own in South Haven, Michigan."

"Splendid," he said, patting his belly. "I'm looking forward to meeting them both."

"Oh, I forgot to bring in the paper," I said, getting up. "Usually, I bring it in first thing in the morning."

When I opened the door and looked out toward the sidewalk, I saw coal scattered from there up to my front porch! It was a horrible sight. What would folks think as they drove by? The timing of this was the worst. I didn't see the paper, so I immediately shut the door and went in to call Cotton. I left a message with Susie to request that he come over as soon as soon as possible.

Taking a deep breath and trying to gather my wits about me, I told Mr. Mills there was no paper and that I'd have to excuse myself to take care of something. I just couldn't leave the mess there. Who knows how long it would be before Cotton would arrive? I went out the door with a couple of trash bags and a broom. It wasn't but a few minutes before Mr. Mills opened the front door and looked at me in wonder.

"Good heavens, Kate," he gasped. "What are you cleaning up? Can I help you?"

I wanted to cry but took another deep breath. "No, I'll get this," I said, looking down. "I'm sorry you had to see this. Every now and then, someone wants to play a little prank on me."

"How awful for you. I wish you would let me help you."

"No, I'll be finished here soon and I have my handyman coming by to help," I said, giving him what I hoped was my bravest smile. "He'll hose this all away."

He shook his head and closed the door.

What must he think? I had most of it cleaned up when Cotton pulled in the driveway. He came running to the front of the house. "This is a bunch of bull! You get inside and clean up. Don't you have some guests?"

I nodded, holding back tears.

"You'd better think about reporting this. Enough is enough!"

"Thanks Cotton." That was all I could say. When I went back into the house, Mr. Mills was reading a book on the sunporch. I left him alone and started cleaning breakfast dishes off the table. I heard a car pull in and peeked out to see Aunt Mandy in her white Cadillac.

"I think you've got company," announced Mr. Mills from the sunporch.

I left the dirty dishes and went directly outdoors to greet my beloved Aunt Mandy. "Oh, I'm so glad you're here!" I said, giving her a big hug.

"Me too, sweetie," she said. "This was quite a lovely drive this morning. You are truly hidden in these beautiful hills, aren't you?"

I nodded and smiled. "It's a great place," I said, taking her by the hand. "Come on in. I'll have Cotton bring your things in later."

She was all eyes as she gazed around the outside of the house. "This place is just as grand as you described, sweetie," she said as she went up the back steps.

"Aunt Mandy, this is Fred Mills. He is staying here for a couple of nights."

"A pleasure," Mr. Mills said as he took her hand. "Your niece has certainly looked forward to your visit. You are quite brave to make that long drive from Florida."

"I've been used to travel, but these days, I just take my time and stay at various places along the way," she smiled proudly. "My caddy and I do quite well together. Where are you from, Mr. Mills?"

"Please call me Fred," he insisted. "I'm from St. Louis and I came to have Thanksgiving dinner with my nephew in Dresden."

"Oh, what a shame you won't be joining us," she flirted as she took off her coat. "You would make a mighty fine dinner partner!"

They both chattered and laughed as I observed them. I wanted to tell her about John arriving later, but I couldn't get a word in between the two of them. Aunt Mandy still had her charm, just like my dad. She was dressed in winter white slacks and a blazer, which was just her style. She had more wrinkles than when I last saw her and now her hair was completely white. All in all, aging had been good to her. I got her settled in with a cup of coffee and then showed her the downstairs. She loved Josephine's guest quilt and couldn't wait to sign her name. When Cotton brought in her things, we went up to the Wildflower Room, which she admired.

CHAPTER 24

Mr. Mills went on his way to visit with relatives for the day, leaving my aunt and me free to visit in front of the fire. I loved hearing her talk because she had a slight southern drawl which fit her perfectly.

When I told her my friend John would be joining us around the cocktail hour, she grinned.

"And what is his purpose in coming to Borna, if I may inquire?" There was an unmistakable mischievous lilt in her question.

"He's a writer and lives on the first floor of the condo I have in South Haven. My condo is on the second floor," I explained in a serious tone. "He's going to write a story about East Perry County for the magazine he writes for. He's also written some books. I was very impressed when I Googled him. You'll love him! It's too bad he's so young." I smiled and she picked up on my message.

"Nonsense, honey," she replied as she crossed her legs. "As you get on in years, those age gaps mean nothing. There can be really old thirty-year-old men, you know. I have a couple of gents that are younger than me at my residence, and we have a grand time!"

"That's great," I said, suppressing a little giggle.

"Tell me, my dear, on a more serious note, how you have gotten on since Clay's death?" she said, turning her head aside.

I wasn't prepared for this question. "After I discovered more darkness in my marriage following his accident, I became pretty depressed and bitter," I explained. "I wanted to literally kill a dead man! Does that make sense? Thank goodness Clay left this house and property to me in his will, because it has saved my life."

She nodded, indicating that she understood. "I thought there was more to your story when I heard you were leaving South Haven," she observed. "If it makes you feel any better, I've cursed a dead man or two in my life."

It felt so good to laugh together.

"Oh, Aunt Mandy, I'm so glad you came," I said, putting my hand on hers. "After losing my relationship with the Myers and Jack living so far away, I really miss not having family around. Getting your letter was so timely."

She smiled at me affectionately. "Say, I happen to know you must have a lot of food preparation to attend to for tomorrow, so how about putting me to work?"

"No, you're company," I resisted.

"I am family, remember," she chided gently.

"Okay, how about you set the dinner table for tomorrow," I suggested, pointing to my cabinet of china. "I'll start some prep work in the kitchen."

"Good idea," she said, getting up from her seat. "I haven't set a pretty table in a long time."

My heart was filling up with love and excitement as we began our duties. I had easily picked up on the dry sense of humor that she shared with my late father.

Mr. Mills returned around five to change his clothes for a family dinner. He didn't hesitate for a second when we asked him to join us for a cocktail before he left. As we relaxed for a few moments, my phone rang. It was John telling me he had just turned onto Road A toward Borna. My heart skipped a beat knowing he was this close.

Just as Mr. Mills went out the door, John pulled into the driveway. I announced to Aunt Mandy that John was here and I was going outside to greet him.

"You're here, you're really here!" I shouted. He enveloped me in a big hug. I pulled back, fearing a kiss would come next. "Come on in! That was Mr. Mills, a guest who is leaving for the evening. My Aunt Mandy is inside and she is dying to meet you."

"I can't wait," he said, holding onto my arm.

Aunt Mandy graciously greeted him when I made the introductions. "Young man, I'll bet you are ready for a cocktail after that long drive. What can we get for you?" Aunt Mandy had quickly assumed the role of hostess!

"I can see that Kate has quickly trained you in the hospitality business, so I'll take a Cabernet, if you have it," he responded happily.

"I'll get that," I quickly interjected. "You two go sit by the fire."

When I rejoined them, I could hardly get a word in! Aunt Mandy was full of questions. John bragged about my ambitious business venture and described how we both enjoyed our condos by the lake. I brought out a light tray of bruschetta, cheese, sausages, olives, and slices of my homemade bread for our supper. It couldn't have been a more pleasant visit.

CHAPTER 25

Aunt Mandy excused herself around eight, complaining that she had enjoyed too many swallows of wine and saying that it had been a long day. I walked her up the stairs to wish her a good night. She gave me a wink when she told me to enjoy the rest of the evening.

When I came down the stairs, John was examining the guest house quilt in the entry hall.

"Where would you like me to sign?" he asked, picking up my designated pen.

"Anywhere you like," I said. "Don't forget to sign only your name. I don't want any clever remarks or artwork."

He laughed. "You can't tell a writer what to write," he teased.

I shook my head and walked toward the living room. "How about a nightcap, Mr. Baker?" I asked as I saw him write his name on the quilt.

"Nightcap?" he gave me a questioning look. "Does the town shut down at the strike of nine?"

I had to chuckle. "Actually, there is a bit of truth to that," I affirmed, going into the kitchen. "Most folks get up early and turn in early."

John joined me as I poured a glass of wine for each of us. "I really like your aunt," John began as he watched me slide his drink closer to him.

"Isn't she sweet?" I added. "I see so much of my dad in her.

I have so many questions to ask her." I paused and took a slow sip. "So, John, now that you are my guest, how about filling me in on South Haven."

He paused. "It seems we are going to have an early winter, unfortunately," he claimed as he took his first sip of wine. "I have to say that I'm pleased with how the condo association keeps up the grounds and provides winter maintenance."

"I'm glad to hear that," I replied as I poked the logs in the fireplace. "Just so you know, Jack may spend some time there before he comes here for Christmas. What will you do for the holidays?"

"I may go see my parents in Wisconsin," he said, stretching his arms. "They can't seem to understand that with all the travel I do, it makes it difficult to visit them more often."

"Why didn't you go there for Thanksgiving?" I was very curious to hear his reply.

He grinned. "Well, I had this commitment to write an article about East Perry County, and then I had this dear friend beg me to come visit her," he explained, a smile perched on his lips.

"What?" I teased. "I never beg for anything!"

He laughed. "I'll have to admit that I was very curious to find out about this little piece of heaven you described," he confessed as he touched my shoulder.

I made every effort to ignore his touch and quickly tried to change the subject. "So, what are your plans tomorrow?" I readjusted my sitting position.

"After breakfast, I'll check out a list of places I want to see," he said, taking another sip of wine. "I want to go by the museum first, and then the Saxon Village has me intrigued. That should be a good photo opportunity. I wish you'd come with me."

"Sorry, no." I shook my head. "If you want to have a nice dinner, I need to be up early to get things going."

"I can hardly wait," he said. "Can I do anything to help?"

"I'll let you know if there is," I said with a wink.

"What time is dinner?" he asked. "I can get carried away with time when I'm into a story like this."

"Cocktails are at five and dinner is at six."

Just then, Mr. Mills entered the front door.

"Did you have a good visit?" I asked as he shook off his coat. "Would you like some wine?"

"It was great. Thanks for asking. But, no thanks on the wine, Kate. I've had my limit for the day. I don't think I can eat another bite for a long time. I forgot about all the good food I grew up with around here."

"I wish I had those kinds of memories," voiced John. "I think we had too many holiday meals at the country club."

"How sad," said Mr. Mills, shaking his head. "Some of my best childhood memories are from around the dinner table. So, did your aunt retire for the evening?"

"Yes, she did." I nodded. "She has had a long day."

"She is a mighty fine lady," Mr. Mills noted. "She's pretty sharp and I'd bet she's had an interesting life."

CHAPTER 26

Mr. Mills retired for the night. When he left the room, John gently lifted my hand to his mouth and kissed it tenderly. "At last, I'm able to have some one-on-one time with you," John said quietly.

I quickly pulled my hand away. "John, the last thing I want my guests to think is that we have a romantic relationship," I said with a serious tone.

John smiled at me. "What would you like them to think?" he asked, teasing me. "I'll certainly do my best to cooperate."

"You know what I'm saying," I stammered, feeling embarrassed.

"Why are you afraid to get close to me?" he asked, more serious now and leaning forward to look into my eyes. "Is there someone here in Borna that you're interested in?"

The question took me by surprise. "No, no, I'm not seeing anyone," I defended myself. "I told you before that I'm not willing to commit to anyone. That's why I like my friendship with you."

"As long as I don't get too close, right?" he said softly.

"You have no business getting close to me in the first place," I countered, raising my voice to a loud whisper. "Don't you want to find someone near your age and get married someday?"

"Hey, hey, I didn't ask you to marry me. I just want to get inside your head and be your friend."

Now I was really embarrassed. "You are my friend, but…," I couldn't find the words.

"Relax, Kate," he said, taking my hand again. "You have nothing to fear but fear itself."

We burst into laughter.

"Am I right?"

"You are right," I admitted. "So, will you be sure to visit the Red Creek Winery tomorrow?"

He nodded. "Nice way to change the subject, but yes, I figure I should still be able to get some color shots from the view out there," he expressed. "The winery has a nice website."

"And the business really deserves some publicity."

"I'll do what I can, boss," John teased. "I guess I'd better turn in. And, I noticed you have the two of us separated by a whole floor."

I had to admit that I enjoyed his attention, sense of humor, and the way he made me feel. I smiled and wished him a good night.

CHAPTER 27

It was dark when I pulled myself out of bed. Luckily, I had planned an easy breakfast casserole, fruit, and blueberry muffins for the breakfast menu. It was a routine I could do in my sleep. Once I had breakfast under control, I could put the twelve-pound turkey in the oven.

I walked down the quiet, dark stairs, hoping not to wake anyone. I welcomed the aroma of coffee, thanks to a preset option on the coffeemaker. After I poured myself a cup, I looked out the back and front doors to make sure I didn't see a pile of coal. So far, I couldn't see any evidence of any such nonsense.

My phone delivered a text sound, so I grabbed it off the counter. It was Jack, saying he was at the airport in New York and was about to take off for a couple of days and would spend them in South Haven. It was good to hear and it confirmed that I had made a good decision by keeping a condo in South Haven for both of us. I texted back, wishing him a happy Thanksgiving and asking him to give Jill my love.

With the turkey in the oven, I ran upstairs to change before any guests appeared. I could hear Aunt Mandy stirring in her bedroom. As I dressed, I had to admit to myself that I was taking extra care to look nice for John. I knew I was fooling no one, because I was the age I was and my girlish figure was evaporating. When I came downstairs, John and Mr. Mills were helping themselves to the coffee.

"Good morning, gentlemen," I greeted them, feeling in good spirits.

We exchanged experiences regarding how well we slept as I proceeded to get breakfast on the table. John wanted to get on his way, so he was the first to eat.

"I'll wait until Mandy can join us," Mr. Mills decided.

"She'll be down shortly," I assured him.

"Smelling that turkey sure makes me wish I was joining all of you this evening," Mr. Mills confided as he sat down at the table.

"Good morning," said Aunt Mandy, looking very sharp in a powder blue skirt and sweater. She always wore pearls, which complemented her white hair. "My goodness, sweetie, this table is delightful and I'm famished. How about you, Fred?"

These two were certainly hitting it off!

John finished his breakfast quickly and said he'd be back by the cocktail hour. While Aunt Mandy and Mr. Mills enjoyed a leisurely breakfast, I stayed in the kitchen making pumpkin pie.

A knock at the door caused me to jump in surprise. It was Ellie. "Come on in, neighbor," I said, giving her a hug. "Happy Thanksgiving!"

"You too, girlfriend," she said, eyeing my pumpkin pie. "It sure smells good in here!"

"John is coming to interview you today," I announced happily. "He just left to drive around the area. He'll be going to the Saxon Village and the museum before he comes to see you, I think."

"Great," Ellie responded. "I just came by to meet your aunt and then I have to get going and help Kelly in the kitchen."

I took Ellie into the dining room and introduced her to Aunt Mandy and Mr. Mills.

"You have been such a gift to my Katy."

"Well, thank you," Ellie blushed. "She has been a gift to me as well. I hope she brings you to the winery before you leave."

"I hope so, too," expressed Aunt Mandy. "I'm anxious to meet that Friendship Circle I keep hearing so much about."

Mr. Mills told Ellie he would be leaving Borna after his family's meal this evening and regretted not having the time to check out her winery on this particular visit.

Out the door Ellie went and part of me wished I would be there with her for her white tablecloth dinner, just as I had been last year. I finally got the pie in the oven before I called Maggie to wish her a happy Thanksgiving.

"A happy day to you as well," she responded. "I'm so glad you called."

"So, what time are you expecting Jack?" I asked with interest. "I am so happy he'll be with all of you."

"Well, dinner will be at six, but I don't know when Jill plans to see him today," she revealed. "Did John make it there?"

"Yes, he did," I said, taking a deep breath. "He left early this morning to interview folks and take photos."

"So, he really is going to make this a business trip?" Maggie asked, not able to conceal her sarcasm.

"Of course," I joked. "I think he's going to fall in love with this whole county!"

"Well, just don't let him fall in love with you," Maggie teased back.

I laughed aloud. "How is your friend, Max?" I inquired,

thinking of how often I'd felt the need to change the subject in the last twenty-four hours.

"We just saw him Saturday night and he asked about you," she answered. "He is still staying at the Carriage Guest House. I think he may have worked out a deal with them."

"My aunt is really enjoying my other guest, Mr. Mills," I mentioned. "It's fun to watch them."

"Please tell her hello for me," Maggie requested.

"Hug my son for me, okay?" I requested.

"I will," she assured me. "Don't eat too much and keep that Mr. Baker at bay, you hear?"

I smiled. "I'll do my best. Love you," I said, ending the call.

CHAPTER 28

A
fter I hung up with Maggie, I made a mental note to call Carla. Mr. Mills said he needed to be on his way. As I watched him say good-bye to my aunt, I got the impression they may have exchanged contact information. He sure had made Aunt Mandy's visit extra special.

Aunt Mandy helped rearrange the dinner table before she excused herself to go upstairs to her room. I stayed focused on my cranberry relish and other menu items. When I felt everything was under control for the day, I went upstairs to call Carla and change my clothes. When Carla answered, she said she was preparing a dinner for her neighbors.

"Maggie said you are entertaining your downstairs neighbor from the condo," Carla baited me for more information.

"Yes, he's been out today working on information for his magazine article."

"When I was cleaning your condo last week, I saw him go into his place downstairs," Carla informed me. "He is a looker, just like Maggie said."

"I think you're right," I said with a laugh.

"Would you mind asking him if he could use a cleaning lady?" she asked tentatively. "I could use another client or two."

"That's a great idea, Carla. I'll ask him."

We said our good-byes and I wished Carla could be here with me as she had been for so many years at my home in

South Haven. I looked at my watch and did a quick makeup check in the mirror. I rushed downstairs to prepare the appetizers before John returned. Since Aunt Mandy's room was quiet, I assumed she was taking a nap. I prepared a cheese ball and a plate of shrimp cocktail, which I placed on the coffee table in the living room. John then returned, carrying a large package wrapped in brown paper.

"Did you have a good day?" I inquired, eager to learn what he had experienced today.

"Very good," he nodded as he took off his jacket. "I would have liked to have had more time. Are we alone?"

"Yes, why?" I said, glancing around to make certain. "I think Aunt Mandy is napping."

"I have a little Christmas gift for you since I won't be here to give it to you then," John announced, unable to hide his excitement.

"No, John," I protested. "That is just not necessary."

"I wanted you to have this so you wouldn't forget South Haven," he said, handing me the package.

As I took it from him, the brown paper easily fell to the floor. I couldn't believe my eyes! It was a painting of the red lighthouse that was the signature destination of South Haven. It was a 9" x 12" beauty in a simple antique frame.

"Do you like it?" he asked, looking into my eyes.

"I love it! It looks like Gene Rantz's work that I see in Michigan," I observed. "This is so special! I don't know what to say. Thank you so much, John." I leaned in to give him a hug. He pulled me closer as I held onto the painting and then gently tipped my chin to place a kiss on my lips. Our eyes met and it was clear that neither of us knew what to do next.

"I'm glad I could make you happy," he said quietly as I backed away slowly.

"This does make me happy, John," I added with a smile. "I will think of you and South Haven every time I look at it."

"That was my full intent."

I walked toward the living room and placed the painting on a chair so I could look at it from afar.

"I'm going up to change," John announced. "Pour me some of that good Cab if you still have some."

I nodded. Just then, I heard Aunt Mandy coming down the stairs. I was grateful for her timing. She saw me looking at the painting.

"What's this?"

"John brought this with him to give to me for Christmas," I explained, feeling suddenly awkward. "I love it, don't you?"

"I've always adored that lighthouse," she began. "I like the frame. Do you have a place in mind to hang it?"

"Not yet," I said, walking back to the kitchen. "Are you ready for a cocktail?"

"That would be lovely and I'm eyeing this scrumptious-looking shrimp," she responded as she sat on the couch and began to help herself.

When John returned, he was wearing a sport coat and looking very sharp. He blushed as we showered him with compliments.

CHAPTER 29

W e finally sat down to admire the succulent, roasted turkey that I had placed in front of John, since he had offered to do the carving. I poured champagne and made sure every dish was in its place with the appropriate utensils.

"I'd like to make a toast to our charming hostess, Kate, who has made our trip to Borna very special," John said, holding up his glass.

"I'll drink to that," Aunt Mandy said in jest. "I'll just embellish a toast to my dear niece and her handsome guest from South Haven!" We raised our glasses again and cheered.

"It's my turn," I insisted, after I swallowed the first drink. "Here's to being thankful for all our blessings, which includes family and friends. Let's hold hands and I'll say grace. I began, "There is so much gratefulness in this room, Heavenly Father. Thank you for bringing me here to Borna and letting me share my love with family and friends. Bless our families who are not with us today. Keep them safe in their travels and bless this food we are about to share. Amen."

My amen was echoed by both Aunt Mandy and John. When I looked at John, it seemed as if his eyes were watering. Was saying grace before a meal new to him? Aunt Mandy coughed gently to avoid her emotions. I was proud that I had held back my tears since I always thought of Jack, so far away, and missed him terribly.

"Who would like white meat?" asked John, breaking the awkward silence.

We dove in, passing the wonderful food and commenting on the fabulous aromas. As Aunt Mandy passed the sweet potatoes, she made a compliment that made me pause and reflect.

"I love the tree carving on the mantle," she commented. "I realized today that it is the image of your lovely maple tree out back."

I nodded, smiling. "Yes, the artist carved it some years back because he admired it so much," I explained.

"What's his name?" Aunt Mandy asked between bites.

"Clark McFadden," I said, swallowing hard. "He's a very well-known artist."

"I'll say," John piped up. "I heard plenty about him just talking to folks today. They are very proud that he is living in the area."

"Yes, they are," I added.

"I understand he did all the custom woodwork in this house," John stated, looking at me for more information. Aunt Mandy looked at me in surprise.

"Yes, he did, and he just finished a lovely, large bar for the banquet center down the street," I said, hoping the subject of conversation would change.

"I guess you got to know him pretty well if he worked here," John said in a teasing manner.

"You might say that," I agreed.

"I hear he is single and would be a good catch for some single woman around here," John continued.

"Is John suggesting something to you, Kate?" Aunt Mandy asked with a wink. "You should pay attention. There can't be too many available suitors in this town!" We all chuckled.

"Okay, you two," I said, getting up to go to the kitchen. "Is anyone ready for dessert?"

"I must have a tiny bit of each, sweetie," Aunt Mandy said. "My figure sure has been put to the test this weekend!"

"Just pumpkin pie for me," requested John. "I get blueberries at home every day, remember?"

"Yes, and I'm very jealous," I said as I listened to him brag to Aunt Mandy.

As I cut into the pie, I wondered how much John knew about my relationship with Clark. Whatever he had possibly heard, I had my mind focused on the fact that my dear friend's health was seriously threatened right now.

We took our coffee and dessert into the living room to enjoy it by the fire. John loved poking the logs and commented about how he wished he had a real fireplace in his condo.

Aunt Mandy headed upstairs after dessert, feeling full and seeking rest. John and I worked together to accomplish the cleanup, leaving us alone to talk. It was good to see John in this setting. He would make someone a good husband one day!

CHAPTER 30

John was up early, preferring only coffee as he prepared to leave for South Haven.

"Thanks for making this trip, John," I said, feeling a bit melancholy. "Now you'll know all the people and places I talk about."

He nodded, giving me a smile. "I envy you a bit," John said as he put on his coat. "I'll let you know when this article comes out. I had a wonderful time. When will you be back in South Haven again?"

"I'm not sure," I said, walking him to the back door. "Ask me after Christmas."

"I'll be waiting," he promised, giving me a hug.

"Safe travels, John." I returned his embrace.

And out the door he went. A little piece of South Haven just went out the door. I took a deep breath, feeling proud of how I had handled his visit.

"Good morning, honey," Aunt Mandy said, sailing into the kitchen.

"Good morning to you," I replied in return. "Did you sleep well?"

"I did until the fragrance of those muffins crept up the stairs," she complained, her smile letting me know she approved. "Our friend certainly got an early start."

"Yes, he only wanted coffee. It sure was nice to have him here."

"Well, sweetie, you certainly know where he lives," she teased.

I wasn't sure how she meant what she said.

"What kind of quiche is this?"

"Bacon and spinach," I said, serving each of us a slice. "Are you still up to going to the Friendship Circle lunch today? It's at Emma's house. I have never been there before."

"Absolutely. I am always up for lunch. It's the highlight of my day back home."

"Great, and if it's not too late in the afternoon, we can stop at Imy's. She owns an antique shop," I suggested. "She is such a sweetheart, and most of my antiques came from her. You may recall that Clay preferred new furniture, so I never could introduce much that was antique. This house begged for period furniture, so its' been quite fun!"

"Oh, honey, you have done a magnificent job here," she gushed. "I wish you were closer so I could give you a few pieces I need to get rid of. I have begun to love bright colors these last few years."

"I decorated the condo differently from this. I wanted it to look like a place on the lake. I've even started a quilt for Jack's room that is all lighthouses. I'm not very far along, but I must show you. Hopefully, I can get it done before Christmas."

"I have an old quilt from your grandmother that you need to have," Aunt Mandy stated. "I'll send it to you when I get home."

"Really?" I asked, perking up. "What's it like?"

"I'm told it's a Feathered Star," she claimed. "It's really in wonderful shape. It's red and green and has such tiny hand-stitched pieces. I can't say for sure that Mother made it. It could have come from my granny."

"It sounds wonderful. If you send it soon, I could display it during the Christmas season."

"I have displayed it a time or two, myself," she admitted. "However, it is ready for a new generation to enjoy!"

CHAPTER 31

Off we went to Emma's house, which took us down the same curvy road that leads to the Saxon Village. Emma's white frame farmhouse sat on top of the hill, sporting a black roof and shutters. On the way, I explained how Emma was the oldest member of the circle and had been somewhat helpful to me with my research of Josephine. When Emma opened the door, she warmly greeted Aunt Mandy and took her to meet some of the early arrivals. The house smelled like cookies had just come out of the oven.

Peggy was the last to arrive, so after my introduction of Aunt Mandy, lunch was served. The large antique dining room table was covered with a lace tablecloth and her mother's china that featured bluebells. Her menu was hot chicken croissants with a side of orange Jell-O salad mixed with carrots and celery and placed on a lettuce leaf. Moving back to Borna reacquainted me with the many recipes that could be made with Jell-O. For dessert, we had a chocolate sheet cake covered with white, fluffy icing.

"First, we must officially welcome Kate's Aunt Mandy. She is visiting here from Florida," Emma announced. "We are so pleased to have you here, but I need to ask your patience as we attend to some business matters."

"Thank you for inviting me, ladies," Aunt Mandy responded graciously.

"We have our list of families for our charity giving," Emma announced. "Please choose one before you leave today. Ruth Ann has generously offered her hall in which to have our wrapping party. Everyone should bring a dish and any wrapping paper you may need for your gifts. Thanks to Kate, this will indeed be a worthy cause and we can really make a difference."

I beamed with pride.

"If I may have the floor, Emma, I would like to ask for as many Christmas quilts as you can possibly find to make sure every business has a quilt to display during the holidays," requested Ellen. "I think this will help our "shop local" campaign and get folks to support our businesses. I think we can quilt the town Christmas, if we try." Some members clapped, excited about the prospect.

"Does it matter what size?" asked Mary Catherine.

"No, we can use all sizes," Ellen explained. "Just drop them off at my house."

"I brought mine with me tonight," Peggy announced, raising her hand.

"Wonderful!" said Ellen with a big smile. "We are going to use quilts wherever we can. Perhaps next year, we can do a Christmas quilt show like Kate had originally intended. There's just not enough time to organize one this year. Now, Ruth Ann, for instance, is putting up Christmas quilts in her banquet hall for the season. It's a marvelous idea! I can't wait to see them! I also want to mention that my girls and I will be having our stollen bake next Thursday. Many of you wanted to help and also wanted to try baking one for yourselves. Just make sure I know you're coming so I can make plenty of space. We have been doing this German tradition for many years."

Aunt Mandy could not believe all the projects our little group had planned.

"I have something to announce," Esther said, raising her voice to be heard. Everyone became silent. "We are going Christmas caroling again this year. We'd like to expand the number of people from last year so we can possibly have two groups. As you know, the elderly in the area really appreciate our visit and it can make their Christmas for them. We'll meet at Concordia's church hall to get our assignments and then return there for refreshments. I'm counting on you, ladies!" The silence quickly turned to chatter.

"Oh, Kate, what a grand Christmas you'll have this year," Aunt Mandy whispered to me.

I nodded and smiled.

After the meeting ended, we left Emma's house behind with the chatter still flowing. "Are you sure you are not too tired to stop by Imy's shop?" I asked Aunt Mandy as I opened her car door.

"I don't want to miss a thing, honey," she quipped. "I can nap anytime and I'm anxious to meet her after everything you've told me about her shop!"

CHAPTER 32

W e pulled up next to another car parked in front of Imy's little shop. Aunt Mandy chuckled at the rustic appearance.

"I heard Kate had a visitor!" Imy said, reaching to shake her hand when we walked in.

"This is my Aunt Mandy from Florida."

Aunt Mandy blushed as she took Imy's hand. "It's so nice to meet you," Aunt Mandy said with a big smile. "What a charming little place you have here!"

"It's a big mess right now, I'm afraid. I'm in the middle of turning my back shed into Santa's Workshop for the holidays. My son made me a nice big sign for it."

"Oh, Imy, what a great idea!" I said, feeling very excited about the prospect. "I love it! So, will it be all Christmas things for sale?"

Imy nodded. "Pretty much. I just have to start unloading some of my things in storage."

"Imy, show us your feather tree and that darling antique village," I suggested. "Have you ever heard of a feather tree, Aunt Mandy?"

"Believe it or not, my grandmother had one in the attic," Aunt Mandy recalled. "She said they would light the candles on Christmas Eve. That must have been a scary sight. Of course, most of her things were sold at her auction."

Imy went on to explain how this was an unusually large

one compared to most. Aunt Mandy fawned over the village when she saw all of the pieces and the picket fence. She watched my excitement as well and told Imy that she would like to buy it for me for Christmas!

"I can't let you do that," I protested. "This is all way too expensive!"

"This should go to someone who appreciates it and has room in a big house for such things," Aunt Mandy stated. "I want to do this for you."

"I don't know what to say," I said, feeling overwhelmed by her generosity.

"You tell her thank you," Imy suggested. "She's right. It does belong somewhere like your guest house. I'll give you the best deal I can."

"That's not necessary," Aunt Mandy corrected. "I've got to spend my money somewhere to help the Borna community."

The purchase turned out to be too large to fit into my car, so Imy offered to deliver the tree.

When we got home, Aunt Mandy went upstairs to rest until dinnertime. Having enjoyed such a big lunch, we agreed to snack on just cheese and veggies during cocktail time.

I checked my phone and a text from John said he was getting close to South Haven and that he had enjoyed his visit. I pictured him going back to snowland and entering his condo. It reminded me of his generous gift, so I went to get the painting and found the perfect spot for it in the kitchen above my coffee bar. The colors were perfect and I would be sure to see it every morning. I really, really loved it!

I, too, felt exhausted from our day, so I went to put my feet up and digest all that had happened today. I made a mental note to email all my Beach Quilters in South Haven and ask them for any extra Christmas quilts they could spare. I knew Cornelia would likely have some class samples I could have or buy. I was getting excited about the stollen bake at Ellen's house. As much as I loved baking, I had never attempted to make a stollen. It was a German tradition that I wanted to include while living in this German village. I made a note of the Christmas caroling. I hadn't done any such thing since grade school and wanted to help Esther accomplish her goal of having two groups.

While I sat there, I took a closer look at the family I had chosen for Christmas gifts. It appeared I had one of many that had a single mother. She was forty-five and her girls were twelve and eight. Her little boy was only three years old. Where on earth was the father? It had been a long time since I had bought for children, but I assumed I could accomplish everything online if I couldn't find it in East Perry.

CHAPTER 33

Toward evening, I made a fire and brought out our veggie and cheese tray. As I poured myself a glass of wine, I remembered the plan to take Aunt Mandy to dinner at Red Creek Winery tomorrow night. When Aunt Mandy joined me, she pointed out the perfect corner in my dining room to place the feather tree. Since I would be having the large, live tree in the living room, the corner location in the dining room was perfect. I told her Cotton had already spotted a tree to cut from my own acreage. I wanted her to meet Cotton and Susie before she left.

"So, what was Christmas like for you and my dad growing up?" I asked, quite out of the blue.

"Oh, honey, I can hardly remember," she said as she sat down in the rocker near the fire. "We didn't have a lot back then, I can tell you that. We were pretty happy with one present, unlike what the kids have today. I do remember spending a Christmas or two with your family, and they spoiled you rotten!"

I laughed. "I'm so glad Jack is coming for Christmas," I said, helping myself to the cheese. "I sure hope he'll like it here. It's so different from New York City."

"How long will he be here?" Aunt Mandy asked, joining me as I snacked.

"Not long, I'm afraid, but that's okay," I answered. "That reminds me that I'd better get his quilt done. I'll go upstairs and get it. Maybe I can make some progress on it this evening."

Aunt Mandy loved that idea.

As I went toward the stairway, I saw a man approach the front door. It was the same man from before that I had assumed was Susan's husband. How could he still be around here? I waited until he rang the doorbell and then I went out onto the porch to talk to him.

"It's me again, Miss Meyr," he greeted. "I'm sorry to bother you again."

How did he know my name? "What is it this time?" I asked curtly as the cold air hit my face.

"Well, I don't believe you were quite accurate in telling me about not seeing a green Volkswagen in the area," he said as he stroked his chin. "We have every reason to believe she is still around here. One fella in Unionville said he was certain he saw her getting gas, and a man at the bar next door to you said he was certain he saw a green Volkswagen parked here at your place."

I shook my head. "I'm afraid I still can't help you. And did you say this person was hiding, as in escaping?" I inquired further.

"Yes siree!" he nodded.

"What's she hiding from?" I asked, mostly to aggravate him. "Is she wanted by the police?"

"You could say that," he said, hesitating. "So you're sayin' you never saw a car here with that description?"

I shook my head. "Just who are you, exactly?" I asked sternly.

"I'm kin to her, you might say," he said, looking down at the porch. "You know you could get in a lot of trouble if you're hiding anything."

"From whom?" I countered, fighting off my aggravation. "You're not the law and there's no one hiding here, so good evening!" I turned around and went inside, leaving him on the porch. Inside, I forgot all about getting the quilt and went immediately to the fire to warm up.

"What on earth was that about, honey? Here, have a sip of your wine."

I took a sip and decided I had to share my concern with someone, so I sat down and told her what had happened with Susan. She listened, horror-struck. She especially squirmed when I told her the man had been here before.

"I had to lie!" I said, pacing the floor. "She may be on the run, but the good news is that she is not with him!"

"Of course," Aunt Mandy said in agreement. "Anyone would do the same thing. Don't beat yourself up over this. The really sad part is that she is still away from her son."

I nodded. "I know," I said sadly. "I just wish she would contact me in some way so I could know she's okay. I really think if he finds her he could kill her, like she said. He is quite determined. I really don't think she's still around here. She talked like she wanted to get away as far as she could."

"Do you think this guy thinks you're hiding her?" Aunt Mandy asked with a worried expression on her face. "You know, he could stalk you for a while just to make sure. You must be very careful these days."

"I know. I'm sorry I spoiled our evening," I said, about to cry.

"Don't you worry. Now, go up and get Jack's quilt!"

CHAPTER 34

It was hard to sleep because I found myself worrying about Susan's safety. Where was she? When I received a late night text from John, it was a nice distraction. I couldn't for the life of me think what John found interesting in me. Why was I even attracted to him? When does a man or woman know what is just friendly behavior between one another and what is actually physical attraction? Perhaps it was just me going through the transition of being a widowed, single person in today's world. Did my early marriage to Clay make me feel deprived when it came to dating? Why did I need any male friends at this point in my life?

Clark had been such a nice and understanding person when I arrived here. He respected my recent hurt and grief. He was understanding and sympathetic at just the right times. He even saved my life from Blade's attack. What was there not to like about a man like this? He was probably comfortable with an independent woman like me. It was obvious he wasn't looking for a romantic relationship, which was fine by me.

After breakfast, Aunt Mandy and I looked over the details of my charity family and discussed what gifts might be appropriate for them. We both agreed that the mother deserved some feminine gifts that she wouldn't buy for herself. We acknowledged that all girls loved clothes, so that would be a good choice for the daughters. The three-year-old toddler would love some books and perhaps a toy that had some moving parts. As we were discussing the possibilities, we were interrupted by a phone call from Ellie.

"Are you both still coming by for dinner this evening?"

"Yes, we plan on it unless the snow becomes heavier," I replied.

"It's not supposed to amount to anything," Ellie replied. "Kelly is planning a good menu, so I hope you can make it."

"We plan on it," I assured her as I hung up.

"Oh, Kate, Imy just pulled in the drive!" Aunt Mandy said as she looked out the bay window.

"Here comes our tree!" I announced as I joined her by the window.

We both cleared the way as Imy single-handedly brought in the feather tree. We told her to place it in the corner before she retrieved the other boxes from her truck.

"I decided you needed some antique ornaments for the tree, so I went through all of mine and brought you some!" Imy shared. "There's a box of little candles that goes to the tree as well."

"That's awesome, Imy!" I cheered. "You didn't have to do that! I forgot it had those attached candle holders on the tree. Thank you."

When Imy finished bringing in the boxes, she joined us for some peppermint tea. She shared more ideas about her Santa's Workshop. We were impressed by her love of Christmas. We told her we would decorate the tree tomorrow morning before Aunt Mandy left to go back to Florida.

Imy said she would be hanging a red and green Pine Tree quilt in her shop for the holidays. She had an extra red and green Nine Patch that she was going to loan to the fire department office next door. Imy, like many others, was the perfect citizen of East Perry that would help us quilt the town Christmas!

CHAPTER 35

Aunt Mandy got all dolled up for our evening at the winery in black wool slacks and a white sweater. Of course, her pearls were perfect for her attire. I dressed much more casually in jeans and a heavy red cable knit sweater.

"I think these snowflakes are sticking," Aunt Mandy announced from the front living room window.

"Don't worry, I think the real snow is not headed our way until a couple of days from now," I assured her. "It'll be our first real snow of the season."

"Well, I need to leave for Florida before that happens, Kate," Aunt Mandy stated firmly. "I've stayed longer than I should have. I am not experienced driving in the snow, remember."

"You're probably right," I admitted. "I just hate to see you go. It's been so great having you here."

"You're welcome to come to sunny Florida anytime, but I don't have much space in my assisted living facility like you have in this wonderful home of yours."

"That's why we have to get you back here as soon as possible," I confirmed.

"Don't you have guests coming soon?" Aunt Mandy asked with concern in her voice.

I nodded.

She persisted, "That's all the more reason for me to get on out of here."

"That's nonsense," I replied. "I only have a mother and daughter coming, and I have placed them in the attic suite. Your being here will not matter. Okay, we must get going. Are you hungry?"

"I'm famished!" Aunt Mandy admitted.

As we drove toward Ellie's winery, I could tell my aunt's nerves were on edge as she observed some of the snow sticking to the ground. Ellie greeted us with open arms as soon as we walked in the door.

"Miss Ellie, your place is quite lovely up here!"

"I'm so glad the two of you decided to come," Ellie said as she gave Aunt Mandy a warm embrace. "Kelly, my cook, has some yummy delicacies for you to choose from. I want you to meet Trout, my right-hand man around here. He can bring you a sampling of our good wines, if you like."

Aunt Mandy grinned.

"We have a table set aside over here with our best view."

"Well, I'm not driving, thank goodness, and I do want to choose a couple of wines to take back home," Aunt Mandy stated as we headed to our assigned table. On the way, Trout embraced her like she was also his favorite aunt. Aunt Mandy loved all of the attention. The place was getting about half full, which was surprising considering the weather outdoors.

We had just finished making our menu choices when Mayor Pelker and his wife walked in the door and said hello. After the introductions, my aunt didn't waste any time telling him what a beautiful community this was. We were all engaged in laughter and conversation when a loud voice from the bar interrupted asking, "What does a guy have to do to get waited on around here?"

Everyone turned around. Clark was standing there! I couldn't believe my eyes. Ellie and I got out of our seats to greet him. Thankfully, Ellie hugged him first, which made it less awkward for me.

"Where in the heck have you been?" Ellie asked after her hug.

"Busy making a buck," he lied.

"It's so good to see you, Clark!" I said, not wanting to end our embrace. Without thinking, I kissed him on the cheek. I didn't care who saw. I could tell he wasn't expecting such a greeting from any of us!

"Please come and join us, Clark," said Ellie.

"Ah, no thanks," he said, shaking his head. "I need to get on home, but I couldn't resist picking up some of Kelley's good gumbo."

"Clark, please come to the table and meet my Aunt Mandy who is visiting from Florida," I said, taking his arm. He slowly followed and rolled his eyes at me.

CHAPTER 36

After all the introductions, Aunt Mandy knew this man had to be special to all of us, and especially to me.

"I have to say how much I admire your work on the carved tree that Kate has on her mantle," Aunt Mandy said. "I'm so pleased I got to meet the local celebrity."

"Thanks, but they all have an inflated opinion about me," he shyly responded.

"Well, you obviously have many talents," she added. "The custom woodwork at Kate's house is very beautiful."

"He doesn't take compliments very well, Aunt Mandy," I said, feeling I needed to explain Clark's behavior.

"I guess she knows you pretty well," Aunt Mandy said teasingly.

"Hey, Clark, your order is ready if you still want it to go," Trout called from the bar.

"Nice to meet you, but I need to be on my way, ladies," Clark said.

"Don't you dare stay away so long again!" Ellie warned. "Will you be here for a while?"

He nodded and turned his attention to Trout.

Ellie looked at me in disbelief. My stomach churned the whole time we were eating. I thought Clark looked thinner, but I was truly happy to see him. Would he contact me soon or would I have to make the next move? I sure wanted an update on his health.

We didn't stay long after we noticed the snow was indeed sticking to the ground. Aunt Mandy reminded me once more that she was not about to drive on the snowy roads. When we arrived home, we turned on the weather channel and learned that the snow was indeed going to melt with the warmer temperatures coming in.

"So, honey, this Clark guy sure is handsome," she began. "I'll bet the ladies around here adore him. Did I pick up on a little magic between you two?"

I snickered. I couldn't believe how observant and outspoken she was. "He's been a good friend ever since I arrived here," I explained. "He's quite different. I liked the way he understood my grief over Clay and how he didn't try to come on to me."

"That is quite commendable, sweetie, but has your friendship grown over time?" Aunt Mandy was obviously fishing.

"Oh, I suppose you could say that, but we both aren't looking for anything more than that," I explained as I was thinking about him.

"Well, you should think about what that means," Aunt Mandy expressed.

"Aunt Mandy, you are something!" I said, laughing. "What time do you want breakfast tomorrow morning?"

"Take it from me, life is better when shared with someone," she said with a big grin. "Eight o'clock will be fine."

We kissed each other goodnight. I went into the kitchen to mix up the quiche she loved so much so it would be ready in the morning. I also took one of Mrs. Grebing's cherry coffee cakes out of the freezer and set it on the counter. As I worked away, Clark was on my mind. I tried to remember if he had lost any hair. He was wearing a baseball cap, so I couldn't really tell. It certainly had to be a great unplanned welcome home for him when he saw all of us gathered in one place.

I turned on the alarm and headed upstairs to bed. Would things be different now that Clark was back? He'd made me feel special before he left by confiding in me about his cancer. Did he regret that?

When I looked out my bedroom window to see if the snow was still accumulating, I saw a pick-up truck pull out of my driveway. Was it just turning around? *There was something familiar about that truck,* I thought.

I brushed my teeth and changed into white knit pajamas. I checked my phone to see if there was a text from John, but there wasn't. It was then that a horrible memory flashed in my mind. The truck I just saw was like the one that pulled into my driveway when I first started working on my house! A grungy man, his wife, and several teenagers had come barging into the house and said they were there to buy it. I quickly found the courage to tell them to get out of the house immediately and that the house was not for sale. I was certain now that it was the same truck. I never did get their license plate number. They had to know by now that I meant business and expected to remain here. What were they doing here? I convinced myself I couldn't do much about anything this evening. I had to remind myself that there were many pick-up trucks in this town and that I may be wrong. I put my pillow on top of my head and convinced myself to go to sleep.

CHAPTER 37

M y alarm went off, causing me to jump. I had been in the middle of having a horrible dream that my guest house was full of noisy, dysfunctional people that wouldn't leave. I put on my robe so I could quickly go downstairs to put the quiche in the oven for breakfast, hoping to forget the dream entirely.

My first cup of coffee brought me back to reality. The thought of Aunt Mandy leaving today was sad. It felt so good having a family connection, even though she was living miles and miles away from me.

When Aunt Mandy came down to join me, she was also in her robe, still looking charming in her favorite color of blue which complimented her so. "Good morning, sweetie," she greeted as she gave me a kiss on the cheek. "You were right; the snow seems to be gone, so I should probably get on the road sometime today."

"We were going to decorate the tree this morning, remember?" I reminded her.

"Well, we can still do that after breakfast, can't we?" she asked. "I'm fascinated with this tree and would love nothing more than to see it in its finest, along with seeing the village set up as well."

"Great," I said, feeling better. "Why don't you consider leaving tomorrow?"

"Now sweetie, I know what you're up to but I do have

things to attend to when I return," she explained kindly.

The knock on the door caught us by surprise. I left Aunt Mandy at the dining room table to see who it was. It was Susie, Cotton, and Amy Sue. "My goodness! Good morning. Come on in."

"We haven't been able to come by and check on you for a while and we were pretty sure this was a day that Susie was supposed to be here," Cotton explained. "I thought I'd drop her off if you still need her."

"Yes, yes, by all means," I remembered. "Please come on in and meet my Aunt Mandy. It's so good to see Amy Sue for a change. We've been so busy with Aunt Mandy's visit that I honestly forgot about you coming. You caught us both in our robes, I'm afraid."

"Oh, Miss Kate, we can come back at another time if you like," Susie offered.

"No, no, please come on in," I encouraged.

When we went into the dining room, Aunt Mandy had vanished to her bedroom to change. "Please join us for some breakfast. We have plenty. I'm sure my aunt just went up to change."

"Amy Sue, how are you, pretty girl?' I asked wanting to hug her.

She quickly got closer to her mother. "She's very shy," Susie explained.

"Kate, does that white Cadillac out back belong to your aunt?" Cotton asked with a concerned expression on his face.

I nodded.

"It's something, isn't it?" I snickered.

"Have you looked outside this morning at all?" Cotton asked.

"No, why?"

"I'm afraid your coal visitors returned," he announced, shaking his head. "They put coal on the hood of your aunt's car."

"What? Oh, no, no!" I said, rushing to look out the back window.

"Don't worry none, Miss Kate, we'll help you clean that all up," Susie consoled me.

"This is horrible!" I said, feeling sick. "She can't see this!"

"I'll go out right now and get started on cleaning this up," Cotton offered.

"Well, good morning, everyone!" Aunt Mandy greeted. "What's all the excitement about?"

Cotton and I looked at each other. "Aunt Mandy, this is Cotton, my good friend that I've told you about. This is his wife, Susie, who's cleaning today. And, this cutie pie is Amy Sue."

"So nice to meet you, folks," Aunt Mandy responded politely. "Kate wanted me to be sure to meet you before I left to go home. Thank you so much for helping my special niece."

"I've asked them to join us for breakfast," I said in a shaky voice.

"Excellent, please do," Aunt Mandy said with a big smile. "How old is our Amy Sue?"

"She's two and pretty shy, I'm afraid," Susie replied. Amy Sue gripped her mother even tighter.

Everyone sat down at the table and I brought out the food. How in the world were we going to explain Borna's mischief to Aunt Mandy?

CHAPTER 38

A unt Mandy was full of questions and compliments as we made casual conversation throughout breakfast. Cotton, Susie, and Amy Sue had arrived earlier and I had convinced them to join us for breakfast. When I saw that Aunt Mandy had eaten most of her meal, I began a conversation about there being a few pranksters in town. She looked at me strangely and I changed the topic. I decided not to tell her about any previous coal dumping but slowly led into the topic about what Cotton, Susie, and I had discovered this morning. I watched her face change as I shared the news. "Don't panic, Aunt Mandy, but someone put some coal on your car last night," I confessed.

"What? Coal on my car?" she asked, like she didn't believe me.

I nodded.

"Don't worry, I'll get it cleaned up," Cotton assured her. "It will be all clean for your trip."

Aunt Mandy slowly got out of her chair and looked out the window of the sunporch. She shook her head in disbelief. "My, oh my, what a disturbing prank that is," she finally responded. "Do you have any idea who could have done this, Kate?"

"I might, but I don't know for sure. I am so, so sorry this happened! It has nothing to do with you."

"I'll go ahead and get started," Cotton said, getting out of his chair. "Susie, you'll need to help me."

"Nonsense," I stated. "Susie, you stay in the house and I'll help Cotton."

"Okay, Miss Kate," Susie agreed. "I'll start cleaning up the kitchen. Amy Sue will be happy if you want to show her this book." She looked at Aunt Mandy.

"I can do that," Aunt Mandy quickly agreed, smiling. "I feel bad for all of you having to do such dirty jobs."

"Let's get started," I instructed Cotton. "I'll meet you outside as soon as I change my clothes."

We all kicked into gear determined to complete our various tasks. When I joined Cotton outside, he had already accomplished a great deal. Our biggest concern was that the grimy coal would leave permanent marks on the hood of the car. While we were outdoors, I told Cotton about recognizing the pick-up truck that pulled out of my driveway late last night. He shook his head and said it was time to report some of this. He thought the family had to be local and were probably carrying a grudge against me when I rejected them the time they stormed into my house.

CHAPTER 39

To our surprise, Aunt Mandy's car cleaned up nicely and looked as good as new. Every now and then, I'd see her looking out the window with curiosity and wonder on her face. Cotton was furious about the nearly constant harassment I had received since I came to Borna. He said he would make an extra effort to keep an eye out for this pick-up truck and would ask around town about who might have access to coal. When we finished, Cotton went on his way and said he'd be back soon to collect Susie and Amy Sue.

"Aren't you two a pretty sight?" I said, grinning at Aunt Mandy and Amy Sue in the rocking chair.

"She is a precious thing, isn't she?" Aunt Mandy admired the child as she rocked slowly. "I sure hate to leave here knowing you have issues like this going on. I think I'll just wait until tomorrow morning to leave."

I smiled and nodded my approval. "Oh, I'm not too worried, and you shouldn't be either," I consoled her as I sat down on the couch. "We'll put all this aside and have a nice dinner as we decorate this feather tree."

"Sounds wonderful," Aunt Mandy agreed. "I think our little darling just fell asleep." Aunt Mandy kissed Amy Sue's forehead. "It's been a long time since I've held a little one."

I picked up Amy Sue and laid her on the couch for us to watch while Susie was cleaning.

"I hate to elaborate on the topic, Kate, but has anyone done things like this to you before?"

I nodded, knowing I needed to decide exactly how much to tell her. I chose to share my theory of the folks I suspected and told her the story of the family that stormed into my house while I was restoring it. The look on her face was one of great worry. "It may be just the teenagers in this family causing this," I guessed. "You know, I have to be careful about how much I want people to know about my troubles. I am trying to run a business and I want to protect my business reputation. It is important that people feel safe when they stay here. Some say this community is made up of those who have and those who have not, but I'm not sure I agree with that. I can see a bit of revenge and jealousy going on here. Sharla Lee from the museum said there are many in this county below the poverty line. The elderly stay in their homes as long as they can on their social security instead of going to a nice assisted facility or nursing home."

"It takes a pretty penny, my dear," Aunt Mandy added. "Thank goodness my husband provided me that luxury. I do understand why you just can't call for help for every little thing. Your location is so visible here on Main Street. I'll bet people try to guess what you are up to every time they drive by."

I nodded. "Yes, that's why someone observed Susan's green Volkswagen in just a short amount of time. It was visible from the street," I acknowledged.

"What has happened here?" Susie asked as she entered the room and saw Amy Sue asleep on the couch. "You must have the magic touch!"

"She seems to be a very pleasant, sweet child," Aunt Mandy said.

"I hope she stays that way, because she's about to have a brother or sister joining her this spring!" Susie announced, taking us by surprise.

"Really, Susie?" I asked, happily. "How wonderful!"

"I guess so," she said, shaking her head in wonder. "We didn't exactly plan it this way, and I don't know how we're going to feed another mouth and make room in that small house we have."

That was not a pretty picture, I thought to myself. "When are you due?" I asked, as I wondered what this meant for me and how it would affect Susie being able to clean for me.

"First part of May, best we can tell," she revealed. "Thank goodness that I'm feeling better than I was!"

"Well, honey, it's a real blessing, no matter how you look at it," claimed Aunt Mandy. "It's never the right time to have another child, and it's great for Amy Sue to have a sibling."

"Well, congratulations," I offered with some hesitation. "How did Cotton take the news?"

She took a deep breath. "Well, he's adjusting, but he had to get the truck repaired and then we had to help my mom with a few of her bills, so he's been under a lot of stress," she confessed. I realized that their situation was just like some of the folks on our charity list who just couldn't seem to get ahead.

CHAPTER 40

I left the two of them chatting as I went into the kitchen to think about Susie's latest news. I knew I was the main source of their income, especially in the winter. I had to do something to help, which meant this would be another charity family to buy for. Cotton arrived a short time later, and before I gave him a chance to report to me, I congratulated him on the news. He didn't say anything, but he did give me a big smile.

"I went to Clem's Auto when I left here," he said, his hands on his hips. "It's where a lot of the locals hang out when they're out of work. I thought I'd poke around and ask a few questions without anyone getting suspicious."

"So, did you learn anything?"

"I may have, but let me check things out a bit before I tell you too much," he said as he scratched his head.

"Just be very careful, Cotton," I warned. "I don't want you to end up being a target."

He smiled and assured me that he would be fine.

The little family left for home as soon as Susie gathered the items she had brought for Amy Sue. Aunt Mandy and I discussed the terrible stress they must be feeling. As we talked, I started some homemade vegetable soup that I knew would be healthy for both of us. It was certain to be a treat for my aunt. While I chopped the veggies, Aunt Mandy started opening the boxes of ornaments that Imy had delivered. We tried to keep the rest of the day light and fun since it was our last day together. I began making homemade bread. Aunt Mandy was amused by the activity and I was beginning to suspect that she had never made homemade bread herself. I made an extra loaf for her to take home.

"Did you cook this way for Clay?" Aunt Mandy asked as she watched me mess up my entire kitchen.

"I did when he was around, but he traveled so much. Plus, we were always entertaining clients and that usually took us to the country club," I explained as I wiped flour from my face.

"Did you resent his traveling?"

"Not really, but looking back, I should have," I said, shaking my head. "I'm afraid I was very naïve."

"What do you mean by that?" She situated herself to give me her full attention.

It was a painful question to answer. "I didn't learn until after Clay's death that he was seeing someone at the time and had a reputation for being quite the ladies' man, according to one of his co-workers."

Aunt Mandy's eyes grew wide, however, she recovered quickly. "I think nearly every woman at one time or another has to bear that cross, my dear," she quipped. "Back in my day, some of us just swallowed our pride and hoped it would go away. The consequences of doing anything about it were just too great."

"Are you talking about yourself?"

"Of course, and to my husband's credit, it did pass," she acknowledged sadly. "He seemed to be truly sorry, and we had a lot of good years after that."

"I'm glad for you," I said slowly, taking this in. I was grateful for the task of putting ornaments on the tree and reached for one as I said, "It's been very frustrating because I couldn't confront Clay after I knew. I had so many questions and so much anger that I wanted him to know about. It's hard to yell and punish a dead man!"

She gave me a hard look. "Oh, I don't know about that," she retorted. "I think you can and should! I'm sorry you had to go through that, honey."

"Well, all was not lost. I inherited this property," I said with a smile.

"That's my girl," Aunt Mandy responded. "You have such great friends, and to own this little gem in the center of this charming town is truly a blessing!"

I nodded.

"Is there anything to put on the top of the tree?"

"We'll find something if there isn't anything in these boxes," I vowed. "Last year, I had nothing but white lights on my big, live tree. I purchased one ornament from the church tour and that was it. My plans for this year are still pretty simple. I want to make sugar cookies and tie them with red ribbons and hang them on the tree. Did you string popcorn and cranberries when you were little? I want to do that."

"Can't say we did, but I knew some folks who did," Aunt Mandy recalled. "You are pretty ambitious."

"I will take pictures for you," I assured her. "You know, you could always come back for Christmas, but I wouldn't advise driving. I could send Cotton to pick you up at the airport."

She looked down like she was sad. "I would love to be here with you, but I have a dear friend Mildred who lives in the same building and she really depends on me," she revealed. "She has no family, and I know she's counting the days and hours until I return. I need to stay with her through the holidays."

"That is very commendable and sweet," I said, patting her arm. "She is lucky to have you!"

CHAPTER 41

Undisturbed, we finished decorating the tree. It certainly was like no other with its fragile and home-made ornaments. There wasn't anything appropriate for the top, but I would think of something. We shared a quiet meal of comfort food and great conversation. I couldn't believe how sharp and wise my aunt was at nearly eighty. She was such a southern lady and so full of life. There were times that her memory wasn't as sharp, but neither was mine!

We went up to bed, feeling sad that in the morning, we would have to say good-bye. In my journal, I had recorded many observations about our visit together. Was Aunt Mandy right when she hinted about me seeking Clark's attention and that life was better sharing it with someone? I honestly felt happy for the first time, being able to be myself for a change. Was it possible for a woman to have it all? Could a woman achieve her own goals and have a husband and truly be happy with that?

I turned out the light thinking about my two best friends, Ellie and Maggie. One was happily single and one was happily married. I accepted that. What would I do without them? It seemed to me that good friends and satisfying relationships of various kinds could certainly be a replacement if a woman did not have a man in her life. Was I just fooling myself?

The next morning, Aunt Mandy and I came down the stairs at the same time. It was early and we were both subdued. "Would you like some coffee to take with you?" I asked. "I packaged some muffins and a loaf of bread for you to take."

She smiled. "You are a doll, honey," she said, shaking her head in disbelief. "I'll bet I've gained five pounds during my visit."

I smiled, thinking that I must have as well.

"I'll help take your things to the car," I said as I picked up two of her bags. "The weather looks pretty good for you today."

When we got outdoors, Aunt Mandy bragged about her clean car. She said I should thank Cotton once again. We hugged and hugged while I wished her a safe trip. She promised to call when she arrived. I saw tears in her eyes and the thought of her leaving choked me up as well. As I waved good-bye to her, I wondered if I would ever see her again.

I went inside and poured myself a cup of coffee to allow myself a moment to get a grip on my emotions. It was good that I had guests coming today because I really needed to get my mind on something else.

I went upstairs to get dressed and then began to strip the linens off of Aunt Mandy's bed. On her dresser, leaned against a lamp, was an envelope with my name on it. I quickly opened it. It read: *"Darling Kate, Thank you so much for the most pleasant visit of my lifetime. I'm so proud of your perseverance in making Borna your new home. Your father would be very proud of you. Please remember to not only open your heart to your guests, but for yourself as well. As always, Your loving Aunt Mandy."* I sat on the edge of her bed and cried. What a special lady she was! It made me realize how family really counts in our lives.

I returned downstairs just in time to see Ellie turn into my driveway. I quickly checked my appearance to disguise my sadness before I went to the back door to let her in.

"I see your aunt has left."

I took a deep breath. "Yes, she just left and I miss her already," I said softly.

"I knew you'd be down. It sounds like you could use some cheering up. Would you like to go somewhere today to get your mind on something else?"

I shook my head. "Thanks, but I have some guests coming this afternoon," I explained.

"Oh? Where are they from?" Ellie asked, interested.

"I think she said Des Moines," I answered. "It's a mother and her daughter. Would you like some coffee?"

"I would," she said, following me into the kitchen. "It sounds like we're going to get some snow again."

CHAPTER 42

We sat at the kitchen island and talked about my aunt's visit and how the projects were coming along for the Friendship Circle. We were interrupted by a knock at the back door. It was Cotton. "Hey, what's going on?" I asked.

"Well, I think I found the truck you were talking about," he said, clearly anxious.

"Hi, Cotton," greeted Ellie, coming out onto the sunporch to join us.

"Hi, Miss Ellie," he said politely.

"Ellie has not been informed about this latest incident, Cotton," I explained. "I'll fill her in later."

Ellie looked at me strangely but did not insist on hearing the details at this moment.

"What did you learn?"

"I was out at old man Carter's farm delivering a motor he needed, and when I got there, I noticed there was a pickup truck parked in front of a rundown trailer next door. It looked like the one you described. When we finished unloading, I asked Mr. Carter who lived there. He called them some unladylike names and said they moved in not too long ago. He said the trailer had been vacant for quite some time before the family arrived. He couldn't believe it was habitable, especially with as many family members as appeared to be living there."

That sounded accurate so far.

"I asked if he knew where the guy worked and he said that, best he could tell, he did odd jobs here and there."

"You didn't approach them, did you?" I asked, concerned.

"No, but what I was about to say was that I pulled my truck up next to his like I was trying to turn around, and I saw some pieces of coal in the back of his truck, along with a bunch of other junk." Cotton revealed. As he was telling his tale, the volume of his voice had increased.

"What's going on here?" Ellie cut in.

I ignored her question in favor of asking one of my own. "So, now what, Cotton?"

"Well, Miss Kate, you'll have to decide whether to report this or not," he stated, shrugging his shoulders. "It may be nothing but a nuisance report, but it'll make someone from the law pay him a visit that may scare the crap out of him. Excuse me, ladies. And, that may be the end of it."

"Thanks, Cotton. I really appreciate all of your trouble," I said affectionately.

"It was just a fluke to drive out that direction," he explained, clearly proud of his discovery.

Ellie stood with her hands on her hips still waiting to be included in the conversation and caught up to date on what had been happening.

"I'll think it over, Cotton," I said with gratitude. "I owe you one!"

"Hey, Miss Kate, I owe you a heck of a lot more," he retorted. "Did your aunt leave today?"

"Yes, thank you. She just left a little while ago. She said to thank you again for cleaning the coal from her car."

"She's a mighty fine lady," Cotton said. "I'll be going on now. You ladies have a good day."

We went back to the kitchen where I gave Ellie the update on my latest harassment. She did remember me telling her about the family that barged into my home. She could not believe they had resurfaced, because I had presumed they were folks just passing through. She thought they were squatters who aim to take over a vacant residence and then refuse to move until they're forced out.

"That's probably what they did to this vacant trailer," I ventured.

Ellie agreed.

"Why on earth do I continue to be harassed here?"

"Forgive me, but I think they don't see you as one of us," Ellie began to explain. "I'm sure the word got out that you were some rich woman from up north who came into town trying to take over."

"What? Is that really what they think?"

Ellie grinned. "Just relax. You've got to understand that no matter how much the folks here love you, you are not native to the area. You aren't related to someone here. You didn't marry someone they know. And, you didn't go to the same church or school as they did. Now, are they happy to take your money? You bet they are! I don't mean to be so blunt, but I think it's that way in many small towns."

"So, in other words, I'll never really fit in here?"

"Don't be silly. You fit in just fine," Ellie consoled me. "The longer you're here, they'll get to know and love you like I do."

"Maybe I should seriously think about going back to South Haven," I said, feeling bummed out.

"Now who would be the loser there?" Ellie teased. "Give me a refill!"

CHAPTER 43

At three, an attractive woman with a teenage daughter arrived at my front door. They seemed very friendly and were complimentary of my house. The mother told me to call her Kim and her daughter's name was Shelley. They told me they had plans for dinner, so after they were checked in, I took them up to the attic suite.

"This is so cool!" Shelley exclaimed. "We need to do this to our attic at home. Look, it's even got a hot tub up here!" There wasn't a corner she didn't inspect. "Does the house have a ghost?"

I was speechless. Before I could say anything, her mother chided her. "Shelley, stop it."

"What time would you like breakfast tomorrow?" I asked, ready to change the subject.

"About eight would be fine, but then we really need to get on the road," Kim stated.

"That's fine. I have some refreshments downstairs now if you need something before you leave," I offered.

"Great, I'll be right down," said Shelley, throwing her belongings onto her chosen bed.

"That's not necessary," Kim said sternly to her daughter. "We'll be going to dinner soon."

"Don't forget to sign my guest quilt before you leave," I reminded them.

"I'll do it now!" Shelly offered.

Her mother shook her head, seemingly worn out by her daughter's exuberance.

We went downstairs together and I made sure she used the right pen I had put aside for the quilt.

"Can I have my own block to sign?" Shelley asked with a giggle.

"Sure. Go ahead and sign right there if you like," I said, watching her closely.

"Just my name, right?" she asked as she wrote.

"That's right," I repeated.

I watched her slowly write her first name and then she put a capitol B next to it, which wasn't the initial of the last name her mother had used when registering. Her handwriting was exceptionally nice, which I told her.

"So, are you serving wine?" she asked, catching me by surprise.

"Are you old enough to drink?"

"Okay, I'm only sixteen, but I am old enough to drink!" she answered with an attitude.

"If your mother agrees, it is fine by me," I replied calmly, knowing I had no intention of serving her any alcohol. I also had a pretty good idea that her mother would quickly refuse any such request from Shelley.

"Okay, a Coke will do," she admitted, also knowing her mother would refuse. She followed me to the kitchen. "There's a ghost in this house," she said, matter of factly. "It's a female, right?"

Was she just playing games with me? "You're pretty bold to say that," I said, keeping my smile. "What makes you say that?"

"I felt her presence right away, and I think I got a glimpse of her," she bragged. "I've always been able to pick up on where spirits are. Mother gets freaked out about it and doesn't like when I tell people what I see. She doesn't take me seriously about anything."

"So, what do you think she looks like?" I asked casually.

"It was just a quick glance, but she had dark hair and it was pulled back. I think she was wearing a black dress and she was smiling at me, which is always a good thing."

I was very taken aback. Could she really have a gift?

"Would you like some of these cookies?" I offered, hoping she would tell me more. "You really have me intrigued with this information, Shelley," I admitted. "Do you remember anything else? Like, was she fat or tall?"

"Skinny. Very, very skinny. Why do you ask? Do you know her?"

I shook my head.

"You do believe me, right?"

I nodded. "I do believe some people are gifted to see spirits," I acknowledged.

"What's going on in here?" Kim asked joining us in the kitchen. "Shelley, why are you eating before dinner?"

Shelley shrugged her shoulders and got out her cell phone.

"I hope you all have a pleasant evening," I said to Kim.

"My uncle is picking us up shortly but I have no idea where we're going, other than it's in the town of Dresden," Kim explained.

CHAPTER 44

Thirty minutes later, Kim and Shelley were picked up and I was left alone to digest what Shelley had said about Josephine. There was no doubt about what Shelley had innocently revealed. Her description fit and there was no other explanation. I think Shelley knew that I knew who she was talking about. I think I was lucky not to have ever seen her, or was I?

I decided to have leftover soup and bread for my dinner. I was trying hard not to be so down about Aunt Mandy leaving today, and Ellie's assessment of my existence in Borna was a bit depressing. Maybe I was taking too much for granted feeling so accepted here. Time would tell, I supposed. Clark always told me to be strong and not let anyone bully me into leaving. I thought putting Blade into jail had accomplished that.

When I finished dinner, I noticed that it had begun to snow. It was a good thing my aunt got an early start. I wanted to call it an early night, I was so mentally exhausted, but I thought I'd better stay awake until my guests returned. I made a fire and decided to work on Jack's quilt. Keeping my hands busy would help. I was certain that with the wintry weather, my guests would not be out very late.

My phone rang, and to my delight, it was John.

"How's my Michigan neighbor doing?" John asked with a teasing tone.

"She is alone and feeling very sorry for herself," I reported.

"Whoa! I must have dialed the wrong number," John joked. "This doesn't sound like Miss Borna speaking!"

I smiled to myself but couldn't muster up a witty reply.

"It's that bad, huh?"

"Aunt Mandy left this morning and it hasn't been too jolly ever since," I said, trying to lighten my mood.

"Well, maybe my little bit of good news will help," John offered. "My boss at the magazine loved the East Perry article and it should be in the next issue."

"That is great news," I gushed. "Maybe I'll score some points around here!"

"Points?" John asked.

"Never mind." I dismissed the idea. "I'm just having a pity party. Why don't you ask me to come back to South Haven now? I think I'm ready."

"What? Did I hear you right?" he asked with a chuckle in his voice. "You know I'd welcome you with open arms if I knew you were serious. I know you're teasing, right?"

"You're right," I admitted with a sigh.

"Maybe you just need to get out of town for a little while," John suggested. "After Christmas, why don't we meet up halfway and enjoy New Year's Eve together?"

I couldn't believe my ears.

"You just say the word and I'll plan it all."

"You are something, John Baker!" I teased. "Don't you have some cutie pie more your own age in that phone bank of yours that you could call?"

"Yeah, maybe so, but I'm asking you," he argued.

"You are a sweetheart, John, but I think you're going to have to wait until early spring before you see me in that condo of mine," I shared. "I'm pretty committed here for a while."

"My invitation stands, Kate," he said firmly. "Don't be in such a hurry to refuse."

"So, all is well with my condo?" I said, hoping to initiate another subject.

"Cold and empty," John teased.

We soon hung up. There was no doubt that I was giddy with his suggestion to meet up. I loved the news about the article.

Around nine, my guests returned, complaining about the roads. Shelley quickly ran up the stairs to the attic and I asked Kim if she wanted to join me for a nightcap. She eagerly accepted when I suggested we have amaretto on the rocks, which was my favorite after-dinner drink.

"So, I take it you're single, Kate?" Kim asked, taking her first sip.

"I'm a recent widow, so finding Borna and this fascinating house has been a gift to me," I explained.

"I'm going through a divorce right now, which is why it's just the two of us here," she confessed.

"I had a few minutes to visit with Shelley this afternoon and she shared with me that she sees ghosts on a regular basis," I revealed. "Was she just pulling my chain?"

Kim shook her head in disgust. "Like it or not, Shelley has always made this claim. I try not to make too much out of it, but I do believe her after all these years. I warned her that people don't always appreciate her comments. I worry that someone will exploit her one day. I told her she needs to keep this special gift to herself."

CHAPTER 45

As I listened to Kim, I realized that Shelley did indeed have a special gift to see things that others did not. There was every reason for me to believe she had seen Josephine. Kim and I parted ways around eleven. It was nice to have company as we shared a drink. She seemed to be a nice person and had a good career in real estate. When I finally crawled into bed, I was glad to end this very sad and challenging day.

The next morning, I was up early to get the muffins baking and prepare a veggie quiche since Kim was a vegetarian. At eight, I still had an empty table, so I assumed they were running late. I peeked out the window and was glad to see they had an SUV which would make traveling in this weather safer for them.

Finally, Shelley came down the steps with an attitude written across her face. She quietly drank her orange juice and only took a muffin. "Mom will be down in a minute," she said flatly as she checked her phone.

"Did you sleep well?" I asked, as I always did with my guests the next morning.

"Yeah, I guess, until your ghost woke me up this morning," she complained as she tossed her hair back.

How should I respond to this? "What did she do?" I asked hesitantly.

"Oh, nothing much, but she was not calling me by my

name, so I ignored her," she sighed, aggravation in her voice.

I smiled. "So what name did she call you?" I asked, curious to hear her answer.

"I think it was Clark," she said, shaking her head. "Did someone live here by the name of Clark?"

I slowly shook my head.

"I probably heard it wrong or she thought I was somebody else," she calmly explained. "It happens a lot."

I had to quickly excuse myself from the dining room and go into the kitchen to get a grip on what she had just said. Why on earth would Josephine be saying Clark's name? Did something happen to him? Or worse, did he die? Why was Josephine talking to her instead of me? Was I ignoring something?

Kim joined Shelley and began eating her breakfast. I desperately wanted to ask Shelley more questions, but I thought it was not a good idea to do that in front of her mother.

An hour later, they were on their way out the door. I was very relieved and yet disturbed by this revelation. As I cleaned up the breakfast table, I kept trying to analyze it all. I really didn't want to make the first call to Clark now that he was home, but this really had me concerned. Since I hadn't heard from him, I thought he may not be feeling very well just yet.

I ignored cleaning the attic suite, leaving it for Susie to do. I could spend the morning Internet shopping for my charity family as well as for Cotton and Susie's family. It would help me get my mind off of Clark. I got myself a coffee refill and settled in at the desk in the reception office. I started by going into Amazon, beginning with the toy section. I found the browsing useless because my mind was miles away. I got up and went to get my cell phone. I had to settle this mystery once and for all. I would just casually call him to see how he was doing and if he needed anything. Isn't that what friends do? I think he would do the same for me. The phone rang and rang and there was no answer. I left a simple message that I had called. With him not home, he must be well enough to be out and about, so that was good news.

My phone rang and I thought it might be Clark returning my call, but it was Maggie. I always jumped quickly to take her calls, but not this time. I let it go to voice mail. My mind was elsewhere.

CHAPTER 46

I heard Cotton outdoors using the snow blower. Maybe he would know something about Clark. I was likely overreacting, but Josephine saying Clark's name was significant. I waited until Cotton was finished, and then opened the back door to motion him in. He gladly accepted my invitation and I quickly poured him a cup of coffee as we talked on the sunporch.

"Did you decide what to do about our coal dumper?" Cotton asked with a half smile.

"No, I haven't, because I have something else on my mind."

Cotton looked bewildered.

"I'm worried about Clark," I confessed as I paced the floor.

"Clark? What's the matter with him?" he asked, concerned.

"It's a long story, Cotton, but something happened this morning and I want to know if he's all right," I explained awkwardly.

"Well, just give him a ring," Cotton said, looking at me strangely.

"I've been calling but there's no answer," I said, frustrated. "Look, I'd like to tell you more, but I'm not at liberty to do so."

"Well, would you like for me to swing by his house on my

way home and check on him?" Cotton offered. "Would that make you feel better?"

"Oh, would you?" I asked, relieved. "Would you call me when you get home and let me know what you find out?"

"Sure," he nodded. "Thanks for the coffee. I'll get going then."

I felt better knowing I had taken a step to determine if Clark was okay. I got my phone off the counter and tried calling him again. Still, there was no answer. Feeling a bit better, I decided to return Maggie's phone call.

"Well, it's about time I hear from you, girlfriend," Maggie teased. "What's going on there?"

"Aunt Mandy left yesterday and just a little while ago I had some other guests leave, so I've been busy," I offered.

"You are the busy one," she joked. "I got your email requesting Christmas quilts from our Beach Quilters. We are all going to drop them off at Cornelia's shop so she can send them all at one time."

"Thanks so much. We can certainly use them!" I exclaimed, feeling grateful.

"Well, we need to be there for each other, even though one of us is out in the boonies," Maggie joked. We laughed. "Is there anything new from your Michigan John Boy?"

I had to giggle at her question. "You're terrible! Yes, as a matter of fact, he called last night to tell me the article on East Perry County will be out in the next edition of his magazine. I can hardly wait!"

"That is pretty cool," Maggie had to agree. "He is trying very hard to please you, my dear."

"That's okay by me," I agreed happily. I couldn't dare tell her he had invited me to meet up with him for New Year's Eve.

She would die! "Please thank all the girls for their quilts, will you?" I said with gratitude. "Now, tell me, is there any word regarding our lovebirds?"

"No, not really, but in regard to Christmas, it sounds like Jack is going to spend a couple of days here to be with her and then leave for Borna to be with you."

"That will please the mamas, won't it?" I said with a laugh. "It's so good to talk with you. I really miss you and Carla. Do you know how she's doing? Did she by chance tell you whether John hired her to clean his condo?"

"Oh, yes she did," she responded. "She is very happy about that, of course. I hope he doesn't hit on her, like he did you!"

"Oh, Maggie, stop," I insisted. "You are the worst! Will you tell her I said hello and that I'm happy about the news?"

"I will," Maggie happily agreed. "I love you, girlfriend." She hung up without seeing the smile on my face.

CHAPTER 47

It was another fifteen minutes before I heard from Cotton. "Well, the bad news is that Clark isn't home," Cotton reported. "The good news is that I didn't get stuck out there. It was pretty treacherous."

"Oh, Cotton, thank you so much," I said, feeling relieved. "I owe you once again. I will make it up to you somehow."

So now I was back where I started regarding my concern for Clark. At least he wasn't dead in his cabin or car. He probably went out of town again, but that possibility seemed rather unlikely since he just came back and it looked like his health was poor. I had to conclude that it was none of my business and that Clark chose to keep his life private. Why didn't I respect that?

Since the weather was bad, I called Ellie, thinking she may be home and we could share dinner together. When she answered, she surprised me by saying she was at the winery.

"What are you doing out there in this horrid weather?" I asked, concerned.

"Well, some of us got stuck here and believe it or not, we have a few customers." I have a cot here, so I'm not going anywhere tonight. Hopefully, the roads will be better in the morning."

"Have you ever spent the night there before?"

"Yes, a few times," she said lightheartedly. "There's always work to do here, and let's face it, I have lots of food and wine!"

"For sure," I replied. "I just thought we could share dinner at one of our places tonight."

"Sorry. Another time, neighbor," she said as we ended our conversation.

Okay, another night alone. Even on this treacherous night, everyone seemed to have plans, but I had none. I actually liked my time alone, but I was still bummed out about Aunt Mandy leaving. After I poured myself a glass of wine, I thought I'd better check to see if she got home okay. I thought she would have arrived and called by now.

"Oh, honey, I was going to give you a call later," Aunt Mandy apologized. "As I told you, my friend Mildred was most anxious to know I had returned."

"That's fine. Did you run into any bad weather along the way?" I asked, getting comfy by my fireplace.

"No, not really," she claimed. "Is everything okay there, sweetie? Did your guests come and go?"

"They did and they were very nice," I added. "The daughter told me I had a ghost in the house."

Aunt Mandy gave a giggle. "Did you tell her your ghost's name?"

"Well, it was all very compelling, let me tell you!"

"Thanks again sweetie for everything," Aunt Mandy said. "I really had a wonderful time. You take care and remember that your auntie loves you."

"I love you, too," I said, ending the call.

I sat and stared at the fire for a while before my stomach started to growl. I went into the kitchen and stared at the inside of the refrigerator. I settled for warming up some of the veggie quiche I had ignored at breakfast. Now it was looking pretty delicious.

CHAPTER 48

I took my dinner in front of the TV, which I seldom do. After I finished, I was about to nod off when I heard someone knocking at the back door. Who could it be at this hour? With all the trouble I was having, I decided to look out the bay window in the dining room to see if I recognized the car.

To my surprise, it was Clark's SUV! I couldn't believe my eyes and I hurriedly rushed to the back door.

"Clark, what are you doing out tonight?" I asked as he stepped in the door with snow-covered shoes.

"It's brutal out there!" he exclaimed, shivering. "I'm on my way home from Springfield and it feels like I have been on the road for days! Your warm, cozy house was just too tempting to pass by."

"Let me take your coat," I said, brushing snow from its shoulders. "Go in by the fire and get warm. "I'll get you something warm to drink. Have you had dinner?"

He shook his head. "I didn't want to take time to stop," he said, rubbing his cold hands together.

"I made vegetable soup and homemade bread. Would you like some? I just had some leftover veggie quiche from this morning. Take your pick."

"How about I have all three?" he joked. "It all sounds good right now."

While Clark got comfortable, I went straight to the kitchen to fix him a hot toddy and warm up the quiche and soup. My heart was pumping with excitement as I thought of him sitting in my house.

"Home alone?" he asked, taking the tray of food I offered.

"Not anymore," I responded with a smile. "I had a couple of guests that left this morning and my aunt left yesterday."

"Eating by this warm fire is great. It doesn't get any better than this," he said appreciatively.

"What would you do without me?" I teased. I hoped he was taking this the right way.

He looked at me, raising his dark eyebrows. "Life without Miss Borna would be quite dull, that's for sure," he teased. "Thank you so much. This looks delicious."

"So, how are you feeling?" I really wanted to know. "You've lost some weight, I see."

"Let's just say that this is what the doctor ordered," he said, ignoring my real question. "This is very good."

I had a whole list of questions to ask him, but I thought he should eat in peace and I also thought that perhaps I had asked my limit for the time being. "You have no idea how I have missed you," I said, staring at him.

He smiled and just kept eating like he hadn't eaten in days. "You really are a good cook," he said between bites.

"Thanks. It's nice to be appreciated. That should put some weight on you."

He smiled and nodded. "Do I look that bad?" He managed a chuckle.

"No, you look fine. So, you've been working again?"

He nodded as he finished his soup. "Bills have to be paid and commitments have to be met," he said, placing his empty bowl on the tray.

"How about seconds? I have chocolate chip cookies for dessert."

He grinned. "Bring them on," he instructed, rubbing his stomach. Trout said you had your neighbor here for Thanksgiving."

The comment surprised me. I nodded. "Yes, he's a writer and novelist." I tried to sound casual. "He was here writing an article on East Perry County. He writes for a magazine and the article is coming out in the next issue. Everyone's excited and he's an interesting young man."

"I heard he is quite smitten with you!" Clark teased.

"Trout told you that?" I asked, wrinkling my nose. "That's interesting. He's almost young enough to be my son."

"Well, I got a little jealous," he admitted, but his voice had a bit of a teasing quality to it.

"You? I don't think you have a jealous bone in your body!"

He laughed out loud.

CHAPTER 49

I tried to get past Clark's flattering remarks and bring the conversation closer to what I felt was normal. I didn't want him to think I was taking his compliments seriously. "Can I get you anything else?" I asked, taking away some of the dishes into the kitchen.

He shook his head and watched me walk away.

When I returned to the living room, Clark's head was tilted back and his eyes were closed. He had fallen asleep! I couldn't believe it. I realized then that Clark had to be mentally and physically exhausted from his trip, especially with the challenging weather. I turned off the nearby lamp, leaving only the light from the fireplace. I placed another log on the fire as I watched Clark sleep into the night.

I pushed him gently aside, so he would be more comfortable. I took the quilt that was draped on my rocker and gently covered his exhausted body. I didn't want to create any movement to wake him, so I sat in the rocking chair to ponder the situation. I couldn't believe that after being so upset about his welfare, Clark was asleep in my house. Had Josephine been saying his name as a word of caution?

As I gazed at him, I saw a grown little boy that needed nothing more than a good meal and some love and attention. Something maternal came out in me. If his mother happened to be watching me from above, she would surely be thanking me for taking care of him.

Another hour passed and I, too, was feeling exhausted from the day. I rocked until I fell asleep. I jumped when I heard the landline ring in the office. I looked at the grandfather clock and it was two in the morning. Clark hadn't moved an inch, remaining sound asleep. I quietly made my way into the office and wondered if there was a voicemail left since it was such an odd time to call. There wasn't one, so I assumed it was the wrong number. I quietly went back into the living room and put a couple more logs on the fire. I couldn't help but wonder who would drive by my house tonight and see Clark's SUV parked here.

I was now wide awake, so I went quietly into the kitchen to clean up some things from Clark's meal. Now and then, I would peek at him to see if he remained sound asleep. He must truly be wiped out. I had to admit, I was flattered that Clark felt comfortable enough to fall asleep in my house.

When I finished about three, I couldn't decide whether I should go on up to bed or watch over my houseguest on the couch. The quilt had nearly slid off of him, so I went closer to situate the quilt again.

In a flash, Clark grabbed my arm and pulled me on top of him. My heart jumped and I wanted to call out in helplessness, but before that could happen, Clark engaged my mouth in a passionate kiss. Was this really happening?

"No more pretending you're asleep, Mr. McFadden!" I said as soon as I could back away.

"Oh, Miss Meyr, I am not pretending," he said, pulling me close once again. "Don't back away from me. I missed you too."

"You're taking advantage of a very romantic atmosphere," I whispered in his ear.

"Relax. Just stretch out next to me for a little while," he sweetly requested. "Thanks for taking care of me. You are the sweetest woman I have ever known."

I blushed and did relax into his embrace.

"I haven't felt this comfortable with a woman in a long time. It scares me when I think about it."

I was glad I was not the only one with these feelings!

"Do all your guests get the royal treatment like this?"

I smiled and looked into his sleepy eyes. "Only wayward souls that drift in late at night," I teased.

As Clark continued to hold me tight, he drifted back to sleep. I kept still, trying not to disturb him and analyze the moment. It had been a long time since I had been this close physically and mentally to a man. Clay hadn't been much for sweet talk and didn't like to cuddle as much as I did. As I heard only the crackle of the fire, I joined Clark in the sleep clouds above.

CHAPTER 50

I was the first to wake up as daylight appeared. Clark remained sound asleep. I quickly made my way upstairs to shower and change for the day. As I proceeded, I didn't know what to make of me and Clark sleeping together. Did I really see a new side of Clark or was he unaware of how much he had expressed his feelings? Luckily, nothing sexual happened. We really were like two close friends that had found solace and comfort in one another. Thank goodness Ellie had stayed at the winery all night. I was feeling like a schoolgirl hoping no one had noticed Clark's overnight stay. When I came back downstairs, Clark was no longer on the couch. Did he leave just like the last time he fell asleep here? I then smelled coffee coming from the kitchen and there he was, pouring some coffee.

"Good morning, Miss Meyr," he said, flashing me a flirty grin. "Are you ready for some coffee?"

I nodded, smiling.

"I've been searching for my favorite blueberry muffins, but I haven't had much luck," he confessed.

"Take your coffee in by the fire while I mix some up," I instructed with a smile. "It won't take me long to make some."

"Is your back killing you like mine is?" he asked as he stretched.

"The shower helped," I said, acknowledging my discomfort.

"Why don't you go ahead and use the shower in The Study while I get the muffins going?"

"Yes, wife, don't mind if I do," he teased.

Why did he use the word *wife?* Was I acting like one? "Wash your mouth out, mister," I teased back.

While I mixed the batter, I also prepared a plate of fruit and made some scrambled eggs. It was fun cooking for someone who would appreciate it. The sun was out and I found myself humming as I worked. I realized that I had truly started my day with someone. It was totally different than meeting my guests at the breakfast table.

"How do you do all of this?" Clark asked, coming into the kitchen after having showered and dressed. "It smells great, and oh, how I have missed those muffins of yours!"

I shook my head and felt embarrassed by all his compliments. "Flattery will get you everything," I replied.

"Not quite everything, but it may be a good start," he teased.

I didn't want to go there!

"That shower has great water pressure," Clark reflected as he started helping himself to the food. "That's something I need to have worked on at the cabin. I'm not sure they'll be able to do very much to improve it."

"I appreciate good water pressure as well," I agreed. "It's the little things in life, right?"

He nodded as he refilled his coffee cup. "Like these delicious muffins," he said as he bit into one. It made me happy to see him enjoy them.

I found myself hungry as well, which I hadn't experienced for some time. As we ate breakfast, Clark asked me questions about what was happening around town. I told him I was excited about Cotton bringing me my Christmas tree sometime soon.

"Very good! Beg my pardon, but that sorry tree you have in the dining room is pretty tired looking."

I laughed and explained the history of the goose feather Christmas tree. He seemed to be impressed.

"I still need to find a top for it," I mentioned.

Clark couldn't believe my ambitious plan to decorate the big tree with cookies, cranberries, and popcorn.

"That sounds like a tree you'd find in a rustic log cabin!" he teased in a complimentary way.

CHAPTER 51

Clark went on his way with just a casual good-bye. I think we weren't quite ready to acknowledge that we were a couple and romantically attached somehow. I probably should have asked Clark's advice about what to do with my coal dumper since Cotton had identified who he was. Clark always gave me sensible advice. Should I take the chance of letting more time pass and getting another unwanted shipment of coal dropped on my property? That was my concern.

I wanted to clear a spot for my Christmas tree today as well as make some purchases online for my charity family. Time was running out. The real challenge on my Christmas list was Jack. Would the quilt be enough? I was also really stumped as to what to get Clark. He was always so generous. Whatever he was in my life, he deserved to be given a gift. What should I do about John? He had already given me a wonderful painting, which I dearly loved. It was the perfect memory of South Haven, so perhaps I could find something for him that would remind him of East Perry County. I thought of Sharla Lee and her museum. I knew they had books about this area, and so perhaps they would have prints and other things.

In between my chores, I received a booking for January and a request for a big family to stay here, which I refused. I had not warmed up to the idea of accepting pets and children at the guest house yet. I certainly saw a need for that in the Borna vicinity, however, I was still just a rookie at receiving adults in this guest house at this point!

Ellie called and asked if I would like to come to her house for chili tonight. I eagerly accepted, as I remembered how yummy it was from before. I told her I would whip up some brownies for dessert. For some reason, I loved having chocolate after a spicy meal. With Ellie's dinner to look forward to, I made good progress throughout the day.

Before I left for Ellie's, Cotton stopped by to clear the sidewalks and front porch. I told him to remind Susie that I could use her tomorrow. I also told him Clark had stopped by so Cotton wouldn't continue to worry about him. As always, I made a gift basket for him to take home containing muffins, fruit, and brownies. It was time for his bi-monthly check from me, so I added on a nice bonus for him doing my detective work. He was thrilled and advised me once again to report the coal dumper.

"Cotton, what would you say if you and I went to see this guy and tried to talk to him?" I thought Cotton was going to choke. "I would just like to ask him directly why he hates me so."

"Have you lost your mind, Miss Kate?" Cotton asked, scratching his head. "First of all, he'd deny it and then he'd come after you with something worse! These are disturbed people who steal and do whatever they feel privileged to do. They feel the world owes them, especially the rich. That's why they were just ready take over your empty house a while back."

"But Cotton, if I report him, there's retaliation I have to still worry about," I expressed, concerned. "What if I killed him with kindness? What if I brought his family Christmas presents? They have innocent kids, for heaven's sake, not to mention that poor wife of his! I saw how he yelled at her here and how quickly she jumped to his demands."

"I've never seen the like of you, Miss Kate," Cotton said, shaking his head. "You're something else."

"Maybe you'll get the Christmas spirit as it gets closer," I teased.

Cotton left not knowing what to think about me. I did have to chuckle at his reaction as I wrapped Ellie's brownies in tin foil. I put on heavy boots and a wool coat to walk next door in the snow to Ellie's house. I hadn't walked there for some time, but my memory served me well, thinking of how warm and inviting her place had been when I first arrived in Borna.

CHAPTER 52

"Come in, come in," Ellie greeted me cheerfully. As always, her place smelled heavenly.

"You are so sweet to think of us having dinner tonight," I said as I handed her the brownies. "Just walking across our yards, I became famished."

"Great! How about some red wine?" she offered. "I have several here to choose from." Ellie pointed to her assortment, all lined up.

"You're the wine expert here. You pick it," I urged.

"Have a seat because this is about ready to eat," Ellie instructed as she stirred the chili. "I baked some corn bread, too. So, what have you been up to? I'm sorry about last night, but staying at the winery was helpful, but not to my back this morning."

I didn't dare tell her I had the same back problem. "I got a lot done today," I began. "I purchased a number of things online for my charity family."

"You're ahead of me," Ellie admitted. "I'm going to get gift cards and then stop at Harold's for a few things since I have a dad and three sons."

"That's a good idea—to keep your shopping local," I said, suddenly feeling guilty about my Internet purchases.

We sat down at her kitchen table, adorned in all blue and white. Ellie had baked the corn bread in a black iron skillet and placed it right on the table. As she filled our bowls, I began to tell her about my evening with Clark. She looked at me strangely when I told her my concern for him came from my teenage guest who had heard Clark's name repeated. When I told her he showed up at my place later in the evening, I really had her attention.

"Well, well, well," she teased. Her face had a look of concern when I told her about his exhausted condition. "What's the matter with him, anyway?" she asked. "He doesn't look good."

"He's dealing with something for sure, but Clark is a very private person." I explained, not telling her he had cancer. "So, long story short, I fed him and he actually fell asleep on my couch. He was so exhausted."

"Goodness!" she gasped. "He stayed the rest of the night?"

I nodded. "I'm sure many tongues are wagging after seeing his car there, but that's all there was to it," I said as I took a bite of the corn bread. "Oh, Ellie, this is so delicious!"

"That's not the first night he's spent there, right?" Ellie stared at me evenly, waiting for an answer.

"I'm not sure, Ellie, but it's complicated," I confessed. "I think he really likes me, but doesn't really want to. Does that sound crazy?"

"Not at all," she said laughing. "I know someone just like him!"

"Who?" I asked innocently.

"You!" she said, raising her voice. "What's the deal with you two? Why don't the two of you face up to embracing a relationship? It's obvious to everyone else, so I don't know who you think you're trying to fool."

I was shocked at her words and tried to process them. "Oh, Ellie, I don't think I agree with that assessment," I said as I lost my appetite. "I am fond of him, yes, but I don't want a boyfriend or a lover. I like my independence. Clark would drive me nuts, I think. He's handsome enough, nice enough, and successful enough, but we lead such different lives."

"So what?" Ellie asked as she poured more wine. "You don't

have to marry him. Hey, you're not hung up on that young, hot neighbor of yours, are you?"

I took a deep breath before answering. "I am attracted to John, I'll admit," I grinned. "That doesn't mean I want a romantic relationship with him. I know he's too young for me, but to be honest with you, John and I have more in common than Clark and me."

"You've got to be kidding," Ellie quickly responded. "You and Clark love this community and he's the most handsome and eligible man in this county. I really think you could become soulmates."

"I don't think that could happen," I argued. "Clark is a loner. Have you noticed that, by any chance? I think that's just the way he likes it."

"Not if he knew he had someone to share his life with," Ellie defended him. "You both are so stubborn! Trout said Clark was clearly jealous when he told him your neighbor from South Haven was here. He had a lot of questions."

"Yeah, Clark brought that up last night," I admitted. "I told him John was here to write an article about East Perry County. Clark doesn't have a jealous bone in his body."

"I disagree," she countered. "Look, I'm the last one to give advice. I'm still moping about my relationship with a married man."

"Have you heard from Carson?" I asked.

She nodded. "Thank goodness for Trout keeping me honest and advising me, or I may have weakened. I am only human, you know!"

I laughed.

"He's just not worth it," Ellie said sadly.

I certainly agreed!

CHAPTER 53

Wе continued enjoying more wine and many laughs as it grew later in the evening. There were no conclusions made and I wasn't in any hurry to leave Ellie's great company. She was the perfect best friend right now. She was single and independent, like me. On the other hand, Maggie was married and would try to understand, but she would still try to steer me toward someone to settle down with.

Finally at one in the morning, I made it home. I hadn't checked or listened to my phone in those hours, but there was a text from John that read:

> Just arrived in Houston where temps are great! I'm interviewing some of the Astro players tomorrow. Thinking of you and your muffins...the blueberry ones, of course.

I texted back only a smiley face. I had to laugh to myself about his sense of humor. I suppose that helped make him a good writer. Finally falling asleep, I had a nightmare taking me to the trailer of my coal dumper. I knocked on the door and Clark answered. He was there having lunch with Maggie and Carla. When I yelled, "No, no, this can't be," I woke myself up hitting my pillow. Fully awake, I got up to get a drink and to hopefully get my mind to settle down a bit.

Morning came too soon. Thank goodness I didn't have any guests to cook for this morning. Susie would be arriving within the hour, so I got dressed quickly. I needed to do some grocery shopping for my Christmas baking and I also wanted to do some shopping at the museum gift shop.

When Susie arrived, she wasn't with Cotton. She got out of a car that I did not recognize. "Good morning, Miss Kate," Susie greeted me cheerfully.

"Good morning. Where is Cotton today?"

"Oh, that darn truck didn't start again today, so my neighbor, Gussie, gave me a ride," she explained. "Cotton is going to get a jump from somebody, so I'm sure he'll be able to pick me up. He thinks we'll have to get a new battery."

"I can take you home, if need be," I offered. "How about some coffee? Sorry I didn't bake anything this morning."

"I'm fine. I'll just get started up in the attic suite like you suggested," Susie said, retrieving the cleaning things from the closet.

"I'm going to run some errands," I informed her. "So, call me on my cell when you are finished."

"I will, but don't you worry none," she said, walking toward the steps.

I finished my coffee and decided the museum was going to be my first stop. Getting out in more pleasant weather was refreshing after being cooped up. As I slowed down to make a right turn onto Church Street where the museum was, I saw a small sign in front of a house across the street that read: *Dresden Inn*. How could I not know about a new inn opening so close by? Sharla Lee would probably have more information. I parked my car and got a better look at the house. It was a large, white framed farmhouse that looked nice enough, but I couldn't wait to find out more.

CHAPTER 54

When I arrived, Gerard was handing Sharla Lee a quilt to hang behind one of the glass counters.

"Well, stranger, where have you been keeping yourself?" asked Gerard. "I thought you'd be at Warren Schmidt's book signing last night."

"Oh! I'm sorry, I forgot," I said, feeling badly.

"Don't you fret, the weather kept a lot of folks away," Sharla Lee explained. "Here's his book, which is quite good. He's done a lot of research in this county."

"I'll take one. Actually, I'm here to do a little Christmas shopping, so this may do for a couple of folks on my list. Do you have any paintings or prints from this county?"

"Heavens, yes," Gerard interrupted. "You'll want to look through this file."

"The paintings are scarce and they go quickly when we get them in," Sharla Lee explained.

"Thanks. I'll look through these," I said as I scanned the room for other gift possibilities.

I knew John would like the book, but I really wanted something for him to look at that was from the area. Too bad it couldn't be something from our famous artist, Clark, but that was not likely to happen.

When I went to the counter to check out, I had three books, five woven shawls that were made locally in Unionville, two cookbooks, a print of the Saxon Village for John, and a clever straw woven star that was perfect for the top of my feather tree.

"We'll likely get more things in," Sharla Lee mentioned as she looked over my merchandise. "We'll be decorating the Christmas trees on Monday. Do you have your theme chosen?"

"Oh, I'm getting forgetful, but yes, I'll be here!" I stammered. "I have an idea for my tree."

She and Gerard giggled. "We sure appreciate you buying all of this, Kate," Sharla Lee said. "Gerard can help take these packages to your car."

"Thanks. Say, I wanted to ask if you knew anything about the house across the street that says Dresden Inn? Do I have competition?"

"Oh, Kate, that house belongs to the Grebing family," Gerard explained with a chuckle. "They only use it for family reunions and when their family comes in from out of town. They finally put a sign out front to make it easier for their kin to find."

"How nice," I responded, thinking of all the Grebings I had already met here in town.

Gerard followed me out to the car with all my packages. "So, is one of those presents for your buddy, Clark?"

I laughed and shook my head.

"They say he's in town again."

I nodded, not knowing what else to say. "Thanks so much, Gerard," I said, getting into my car.

Heading to the grocery store, I had two things on my mind. I needed to plan my museum tree and that meant putting my own tree decorating aside for a while. The other topic on my mind was this assumption that Clark and I happened to be an item in town. I wasn't quite comfortable with that picture, nor could I explain it to anyone.

CHAPTER 55

Grocery shopping was not my favorite thing. I was nearly finished when I ran into Ellen coming down the aisle. "So good to see you, Kate," she greeted me. "Did your lovely aunt go back home?"

"Yes, I really hated to see her go," I replied, still feeling sad about her leaving. "You'll be happy to know that I should receive quite a few Christmas quilts from my quilt group in South Haven!"

"Oh, Kate, I can't thank you enough. That will be such a big help. I'll be glad to pick them up."

"I'll let you know when they arrive. I'm trying to get started on my tree for the museum."

"I'm going to do a snowman tree this year," Ellen divulged. "I did all angels last year. Do you have your theme chosen?"

"I'm chewing on it," I said with a grin.

We said good-bye as we each got into a different line to check out. How could my tree possibly compete with Ellen's creation? When I arrived home, Susie was finishing up so she helped me unpack my groceries. "Susie, I think I could use your help," I began.

She looked puzzled.

"I have to decorate one of the trees at the museum this year," I shared. "I have a theme in mind of sugar cookies and garlands of cranberries and popcorn like they used to decorate with years ago."

"Oh, my goodness!" she said, lighting up. "How wonderful that would be."

"I think so too, but it really was my idea for my tree here at home, so if I decorate both of them like that, I'll have a lot of work to do."

"Are you asking me to help you?" she asked, her voice filled with excitement.

"I am, but you have Amy Sue and Cotton to consider," I noted. "I really need to start soon, like tomorrow."

"You can count on me. It will be such fun. I'm sure that between Cotton and my mom, Amy Sue will be taken care of."

I felt a sense of relief as we laid out a plan, starting first thing in the morning. When I opened one of my kitchen drawers, Susie marveled at all the cookie cutters I had accumulated over the years. "I haven't made Christmas sugar cookies since Jack was a little boy," I admitted. "I think he would get a kick out of seeing some of them when he comes here for Christmas."

We'll make enough for both trees, Miss Kate. Don't worry," Susie bragged. "You get that oven cranked up good and early tomorrow. Gussie, my neighbor, should be here any minute to pick me up."

Before she left, I showed Susie my straw star for the top of the feather tree.

"I didn't get anywhere near that tree to clean, Miss Kate," she declared. "I'm so afraid of knocking off one of those fragile ornaments. I've never seen anything like it."

Her honesty made me smile.

"What will your tree be like?"

"Cotton will cut a fairly small cedar tree from our neighbor's farm, like always," she stated. "We usually put it on a table, because we just don't have that much room. It will keep Amy Sue at bay, too. We've got some handmade ornaments my mom gave us and a silver garland we've had for years. I can't wait to celebrate with Amy Sue this year. She was too little last year."

"What can I get her for Christmas?" I asked, not having a clue.

"That's mighty nice to ask, but anything is fine," she answered, blushing. "This time next year, we'll have two little ones to buy for."

That reminder made me realize I had to plan ahead for this little family.

CHAPTER 56

Susie's neighbor pulled in the driveway the same time as the UPS delivery truck. Susie and I went outdoors together and agreed to meet up in the morning. I happily accepted a big box from Cornelia's Quilt Shop and a box from Aunt Mandy. She had promised to send me her red and green Feathered Star quilt.

I ran inside and quickly started tearing into the boxes. I was pleased to see there were twelve Christmas quilts from my Beach Quilters. They all were unique and of various sizes. I was pleased to see that Aunt Mandy's quilt was in near perfect condition. I'd have to really give some thought about where it would look best. Hanging it was a job for Cotton, for sure!

I didn't waste any time calling Ellen about the quilts, and I offered to deliver them to her house. She was elated and confirmed that she and Oscar would stop by to pick them up when they went out later in the day in order to save me a trip out.

I had decided to place all my Christmas gifts in The Study guestroom as they arrived. I hoped that as early as tomorrow, I would have all the gifts for my charity family.

Darkness was arriving earlier and earlier each day. It was also getting colder, so I made a fire. I arranged my crafting supplies around the rocking chair so I could be near the fire. I tried to get comfortable but felt uneasy, as if someone was watching me. Could it just be Josephine? I got out of my chair and at that very moment, I thought I saw someone looking in the bay window. I went directly to the back door to see if there was anyone there. My back light was on and there were no cars on my property, so I had to assume it was my imagination.

I closed the door and rushed to the front of the house and turned on the front porch light. I closed the door and went into the reception office to peer out the side window. In that second, I again saw some movement. Oddly, I was getting angry instead of scared. This was another new experience that I did not need! I returned to the front door, stepped outside onto to the front porch, and yelled, "I know you're there. I saw you! Get off my property right now!" Feeling a little better, but freezing cold, I shut the door and went back into the house. I couldn't get back to the fireplace soon enough.

I took a sip of wine and wondered who would be frightening me without a vehicle in sight? I sat down in the rocker to pull my thoughts together. I wanted to call Ellie, who always had a good view of my house, but she was working at the winery. Impatiently, I got up from my chair and decided to check all of the locks on the house and make sure my dawn-to-dusk light was working. I ruled out the coal dumper because there wasn't a pick-up truck in sight, and there was no sighting of coal thrown anywhere.

I went upstairs, thinking I might have a better view of the outdoors from there. It turned out to be a ridiculous move because it was so dark outside. The only exception was an occasional car going by.

Frustrated, I decided my evening was being wasted and I needed to get back to my project and quit being a "fraidy cat."

As I came back down the stairs, I thought I heard someone trying to get into the front door. It sounded as if they had a key that wasn't working properly. I rushed down the stairs and stumbled on the last four steps. That was not helpful, and my knees smarted from the impact. The ornate oval glass in the front door showed total darkness, which was mystifying because I distinctly remembered that I had left the porch light on just minutes ago. Summoning my courage, I opened the door to look around and glanced up to see I no longer had a bulb in my porch light socket! Surely this was out of the ordinary.

I had to decide whether to call someone for help. With nothing happening, I didn't relish waking up the whole town with a visit from the county sheriff. Maybe it was just some kids out for a night of fun. I'm sure they liked picking on single women like me. I told myself I was not one to scare easily, so I grabbed my needle and thread and threaded the first cranberry onto what was going to become a beautiful garland.

CHAPTER 57

What was that noise? It sounded like a door slamming outdoors. It must be coming from my cellar door. I had no idea if that door had a lock on it or not. Could someone be coming in through my basement? I really had no desire to go down and find out! I always had an eerie feeling when I went down there. I certainly did not want to go down there now! However, I again summoned my courage and slowly opened the basement door off the kitchen to listen for any noise at all. Of course, the light would be shining from my kitchen, so they would know I suspected something. I tried hard not to take a peek.

I knew I had to make sure the basement was secure, so I slowly opened the door and turned on the light leading down the concrete steps. I took one step at a time. Was this brave or foolish? If something happened to me, no one would find me down here for some time. Should I call out to perhaps scare them away? As I got closer to the bottom, I grabbed a flashlight I had placed nearby when I had previously explored the darker rooms. As I looked around nothing looked unusual, and thankfully I had very little stored down there because it was so damp and cold.

I glanced at the cellar door, which was shut. Even with my flashlight, I didn't know what I was looking for, because if someone was in here, the only way out was up the basement stairs. The area I dreaded most was looking in the back room. I don't remember it having a light. It was where I had discovered the year 1915 written in the foundation. I can also remember that, no matter how hard I tried, my camera would not let me take a photograph of it. I had even talked to Cotton about putting in a wine cellar there because it was totally dark and there were many existing shelves. The more we discussed it, the more I decided it wasn't a good idea for right now.

I got to the door entrance and shined the light around the room without going inside. Of course, someone could easily be hiding in there, but I wasn't going to make it easy for them to capture me in that room. I was done and getting more frightened the longer I tarried in the basement. I raced back up the stairs and slammed the door, latching it firmly. Seeing my cell phone on the kitchen counter reminded me of how careless I had been by not having it with me.

I went into the living room to retrieve my glass of wine. I took two generous gulps. It was time to determine what to do next. I could almost convince myself I was imagining things, but I sure didn't imagine that my front porch light had been removed!

Feeling a bit calmer, I decided to walk around the inside of the house and double check the locks. I knew that if someone really wanted to break in, there were plenty of ways to do that. I lived on the busiest street in Borna and sometimes it felt like everyone in town knew my comings and goings, yet no one had seemed to notice a bad guy creeping around my property. Ellie and I were supposed to be there for each other, but that wasn't panning out so great with her late hours at the winery recently.

I went back to the rocking chair. It was only eight. I picked up my needle and string to calm my fears. One cranberry followed by three kernels of popcorn was the pattern I had chosen. My hands were not steady, which caused me to prick my fingers over and over. This was not fun like I had hoped. Susie would be asking about my progress in the morning.

I turned on the TV and kept the sound low so I could hear anything unusual. I was safe in my own home, I told myself over and over. I was losing count and squeezing the cranberries way too tightly, causing my fingers to get very red. I knew that every time I'd look at this garland on the tree, I'd think of this horrid night.

I wondered if Josephine would help me if I got attacked in this house. When Blade broke in shortly after I arrived here, it was Clark who came to save me. Who knows if Josephine had anything to do with it, but I was grateful, regardless. I kept rocking and stringing. If someone was watching me now, I would be an easy target. I don't think my needle would have much use as a weapon unless I poked them in the eye! Oh, that was not a pleasant thought. I wanted to drift off to sleep, but I couldn't let that happen. I got up and put two more logs on the fire. I pulled my quilt off the loveseat and took another sip of wine. I could no longer hold the needle straight, so I let the garland slip to the floor. The warmth of the fire helped me to escape into a dreamy darkness, where I would spend the rest of the night.

CHAPTER 58

I jumped when I heard the banging of the trash truck in the still-dark early hours of the morning. The fire had gone completely out and the garland was still there where it had fallen to the floor. The good news was that I was alive, unharmed, and fairly rested from spending the entire night in a rocking chair.

I got up to stretch and noticed that it was only five in the morning. I ached all over as I made my way to the kitchen to make some coffee. I was second guessing my choice not to go up to my bed last night, but if someone was indeed watching me, perhaps it kept them from taking further action. I really felt I would be okay once I had my first cup of coffee. A good, hot shower and some clean clothes would prepare me for my big day of baking. If anything could make things better, it would be spending time baking.

I picked up the garland and surprised myself with how many yards I had produced. My fingers were red and sore, but hot water and soap would take care of that. I would have Cotton inspect the outside of the house when he dropped Susie off this morning.

Somewhat energized, I went upstairs to begin my day. I took a minute to check my cell phone. There was a voice mail from Ellen saying something had come up and she wouldn't be able to pick up the quilts. In addition to that, a text had come in from John.

It read:

Coming home tomorrow. I got some good stuff. Wish you could have been here. John.

It was probably a good thing that I didn't read this last night or I would have sent him an SOS message!

I went downstairs refreshed and turned on the oven. I cleared the dining room table so we could spread out all of the cookies, decorate, and let them dry there. Between sips of coffee, I laid out all of the ingredients necessary for preparing the dough. I always enjoyed this process.

By seven, Susie and Cotton arrived in their pick-up truck, which I was pleased to see was back in running order. "Are you ready to rock and roll?" I asked Susie.

"Why sure, Miss Kate," she said, laughing. "It looks like you've been up all night getting this set up."

Little did she know. "How about some breakfast, you two?"

"Not for me," Cotton answered. "I've got to get to Harold's and do a little job for him this morning."

I couldn't let him leave without asking him to check around outside, so I briefly told them what my night was like. Cotton's face turned red with anger.

"Just quickly check around the outside and look at the cellar door for me before you leave," I pleaded.

"Of course I will," Cotton said as he shook his head in disgust. Out the door he went.

"Miss Kate, you need a dog!" Susie stated. "A dog would have scared the livin' daylights out of this person. You would have felt a lot safer!"

"I know. Don't tell me," I rebutted. "There really was someone there. I heard them try the door, and then they removed the light bulb from the front porch. I had that light on just minutes before. I don't scare easily, but someone was testing me."

"For cryin' out loud, you should have called someone," Susie scolded. "Cotton would have been over here in a flash if you didn't want to call the law."

"Ever since I arrived here, someone's been unhappy," I said, anger seeping into my voice. "I'm new and not one of them. Okay, I get that, but I'm not going to report every single little thing that happens!"

Susie shook her head in wonder.

CHAPTER 59

Susie marveled at how organized I was with my plan to make hundreds of sugar cookies. We selected ten shapes out of the many choices. We picked a Santa, Christmas tree, candy cane, snowman, ornament, reindeer, star, sheep, bell, and an elf. I rolled out sheets of dough, and Susie did the cutting. Each cookie had to have a hole poked with the end of a pencil to make room for the hanging ribbon. As they came out of the oven, they were placed on the dining room table to cool before decorating.

When Cotton came back inside the house, he was in awe of our progress. "Holy cow, ladies!" he said as he wiped his shoes on the rug. "You sure know how to make a big mess!"

We laughed.

"It does smell mighty good in here!"

"You want to help?" I asked, teasing him.

"No siree!" Cotton replied, shaking his head. "I need to tell you, Miss Kate, that last night you did have some kind of prowler. Someone did break the padlock on your cellar door and then I discovered something else." Cotton pulled a light bulb out of his coat pocket. "I found this in the bush by your front porch."

I took a deep breath. "Oh! It's just as I thought," I said in despair.

"Well, with all the folks going by here, he couldn't take a chance being seen in the light," Cotton explained. "He couldn't break the bulb because of the noise. You've got some pretty good light in the back of the house."

"Do you think he got in the basement, Cotton?" I asked with some hesitation.

"He very well could have," Cotton noted. "When I go to Harold's, I'll pick up a new lock and get it fixed yet today. I didn't see any damage to your front door, but I would keep that porch light on all of the time, if I were you."

"Thanks, Cotton, I'll do just that," I said wisely. "Tell Harold to put whatever you need on my house charge. Would you do me another favor? I need you to drop off this box of quilts at Ellen's house down the road. I know she's anxious to get them."

"You bet," he nodded. "Is this the box you mean, sitting by the door?"

I nodded once again.

Cotton went out the door and before he got into his truck, Clark pulled into the driveway. It put a smile on my face until I saw Cotton approach him. I could tell from their faces that Cotton was spilling the beans about what had happened last night. I wanted to go out and interrupt, but I had two sheets of cookies about to come out of the oven. Susie was quickly catching up with me. After ten minutes or so, I heard Cotton's pick-up truck finally leave. Clark knocked at my sunporch door.

"I heard Santa's got his elves making cookies in here," Clark said with his sexy grin. "I could smell them down the road!"

I smiled.

"Hey there, Susie, how are you?"

"Just fine, Mr. McFadden," she responded politely.

"I guess you heard plenty from Cotton before he left," I said, shaking my head in dismay.

"I know I can't protect you around the clock, but there's no reason you have to put up with bull, little lady," he said with some anger in his voice.

"That's what I told her, Mr. McFadden," Susie chimed in.

I ignored both of them and took more cookies out of the oven. "I still have coffee on. Would you like some?" I asked. I was eager to get off the topic at hand.

"Thanks, but I really don't have time," he explained. "I'm on my way to Perry, but when I saw Cotton's truck I decided to stop and ask him to help me with something. Now don't worry, he knows you are his top priority!" He snickered.

"With this time of year and no snow right now, I don't have much for him to do," I explained. "I'm sure it's fine with you, Susie, right?"

She grinned and nodded.

"I'm helping Anna at the Saxon Village right now," Clark shared. "She wants to display the manger scene, but last year, someone stole the cradle and baby Jesus, so I'm rebuilding one for her."

"How awful," I remarked. "Who would do such a thing?" I guess I wasn't the only one with problems. "Why didn't anyone tell me there were so many bad guys in Borna when I moved here?"

They laughed, knowing I was joking.

"Well, when a beautiful lady comes into town wearing rose-colored glasses, everyone in town wants to please her so she won't leave. We didn't want to let you know about any bad stuff," Clark teased. "If I don't get to steal one of those cookies, I think I'm going to leave you ladies." At that moment, he quickly grabbed a star-shaped plain cookie and went out the door.

CHAPTER 60

"I'm tellin' you, Miss Kate, that guy's got a thing for you," Susie teased.

Just then, I saw the mailman come to the front door with a package. "This is for you, Miss Meyr," the mailman announced with a smile. "The Christmas season is upon us!"

I smiled and took the package as well as a small stack of envelopes and closed the door.

"Oh, Susie, I haven't even thought to send Christmas cards this year," I complained. "I can't believe I've got some here in the mail. Do folks around here do this still?"

"Oh, for sure!" Susie cheerfully responded. "I love them! I keep them every year and decorate with them."

I sat on one of the dining room chairs and proceeded to open the package. It was from Aunt Mandy. The note inside read: *Here are some of Mother's old ornaments I thought you might like to have for your feather tree. I have fond memories of them. Enjoy! Love, Your Auntie.*

Susie and I got the biggest kick out of examining the handmade ornaments. They used tin foil, pipe cleaners, and whatever else they could find to create such beauty. There was only one breakable one, and it survived the journey safely.

Before I could open my Christmas cards and bills, Ellen called to thank me for the generous shipment of Christmas quilts from the Beach Quilters. I knew Ellen was pleased that I took her request seriously.

I had to admit that opening each card, especially ones from some South Haven friends, was very special. Aunt Mandy was always religious about sending a card to me. I was feeling guilty about my neglect. Maybe it wasn't too late.

As we continued to work, Susie mentioned how she was hoping Cotton would go with her to the Obrazo Christmas walk. "It's really nice, Miss Kate," she bragged. "My friend Jenny and I went last year. I'm sure my mom will babysit for us. It lasts past Amy Sue's bedtime, for sure."

"Well, good luck with that, because some men just don't go for that sort of thing," I reminded her. My cell phone buzzed and showed Ruth Ann's name. I answered the call.

"Kate, you just have to stop by before our wrapping party to see all the Christmas quilts on the wall," she encouraged me. "The whole place is magical! It's too bad that I'm not having many parties this year."

"Well, when all the employees from the East Perry Lumber party see what you have to offer, you'll be turning folks away next year," I assured her.

"I called to see if you wanted to meet up for a burger at Marv's tonight. I deserve to get out of this place. I was as busy as a bee today!"

"I suppose I could, but it'll have to be later. I have Susie here helping me bake sugar cookies for my museum tree and the tree here at the house. The place is a mess, but I'll be ready for a break as well."

"Well, let's say seven. Will that work for you?" she suggested.

"Sure. I think we'll be done before then," I said, thinking ahead. I had to smile at the thought after this very full day.

"Cotton will be here soon, Miss Kate, but I'll stay as long as you need me," Susie offered. "I can come back in the morning, too, and help you get this all cleaned up."

"Not necessary," I stated with gratitude. "I can deal with this."

"I can take some of your garland home with me if you need help," Susie offered with a big smile.

"Now, that I may take you up on because the big tree will need quite a bit."

"It'll be fun, and I'll make Cotton help me," she joked.

"Good luck with that, too," I said, picturing the sight.

Cotton arrived and off they went, leaving me with a sight to behold! I could always clean up much better alone, so I got busy right away in order to make it to dinner on time.

When I went upstairs to change, I wanted to crash across my bed. I was so tired from the night before and after today's many accomplishments. However, it would be fun to visit with Ruth Ann, I told myself. I wanted to be out of the house tonight, despite feeling safer with Cotton's repairs.

CHAPTER 61

I decided to walk down to Marv's. Feeling very refreshed, I put on my heavy, cable knit sweater, clean jeans, and my best boots. When I passed Ellie's place, her car was gone. She sure was working a lot at the winery, considering it was the winter season. I hoped that Carson was not back in her life.

When I walked in, I forgot how crowded and noisy the place was on a weekend. I didn't see Ruth Ann, so I looked for a small table for two and grabbed it. The music was louder than I ever remembered and there were a few couples dancing throughout the room. I was really thinking that perhaps this was not a good idea when I saw Ruth Ann walk in the door. She rolled her eyes when she saw me. I knew what she was thinking.

"Do you just want to get our order to go and eat back at my house?" I yelled at what seemed like the top of my lungs.

"Yes, great idea!"

I nodded. "I'm not in the mood for any drama tonight."

We each ordered a beer while we waited for our order.

"This business really attracts all ages, doesn't it?" I said, looking around the smoky place.

"It is pretty popular and Marv said many come from some distance away.

"What are you two good lookin' ladies doin' in a place like this?" asked an older guy with a mustache and a cowboy hat.

Before I could respond, he said, "I'll bet you're here to party like the rest of us, huh?"

Ruth Ann and I looked at each other in hopes of not laughing too hard.

"Thanks for the compliments, but we're just here to pick up some hamburgers to go," I explained, looking frantically for our waitress.

"Well, you don't have to rush off none." His voice slurred from too much alcohol.

I don't know how he managed to stand up.

"I'm a really good dancer." At that, he grabbed Ruth Ann's arm to take her away and she twirled around to successfully break his grip. He didn't even know what happened. He was so drunk.

I stepped in front of him. "Why don't you leave us alone and go have yourself a drink on us?" I said nicely as I tucked a five-dollar bill into his shirt pocket.

"Here ya' go, ladies," yelled the waitress, holding our dinner bag above the crowd. I quickly secured the bag, gave her a twenty-dollar bill, and told her to keep the change. We were out of there! When we got outside the door, we doubled over laughing like two teenage girls.

"This was the last thing I needed today!" Ruth Ann said as she tried to catch her breath. "We'd better get out of here quick. You want a ride?"

"No, I'll probably get home before you will," I said, walking quickly up the side of the hill to my house.

As I got to Ellie's house, I noticed two young men or boys running from my house and heading across the street. When I got home, I went to Ruth Ann as she was getting out of her car and asked if she had seen the boys crossing the road.

"Yeah, why?" she asked, looking at me.

"They were running from my house!"

"So what? This town has folks running all over the place on a weekend, especially around these taverns. What's wrong?"

"I'll explain later. Let's get in the house," I said, frantically unlocking the back door. When I got inside, I looked out the front windows to see if I could see anything strange or to see if the boys had returned.

"What is going on?" Ruth Ann asked as she took off her coat.

"You want wine or beer?" I put our hamburgers and fries on plates.

"I think I'll have another beer," she answered. "The one at Marv's tasted pretty darn good."

I joined her with a beer as we started eating our food in the living room. Ruth Ann sat in the rocker and listened intently about the nerve-wracking night I had experienced the night before.

"I guess I was thinking that maybe those boys were the ones who tried to break into my place," I confessed. "I just have to be so careful now."

"Well, I can understand," she said sympathetically. "Folks can see you so plainly here. But no one has ever tried to break into my apartment that I know of. Have you reported this?"

"Unless it's something really serious, like I had with Blade, I can't afford to," I said, taking a deep breath and another sip of beer. "This is a guest house, a place where I want people to feel safe. I can't let the slightest rumors get around town. You know how it is."

She nodded. "Oh, I totally agree. I had an incident with a small party in my side room last week where someone had gotten really drunk. He started to make everyone uncomfortable, so I suggested that he leave. I asked if he had a ride home and he got very ugly with me, so I walked away. I don't have a bouncer or man around to handle things like that. Thankfully, awhile later, someone got him out of there. I was also afraid he was going to throw up in my place."

"That must have been awful for you." I tried to picture what she had described.

"At least you can control who can stay in your house," she noted.

It was so good to share my troubles with someone who truly understood. Ellie, of course, would also, but I hated to always burden her. I'm sure she had many concerns of her own, owning a winery.

"You should have called me," Ruth Ann suggested. "I don't know what I could have done, but a signal of sorts would be good for both of us to use if we have a scary situation. We would at least know that one of us was in trouble. We began joking about the code or word we could use if one of us called the other. We finally settled on "pink flamingo" and rolled with laughter. It ended up being a fun evening.

CHAPTER 62

The next morning, I dragged my tired body downstairs somewhat later than usual. I stared at the hundreds of sugar cookies. Right now, I didn't think I could eat or look at another cookie in a long, long time. The house was chilly, so I took my coffee to the fireplace where I would get a fire going to keep me warm for a day of decorating. I pulled my robe close to me before going out to the deck to get more firewood. As I glanced across the backyard, I saw beer cans scattered on the white snow. I assumed they must have come from the young men I saw running from my place last night. I closed the door to the cold air and rushed to look out the front of the house. There were about six more cans in plain sight. Could it simply be excused by saying they were just here to party? Why here?

I sat in the rocker and tried to size up my problem. Should I just go to church this morning and forget all this nonsense? Oh! The thought of people driving by here on their way to church made me realize I needed to get out there quickly and pick up what I could. I dashed upstairs, threw on jeans and a sweatshirt, grabbed a trash bag, and headed out the door. This incident reminded me of when Blade dumped trash in my front yard. Ellie and I had gone out on a cold, snowy day before dawn to get it all picked up. Was this going to become the norm for me living on Main Street in Borna? It was certainly different than living in my prestigious neighborhood in South Haven!

The passengers of one car honked at me as they passed by. It was likely someone I knew, but I wasn't going to acknowledge them. I eventually worked myself around to the backyard and told myself I probably needed to check every morning for things like this. Next week was the church tour and many cars would be traveling by.

When I got inside, I heard the phone ringing. It was Cotton. "I hope you'll be home today, Miss Kate, because my friend Arnie is available to help me bring your tree," he said, excitement evident in his voice.

I smiled at the thought. "Sure, bring it on! I'll be here decorating cookies all day." Now I felt it was going to be a fun day, so I cleared a path for them to bring the tree in through the front door where it would be closest to the front window.

Still drinking my morning coffee and nibbling on fruit, I started mixing icing colors for the cookies. They were all getting a white base which had to dry before I could do any detailing. I got interrupted by my usual Sunday call from Jack. He was in good spirits as he repeated his plans to go to South Haven before coming here.

"You don't mind me getting there on Christmas Eve, do you Mom?" Jack asked politely.

"I'll take you whenever, son!" I teased, delighted at the prospect of seeing him at last. "I can't wait!"

"Do you have any guests staying there over Christmas?"

"I hope not, but would you object?"

"Absolutely not! I look forward to seeing my mom in action!" he teased. "You're not going to charge me while I'm there, are you?" We laughed and I wished I could hug him. I was so eager to see him in person.

"Please tell Jill I wish her a merry Christmas," I reminded

him. "Do you have any idea what I could get her for Christmas?"

He paused. "Well, she's quite the reader and I know she's a fan of Jane Austen, if that helps," he hinted.

"Oh, it does. So what are you going to get her?"

"I want it to be a surprise, so does that give you enough information?" he said with a silly laugh.

"No! You're not!" I shouted. "Is it what I think it is?"

"I'm not telling you," he teased.

My heart leapt for joy at the possibility that Jack might give Jill an engagement ring. This was a dream Maggie and I had for them all of their lives. I could only hope I had guessed correctly. Surely Jill would say yes. Growing up, she was always fonder of Jack than he was of her. I wanted to pick up the phone and call Maggie, but didn't dare. Jack would kill me!

I had just finished with all of the white icing when Cotton knocked on the back door. When I rushed to look out the door, I couldn't believe the large tree on the back of his truck!

"Miss Kate, this is my buddy, Arnie."

Arnie tipped his ball cap to acknowledge me.

"Nice to meet you, Arnie, and you are so kind to help with this," I said, wiping my hands clean. "I'm ready for you, so I'll open the front door. It goes in the same place as last year."

CHAPTER 63

After Cotton and Arnie put the tree in place, we admired its beauty. It looked as massive as any tree I had seen in the churches on the Christmas tour! It nearly touched the top of my tall ceiling. However, there was plenty of mess to clean up from its path into the house.

"Miss Kate's gonna put all these cookies on this tree," Cotton explained to Arnie. "Isn't that something?" They both laughed in amazement.

"My little one would love to have a tree decorated like that," Arnie responded. "Amy Sue would too, I'll bet."

Cotton nodded.

"They won't taste very good, I'm afraid," I warned. "When I'm finished with the decorating, I put a glaze on them so they won't crumble into pieces."

"Oh, my! Thanks for tellin' me," Cotton said as he moved the ladder.

I offered them a beer and gave each of them a fifty-dollar bill before they went outdoors. They were thrilled! After they closed the door, I immediately watered the thirsty giant. The smell was divine. I couldn't wait for Jack to see such a sight on Christmas.

My cell phone rang and it was Sharla Lee checking on when I planned to come decorate my tree for the museum exhibit. I explained that I was putting the last coat on my cookies, so it wouldn't be until later in the day before I could arrive. She said she'd be there until five, and I assured her I would make it before then.

I had plenty of garlands for the museum tree and plenty of precut ribbons to tie on the cookies. Sharla Lee said she had signs made up for each tree. For a tree representing my guest house, I wanted to convey a warm, welcoming feeling, as if it were a tree in someone's own home. I worked diligently the rest of the day, only taking a small break to eat a cup of soup. I was starting to layer the cookies in boxes when I saw Clark's name appear on my cell phone. This couldn't be! He never calls!

"Are you sure you have the correct number?" I asked Clark in a teasing tone.

"Is this the cookie lady, by chance?" he asked, using the same tone.

"It is," I happily admitted. "I'm just about ready to deliver my cookies to the museum."

"I've never seen all their trees, but I've heard it's quite a spectacle."

"It'll be good advertising for my guest house, I hope," I added.

"Well, I'm calling for a reason," he stated, his tone suddenly serious.

"I figured as much," I responded.

"Tomorrow night they're throwing a surprise birthday party for Trout at the winery," he announced. "Did Ellie already tell you?"

"No, she didn't, but what a great idea. I like Trout a lot."

"I do, too," Clark agreed. "He's been a good friend, but the thing I'm getting to is…," he paused. "I wondered if you'd like to go to the party with me."

I considered fainting from pure shock. "Do you mean, like a date?" I asked bluntly.

He paused. "Call it what you like," he mumbled. "Maybe I should have just asked if you wanted a ride to Trout's party. Would that have been less scary?"

We chuckled.

"Wow! Well, did you hear the weather forecast?" I asked.

"Yeah, it's not good, and Ellie told Trout they would be closed, so she's working on a reason to get him there," he confided. "She said if she called for his help, he'd show up, no matter what."

"What a nice thing to do for him," I mused. "So, Clark, does this mean you will come to my door to pick me up? You know, folks will see us together."

He snickered. "Well, since you put it that way, I might have second thoughts," he teased.

"I'm truly flattered, Mr. McFadden," I gushed. "I haven't had a real date since I moved to Borna." Thank goodness he didn't know about my last visit to South Haven!

"Well, I am the lucky one," he bragged. "How does seven-thirty sound? Trout's arriving about eight."

"That's perfect. I love parties," I added, already feeling excited about the prospect of Trout's party.

"I guess it's a date then," he said, ending our conversation.

A real date with Clark McFadden! It was hard to believe. Yes, I did have lunch with him one day when he was here working. Then there was the time he fixed dinner for me out of sympathy, but it was nothing like a real date. My adrenalin was pumping with the excitement of it all. This gave me the boost I needed to get my cookies packed and on their way to the museum.

CHAPTER 64

Iknew I was the last person to decorate a tree at the museum. Most of the other decorators were leaving when I arrived. "Hi, Sharla Lee," I greeted her hurriedly. "This won't take long, I promise."

She grinned and waved her hand like it didn't matter.

It was a Christmas tree wonderland! I hoped I could do the exhibit justice with my cookie tree.

"Kate, your tree is over here on this side of the room," Gerard said as he guided me there. "You are next to Ellen's snowman tree, which is pretty amazing. She even made a snowball garland out of marshmallows!"

Wouldn't you know that my tree would have to be placed next to Ellen's tree. "That's a lot to compete against, Gerard," I remarked as I put down my cookie boxes.

"I tell you what, Kate, there's not a bad looking tree in the place," he bragged. "Different strokes for different folks, you know." He went away laughing as I stared at my lackluster tree. Thank goodness everyone was gone except Sharla Lee and Gerard. It would have made me nervous to decorate with others watching. I took a deep breath and started at the top. I brought way more cookies than I would need, but I didn't want to have to return home to get more if I ran short.

As I worked, I had to smile as I situated each cookie in just the right place. It was weird how no two cookies were exactly alike. The addition of the red ribbons made the tree come alive. As I added the finishing touch of the cranberry and popcorn garland, I couldn't help but think of that scary night when I fell asleep in the rocking chair with my garland. I didn't have a tree topper, so I quickly made a large bow from the same red ribbon. I placed it on the top and let the streamers fall in cascades. I had to say that it was looking mighty nice!

"How are we coming, Kate?" asked Sharla Lee as she walked up to me. "Here's your sign."

I held my breath as I watched her judge my tree.

"Oh, Kate, this is absolutely charming!" she said loudly. "Gerard, come take a look at this! You certainly have the touch, and the folks will love this!"

"Well, I'll be!" Gerard said with his hands on his hips. "I can see those cookies disappearing when all the kiddos come through!"

"Oh, no, you don't mean that!" I said, concerned.

Gerard erupted into laughter. "I'm just pulling your leg, Kate," he teased. "I'll watch your tree like a hawk. I think you have a really good shot at being the best of show here, by golly!"

"You are both too kind! I must warn you, though, that someone could easily break a tooth if they bit into one of these!"

They teased me and ventured guesses about what I may have mixed in the dough. I left feeling like my tree was competitive. Now, I could concentrate on going home and decorating my own tree.

Arriving home I suddenly had an appetite, so I fixed a tuna sandwich and opened a can of tomato soup. It would hit the spot on such a cold night. Snowflakes were starting to fall.

While my soup was warming, I decided to build a fire in the fireplace and prepare to decorate the tree. My goal would be to get all the white lights strung on the branches. I also put on a Christmas CD to get me in the spirit of Christmas. It was perfect!

As I ate dinner by the fire, I told myself I was not going to be frightened by anything tonight. Before I concentrated on the tree, I checked all the lights and locks to reassure myself. If anyone peeked in my windows tonight, they would see a happy woman enjoying her tree. Surely no one would want to spoil that! When Ellie knocked at my back door, it did make me jump. With all the outdoor lights on, I felt relieved and happy when I saw my good friend and neighbor.

"Merry Christmas!" I greeted her happily. "Please, come in!"

"It sure smells and looks like Christmas in here," she responded. "I saw your tree from the outside window."

"Your timing is perfect, my friend. I was about to get on this ladder and begin stringing the lights. Do you remember how you assisted me last year?"

She laughed and shook her head. "I guess it's officially a tradition then, right?" she kidded.

"I'll bet you stopped by to invite me to a special party tomorrow night," I said, surprising her.

"Who called you?" she asked, picking up the lights. "I'm sorry I'm getting to you so late."

"Someone called to see if I wanted to go," I revealed.

"Was it Clark?" she immediately guessed.

I nodded, smiling.

"Wonderful, my friend!" she replied. "Is this a real date with Clark McFadden? Did I hear this correctly?"

"I think so," I said, laughing. "I had to tease him a bit about it. This is my first real date in Borna. How about that?"

"I just hope I can pull this off because the weather is going to be a problem," she admitted. "Trout may refuse to come out without me telling him why. Please don't bring a gift, by the way. He would really hate that scenario."

"I hear you," I agreed. "Hey, give me a hand here." I reached for her strand of lights as I climbed higher on the ladder. Ellie stayed a good forty-five minutes before she said she needed to get home to make some food for the party. I offered to bring something, but she wouldn't hear of it and said it wouldn't be cool to do so on my first date.

The evening was too pleasant to tell Ellie about my previous haunting the night before. She had enough on her mind. The tree lights were in place and the results were spectacular! I left the tree lit because I was already seeing lit displays throughout town. The city always placed a bright nativity scene in Ellie's large front yard because it was so visible coming around the corner into Borna. Tonight was its debut, just as it was for my Christmas tree.

CHAPTER 65

Iawoke early the next morning to blistering winds and frigid temperatures. It was snowing! I remained in bed wondering what this weather would mean for the party this evening. I reached for my cell phone on the nightstand and the weather report showed it would clear up in the afternoon. I tried to picture what Clark and I would look like together at the party. What would people think? I wasn't totally comfortable with the townspeople thinking of us as a couple. Why was that? I guess some folks, like Harold, were already thinking of us that way.

My plan for the morning was to organize my charity gifts to take to the wrapping party. I needed to check my entire Christmas list to make sure I had everyone taken care of. Susie and Cotton were still a challenge because they needed everything. Maggie and Carla were getting Red Creek wine and the handmade shawls I had purchased at the museum.

Bundled up, I came downstairs to start a new fire in the fireplace. What would I do without it? It was a good thing Cotton kept the firewood stacked high and handy! I could hardly see out the windows from the blowing snow clinging to the window panes. I hated winter, but it had its special beauty here in East Perry County. I turned on the tree lights and reminded myself that I needed more garland for the tree. I was counting on additional yardage from Susie, who had offered to make more at her home. I was in the kitchen looking for a breakfast idea when my cell phone rang with John's name showing up. He got my first smile of the day.

"What's this about East Perry getting lots of snow?" he asked when I answered.

"I know, and I hate it," I complained.

"I'm home for a few days and I'm again reminded of my absent neighbor, so I decided to call and hear your voice," he confessed. "A text from you isn't quite the same."

I agreed. "Here I am," I responded. "So, where do you travel next? I hope it's somewhere warm."

"That it is!" he replied. "I leave for Charleston, South Carolina, which is one of my favorite cities. You should meet me there. You would love the old plantations and southern food. I'm staying in a 1790s B&B. Does that sound tempting to you?"

"Charleston is awesome," I cried. "I am jealous. I was there with Clay many years ago."

"Well, I'm serious about my invitation," he reminded me. "I think it's time to have another visit."

"Thanks, but the next visit needs to be to South Haven when this winter weather breaks," I explained with a sigh. "How long will you be gone?"

"A whole week if can stretch it that far. Will you at least think about my offer? The weather will be a plus, even if I'm not!"

I chuckled. He knew my answer was firm. "John, you are something," I joked. "Where will you spend Christmas?"

"Well, since I didn't get an invitation from you, I haven't decided yet," he stammered.

I ignored his complaint and aimed to change the subject. "My big tree went up yesterday," I announced. "I'll send you a photo. It's spectacular!"

"Please do that," he encouraged me. "Do you have any guests right now?"

"No, it's been slow. Part of me doesn't want to have guests during the holidays because I'm so busy with things going on here in Borna, but part of me wonders why no one is calling."

"Hang in there, babe," he said, being cute. "You can always call me when you get lonely. Perhaps if I run into your son, he'll encourage me to visit."

"Don't even go there, John," I warned. "You watch what you say around him."

"Why are you playing so hard to get?" he ventured, teasing me again.

"Because, I don't want anyone to 'get' me," I responded firmly.

"Okay, I get that, but is it just me?"

He had put me on the spot and he knew it. I thought of Clark. "I'm happy with the way things are," I stated. "Isn't that okay?"

"Well, I guess I just worry about you," he said in a more serious tone.

"No need to worry, dear friend. Hey, I need to run. It was nice of you to call and harass me!"

He laughed as we hung up.

I stared at my phone in wonder. Why did he keep pursuing me? Was he confident enough to know that I wouldn't take him seriously? Unfortunately, he did pick up on me liking his attention, and who wouldn't, at my age?

I went into The Study with my coffee and began putting names on the charity gifts before putting them in a large trash bag for travel. I was then interrupted by a phone call from a man who introduced himself as Herman Lottes. He said he learned on my website that I was living in Doctor Paulson's old house in Borna. He was fascinated that it had become a guest house. He claimed to be distantly related to Josephine Lottes Paulson. I couldn't believe it! I asked if he was coming to the area but he didn't think that would occur anytime soon. We visited a while longer and he promised to make the visit in the spring or summer. I let him know how interested I was in Josephine and that if he could find out any information about her, I would appreciate it. We exchanged contact information and I hung up, feeling energized about my mysterious Josephine.

CHAPTER 66

There was no word of Trout's party being cancelled, so I got dressed for my big date. Dressing for a party in Borna in the dead of winter just meant more jeans and sweaters. Trout and his friends were certainly casual, so I proceeded accordingly. My boots were being worn twice as much here than they were in South Haven. I desperately needed another haircut from Norma, but since that wasn't happening anytime soon, I played with my hair to achieve a different look. I doubted whether Clark would notice, but I needed a change.

It was getting close to Clark's arrival and I wondered whether his behavior would be any different tonight. I probably should have told John I was going on a date so he would start thinking of me in a different way. I certainly expected him to be dating, especially at his age. Did he think I was too old to be having dates at my age so his attention would be flattering to me?

The snowplow had made some passes on the road which made me feel a little bit better about going out for the evening. Since Ellie didn't have a garage, I could always see clearly whether she was home or not. Her car wasn't there, which meant she was at the winery. I made sure the fire was completely out and rechecked all the locks and lights before leaving. I left the tree lights on to give an appearance that I may be home. I heard Clark's SUV pull in the driveway, so I put on my coat and gloves and greeted him at the back door. We smiled at each other when our eyes met.

"Just make note, Miss Myer, that I am picking you up at the door, like a real date," he teased. "I thought about honking my horn, but I didn't know if you'd respond." He laughed and I gave him a smirk, knowing he was teasing.

"How are the roads?"

"We'll have to take it slow," he cautioned. "I'm mostly worried about the hill at the winery."

Clark graciously opened the car door for me and we were off. We made small talk about who we might expect to see at the party. I wanted him to keep his eyes on the road, so I wasn't very chatty.

We got to the entrance of Ellie's winery and someone stopped to instruct us about where to park our car so we could ride up the hill in another vehicle. Clark thought it was a great idea, as Ellie's parking lot was where everyone would be most likely to get stuck.

We waited our turn in the cold, and Clark put his arm around me to keep me warm. It was very endearing, but as others arrived, it made me feel uncomfortable. They all greeted us warmly, and Milly and Harold were especially glad to see us together. For ages, Harold had been teasing me about Clark. We slowly moved up the gigantic hill in a four-wheel drive vehicle with three other couples. This grand entrance to the party made it seem extra special.

Ellie happily greeted us, along with Trout's sister, who was young and charming. The place looked amazing. Ellie, or someone, had taken the time to decorate the winery in a fishing theme which reflected Trout's interests so very well. To my amazement, someone had created a fabulous birthday cake that looked like a real fish. Ellie gave Trout's sister credit for finding the bakery.

Clark immediately asked me what I preferred to drink as he continued in his role as my Mr. Date. When Clark removed his coat, I saw he was sharply dressed in a light yellow cable knit sweater that made his dark hair and eyes shine. I could tell he had gone the extra mile to look especially good for the evening. I was impressed, which was likely his goal.

I was pleased to see Ruth Ann and Betsy arriving together, as well as Anna and her husband. Our Friendship Circle was well represented.

"I like your hair tonight," Clark remarked. "Did you braid it yourself?"

He looked so serious. Sometimes men ask the dumbest questions. "Thanks," I answered with a chuckle. "It is nice of you to notice." I had to look away because it felt as if he were looking through me.

"Here he comes!" announced Ellie as soon as she got word on her cell phone. "He's not happy about coming up this hill!" Everyone laughed. We remained quiet until Trout made his entrance and everyone greeted him with a resounding, "Surprise!" His choice of some profanity told us he was indeed surprised. Clark quickly asked Trout if he could bring him a drink, which was a nice turn of events since Trout was always waiting on us!

CHAPTER 67

When Clark went to get Trout a drink, Ellie headed my way. "How is your evening going?" she asked, like I was a teenager on my first date.

"Fine," I smiled. "I'm a little self-conscious about folks seeing us together, that's all."

"Get over it," she quipped. "You're just coming with someone to a party, not announcing your engagement. Ruth Ann is a bit shocked since you didn't say anything to her the other evening when you were together at Marv's."

"So, is she jealous?" I couldn't resist asking.

"Probably, but so what?" Ellie joked. "Anna is thrilled to see the two of you together, by the way. Did you know Clark built a new crib for the manger scene and didn't charge her a dime?"

"I could see Clark doing that," I acknowledged. Clark was now approaching us.

"Nice party, Ellie. You went to a lot of trouble."

Clark could certainly be charming at times.

"It's just nice to have the two of you here," Ellie said with a grin. "Please help yourself to the food. Don't worry, we won't be playing games or anything. We just want everyone to enjoy themselves."

Clark led me to the fabulous food table, once again putting his arm on my shoulder. He was much taller than Clay, so this was a new feeling for me. When we found a table for two, Clark seemed to sense my feeling of awkwardness. The food was amazing. The shrimp were the biggest I had ever seen and the cold salmon was perfect, as were all of the side dishes. The oysters and crab cakes were better than I'd ever had from my former fancy country club. Ellie had a huge wooden bowl filled with salad greens, which was a meal unto itself. Trout had to be overwhelmed by it all.

"This is really a treat," I said, enjoying every bite. When I mentioned to Clark that there wasn't fried catfish like we'd had at the fair, I thought Clark was going to choke while laughing.

"What's going on over here, you two?" Trout asked as he pulled up a chair to join us.

"This is a first-class birthday party," I replied. "I'm honored to be included as one of your friends."

He gave me a big grin. "I'll never forget the first time I met this good lookin' lady," Trout recalled, looking at Clark. "She was city green and I got the biggest kick out of talkin' to her."

Clark chuckled. "Were you the one that convinced her to stay in Borna?" Clark asked with a teasing tone.

"Nope. I have to say it took a village," he said with a laugh.

"You made me feel so welcome, right from the start," I said, smiling. "Ellie is so lucky to have you."

Trout leaned closer to me. "I know you and Ellie are very close friends, so I'm just gonna say this once," he whispered. "Carson's got to go. Permanently!"

I was speechless. Trout then left us and Clark looked puzzled since he didn't hear what Trout had told me. I told him I would explain later. Ellie turned down the lights and turned up the sound of country music. Ellie nabbed Clark and took him to the small area they had prepared as a dance floor. A few others joined them and I was entertained just seeing those two together.

The next song had a slow tempo and many couples crowded onto the dance floor. I hated country music but it was certainly fitting for the occasion. Clark reached for and took my arm like he was totally in control. I felt as if the whole world was watching as he pulled me close. I couldn't remember the last time I had danced with a man. Clark was feeling relaxed, which was good to see. He leaned back with a big grin.

"I wondered what this would be like," he said, teasing me.

"So, what's it like?"

"It's like discovering something is much better than you ever expected," he said, employing a serious tone.

I didn't respond but I could feel the eyes of the party guests watching us. After the dance, we joined a bigger table of folks that Clark seemed to know. Clark made sure I was introduced, and when he mentioned Josephine's Guest House, compliments came my way. They were having a lot of fun, so I excused myself to head toward Ruth Ann. She had her coat in her arms like she was leaving.

"How long has this been going on?" she asked with a funny look on her face.

"Only about a few hours," I answered lightly. "He just wanted to know if I wanted to go to the party tonight, and with the bad weather, I wasn't planning to go at all." I could tell she relaxed a little more.

"He acts like he's really crazy about you."

"Ruth Ann, you know Clark and I really well," I began to explain. "Neither one of us is looking for a serious relationship.

We are both very independent."

She nodded, but I can't say that she looked totally convinced.

"Hey there, Ruth Ann," Clark called out as he approached us. "Are you leaving us so soon?"

She nodded and smiled. "It's been nice, but I'll feel better once I'm home. I have to drop off Betsy, too."

"Well, I'm not ready just yet," Clark said, grabbing my arm. "I just discovered what a great dancer this gal is! We'll see you later!" Clark nearly pushed me toward the dance floor and I realized he was totally absorbed in the lyrics and the sound of the music. This was a side of Clark I had not seen before. He was truly having a good time.

Admittedly, it felt awkward leaving Ruth Ann like that. Her reaction was more than evident since she thought she had a chance with Clark at one time. This would not be good for our friendship, which I valued very much.

CHAPTER 68

I had never seen Clark this relaxed before. From what I could tell, he wasn't drinking very much. We eventually left, along with some others, to head back down the hill in the cold. When we got back in his SUV, he put his arm around me as the heater got going. "Where did you learn to dance like that?" he asked, grinning.

"Now that you mention it, I was voted the best dancer in my senior class," I bragged, giving him a smile.

He gave me a second look as if he were second guessing my comment. "Well, I'll just say you are as easy on your feet as you are on my eyes!"

We laughed.

"It's been a long time since I've danced. We didn't do much of it when I was married. I guess it's like riding a bike. It comes back to you."

Clark pulled into my driveway and turned off the engine. "Is this where we make out or is it when you ask me in?" he teased.

I had to laugh. "Are you giving me a choice?" I found myself flirting with him.

"They both sound pretty darn tempting," Clark said, moving closer.

"Since I'm no longer sixteen, would you like to come in, Mr. McFadden?"

We hurried inside to get warm. I immediately asked if he wanted coffee and he eagerly responded in the affirmative as he shivered.

"You want me to make a fire?" Clark offered.

"Oh, I would love that, but you'll need to bring some firewood in from the deck."

Clark looked out the window and suddenly took off like lightning as if he were after someone! He flew out the door, leaving it wide open. When I scurried after him, I saw he was chasing a young man toward the front of the house. Without a coat, I followed in the direction of where I heard yelling and screaming. Clark had won the chase and had pulled the person to the ground where they were struggling in the snow. Thankfully, Clark was nearly twice his size and eventually pulled him up by the collar. He then started yelling at him to get in the house. I followed, shocked at the events of the last few moments. They were both covered in dirty snow and the young man's nose was bleeding.

Inside the house, Clark wasted no time getting to the bottom of what was going on. "You want to start explaining?" Clark asked in a heated tone.

The young man mumbled something unintelligible.

"You'd better start explaining why you're looking in the windows of this house. If you don't start talking, I'll tie you to this chair and we'll wait for the sheriff to come out here."

I grabbed a wet towel so he could wipe his nose. It was a disgusting sight. "Who are you?" I asked sternly. "Were you here the other night?"

He remained silent.

I continued, "I'll bet you were here Saturday night leaving a few beer cans in the yard as well, right?" I was so angry! "Who else was with you?"

"Okay, go on and be the big hero here while I tie you up,"

Clark threatened. "Call 911, Kate! I bet it's going to cost a pretty penny for your dad or someone to get you out of jail on bond. Maybe they'll just leave you there. I'll bet there will be a lot of angry people just waiting for you!"

I could tell Clark was getting to him now. I picked up my phone.

"Okay, okay, don't call," the young man mumbled in a low voice, looking down at the floor.

"So, what's the story?" Clark asked, grabbing his collar again.

"We didn't mean no harm," he said finally. "We just wanted to scare the bitch."

"What did you call her?" Clark yelled at the top of his voice. Clark gave him a hard nudge and he jumped. "You'd better say you're sorry to the lady, for starters!"

He grunted something.

"I didn't hear you!"

"Sorry," he mumbled.

"Do you have a truck or car somewhere?" Clark asked. "What are you doing out on a night like tonight?"

He shook his head. "My brother was gonna pick me up."

"He dropped you off here?" Clark pressured him for more details.

"He was gonna pick me up down at Marv's parking lot," he said, wiping his nose again. "He's gonna wonder where I am."

"Well, why don't you invite him in to join us?" Clark asked sarcastically. "Do you have a phone?"

He shook his head. "We don't have no phone," he stated plainly, proving he could do more than mumble.

"So why are you targeting this woman?" Clark asked. "What did she do to you?"

He instantly formed a mean look on his face and stared at me.

"You don't remember me, do you?" he practically growled.

I shook my head slowly, all the while trying to recall where I might have seen this young person.

"This high and mighty so and so," he said, and then paused for a moment before he continued, "she chased our family out of this house when my old man was gonna buy the place. Don't act like you don't remember." The look on his face was full of hatred.

"What?" I asked, slowly realizing who he was. "Don't tell me you were part of that family in a pick-up truck that barged into my home without permission." I recalled the scene. In an effort to explain, I offered, "He wasn't going to buy this house because it wasn't for sale!"

"There was a sign in the yard!" he yelled. "My old man never forgot you! You're lucky he hasn't...," and his voice came to an abrupt stop.

Clark was shocked. He recalled me telling him about the family's intrusion.

I took a deep breath. "I think I was at your house last week," I countered.

He looked at me strangely. "What are you talkin' about?" the young man asked.

"Does your father have a pick-up truck that happens to unload piles of coal at people's houses that he doesn't like?" I asked, feeling my blood pressure increase.

He wouldn't answer.

I continued anyway. "I saw where you live in a trailer, and I saw coal in the back of your truck. You're all lucky I didn't bring the sheriff to your place and show him the evidence!"

"You aren't leaving this place until we get some answers, young man!" Clark threatened. "Kate, write down his name along with the others in the family."

The young man was learning that if he wanted to leave the house, he would have to tell all.

"You'd better be telling us the truth. What is your father's name?"

"Mosely. Hector Mosely's my old man," he said in a low voice.

"Your name?" Clark asked firmly.

"They call me Measles. My name is Michael, but no one calls me that," he confessed.

"Do you have a brother? What's your brother's name?" Clark pressed him for more information.

"Jimmy," he stated, frustrated. "Now will you let me go?"

Clark shook his head. "What's your phone number?"

"I told you, no phone." He shook his head again for emphasis.

Somehow, that didn't surprise me, considering their living conditions.

"Well Michael, you'll have a lot of explaining to do when you get home," Clark announced. "The first thing you'd better do is make clear to that family of yours that they are never to set foot on this property again or you're all going to jail. I have a feeling your mother won't want to hear that. There are two witnesses who heard your confession and I caught you in the act. It won't be easy for you all if we report this to the sheriff. I figure you'll come up with something to save your hide at home. If I were you, I'd get out of that environment you're in and make something of yourself before you end up in jail. Now get the heck out of here and don't come back!"

He quickly got up from the chair and headed toward the door knowing he got lucky, at least for now.

CHAPTER 69

I was mentally drained as I sat down on the kitchen bar stool. Clark, in wet and soiled clothes, looked at me and shook his head in disgust. "What does a man have to do to get a good cup of coffee this time of night?" he asked, successfully breaking the tension. I had to smile at his unexpected humor. I put my head between my hands and leaned my elbows on the counter. Clark took off his coat, pulled me to my feet, and held me in his arms. It was exactly what I needed. There were no words. I couldn't control my tears. This wasn't at all what the two of us had planned for the evening. Clark was patient as I gathered myself together. What would I have done without him here this evening?

After I made coffee, we moved into the living room. Clark started a fire and we remained silent for the longest time before I observed, "It's so sad that the Mosely boys are trying to please their dad who has such a warped opinion of life," I said in a sad voice.

Clark nodded. "You do have legal options here, Kate," Clark reminded me. "It's unfortunate that we didn't scare Mr. Mosely himself tonight! All we did was get his sons in trouble when they get home. That's why I think I need to stay here with you until morning at least. With a dysfunctional family like that, you never know how they are going to react when those boys get home. I would bet he's abusive to that wife of his as well."

It made me think of Susan and what she was going through. Oh, how I hoped she was safe, as well as Mrs. Mosely! "I have a real problem with making more problems for that family," I said, frustrated with the entire situation. "There's got to be a better way."

"I wouldn't stress about it tonight, Kate," Clark advised. "You're exhausted. Think about it for a while. I want you to get some sleep. I'll stay downstairs and you should go up and get some sleep."

"How can I possibly sleep?" That question came out at a higher pitch than I intended.

"Come here," he said softly as he pulled me close. I could feel his heart beat as he kissed my forehead. It truly relaxed me.

The next thing I knew, I had fallen asleep on the couch and was covered up with my quilt. I looked at the clock. It was five in the morning and still dark outside. Where was Clark? I got up and went to The Study bedroom, where I saw him stretched out on top of the bed, covered with the spare quilt I kept on a quilt rack in that room. He looked so sweet and innocent. He had come to my rescue twice now. I didn't want to disturb him because I knew he needed rest, but I found him irresistible. I slowly crawled in beside him as quietly as I could. As I placed my head on the pillow and closed my eyes, Clark's arms embraced me from behind. His large, strong arms clung to me as if he would never let go. I couldn't move, nor did I want to. We drifted off to sleep together as we waited for dawn.

My natural body clock awoke me the next morning. Daylight was creeping in between the curtains. Just as I had slipped into this bed, I slowly slipped out, careful not to disturb Clark. I quietly made my way to the kitchen to make coffee.

Once that was done, I went upstairs to change. Meanwhile, my head was reminding me that I had just spent the night with Clark McFadden. This was not going to look good as cars drove by. My overnight stay last year at his place was because of being snowed in. This overnight was completely different. When I returned downstairs, Clark was pouring himself a cup of coffee.

"Good morning," I said cheerfully. "We survived. You kept us safe."

"I did do a heck of a job, didn't I?" he joked. "I was a good boy minding my manners with a beautiful woman and I kept the bad guys away while we slept! Why did it take you so long to crawl into bed last night?" He winked.

"It was five this morning," I added as I poured myself a cup of coffee.

"How about I make us some pancakes?" Clark offered.

"Really? That sounds great! I have frozen blueberries from South Haven if you'd like to add them. I can fry us up some bacon."

"Oh, baby, you know what I like!" he said, opening my refrigerator.

CHAPTER 70

It was interesting sharing the kitchen with someone as we prepared breakfast.

"I was thinking about having some kind of Christmas party this year, but after Trout's lovely spread of food last night, I don't think I could compete," I confessed.

"It was fun and it couldn't have been for a nicer guy," Clark added as he flipped his first pancake. "I wonder how long the party lasted."

"What are your plans for Christmas, Clark?"

"I'm still not sure and I don't like to plan too far ahead," he explained. "If my work and schedule allows, I may go see my father. He's not getting any younger, but I really hate to fly."

"So why not drive?" I suggested. "My aunt took her time and actually enjoyed it. She wouldn't try it this time of year, of course. That's the only risk. I sure wish she would be here with me this year. We had such a grand time together, and I'd love for her to see Jack again. I can't wait for Jack to meet you."

He looked at me like he hadn't heard me correctly. "You wouldn't be paranoid about that?" he asked with a grin.

"Of course not," I said with a big smile. "He knows there is a man here in Borna named Clark that's been helping me at the house."

"Well, does that mean he'll be meeting your handyman, or do I get to hug his mother and give her a big kiss if I want?" He reached across the counter and kissed me on the cheek.

"You'll have to behave yourself, if that's what you're asking," I cautioned as I threw a dish towel toward him. "No son wants to see his mother manhandled."

He laughed. "Oh, I see," Clark responded as we enjoyed our food. "Is he protective of you, or is it you wanting him not to think there's anything between us? Moms don't have boyfriends, right?"

That was a good question. "I'm too old to have a boyfriend," I said, surprising him.

"What would you like to call me?" he asked, swallowing his coffee.

Now I was put on the spot. "I think I will introduce you as a close friend," I guessed. "Okay, a very, very close friend." I had to snicker as I watched him remain serious.

We enjoyed our meal and Clark was helping me bring some dishes to the counter when he pulled me close to him. "I've got to leave," he said before his lips touched mine. "Are you going to be okay?"

I nodded and let him kiss me again. "You are wonderful and I can't thank you enough for last night," I said, still remaining close to him. "I'll be fine."

"It wasn't quite the ending I had in mind for my big date, but I did get to sleep with the prettiest woman at the party last night," he teased.

"Okay, Clark, time to get out of here!" I said, pushing him away. "Don't you dare tell anyone you spent the night!"

"It's going to take a lot of loving attention to keep me quiet, I'm afraid," he said, giving me a quick wink. We laughed as he got his dirty coat on to leave. I waved good-bye to the longest first date I ever had. It had contained every emotion from fear to affection!

After I finished cleaning up the kitchen, I looked out the office window to see if Ellie was still home. She was probably exhausted from the party, so I didn't want to disturb her. I could catch up with her at the wrapping party this evening at Ruth Ann's house.

We were to bring a potluck dish to share tonight, along with our gifts and wrapping paper. I decided to bring a German cheesecake since it serves quite a few people. As I prepared the batter, I thought of Trout warning me last night about Carson still being in Ellie's life. That really surprised me. I was certain she had broken it off completely. Perhaps Trout was wrong in assuming the relationship was continuing. I would have to approach her carefully about that topic.

As I put away the rest of the dishes, I smiled to myself about dancing last night with Clark to the tune of some twangy music. If Maggie could have seen me, she wouldn't have believed it! Was Borna in the process of changing me, or was it Clark McFadden making the changes that I felt inside?

CHAPTER 71

Iwas excited and a bit nervous about the luncheon wrapping party, since it was my idea. Ruth Ann was such a dear to offer her banquet meeting room and kitchen. I was hoping Ruth Ann wasn't feeling any resentment toward me since seeing Clark and I together at Trout's party.

I piled two large trash bags of gifts in my car, along with wrapping paper and my cheesecake. When I arrived in the parking lot, I walked in with Mary Catherine and Betsy. Ruth Ann happily greeted us and showed us where to put our gifts. The cheesecake joined the other yummy-looking dishes that were lined up along the counter. I marveled at her sterile, stainless steel commercial kitchen.

We were chatting and helping ourselves to the big assortment of beverages. I chose iced tea due to having had plenty of wine the night before. After everyone arrived, Ruth Ann tapped on her glass to get our attention. "Kate, would you like to explain how this should work today?" she requested as they got quiet.

"I'd be happy to," I began. "First of all, Ruth Ann, let me thank you for letting us meet here. This is so festive with all the Christmas quilts you have on the walls. This should put everyone in the Christmas spirit!"

Everyone clapped.

"As you know, after my conversation with Sharla Lee, I felt bringing a better Christmas to the unfortunate in this county was certainly better than creating another event for those more fortunate."

Many were nodding in agreement.

"After we eat, I'll begin by describing my family and what I decided to purchase for them. Then we'll hear from everyone else. I'm anxious to see what everyone purchased. I really appreciate the expense and time you have given to this worthy cause."

"So tell us, Kate, how will the gifts get delivered to the families?" asked Mary Catherine.

"Sure," I continued. "First, we must get them wrapped and put back in the containers in which you brought them. Please help those who may need some assistance. You will then attach your family's information to your bags and Sharla Lee and her helpers will pick them up from here. I'm not sure when they will be delivered, but your names will remain anonymous, of course."

"It all sounds good, Kate," Ruth Ann said enthusiastically. "This is pretty exciting and a first for our club! I have more wrapping paper here on the counter if anyone needs it. Now, let's eat before some of the dishes cool off." With that explanation and the wonderful aromas, the room erupted into conversation and laughter.

"This was such a good idea," praised Esther. "I could see this really growing year after year."

"Thanks," I nodded. "We'll have to see how all this works. By the way, I've wanted to call you to set up a haircut, if you'll have me."

"It looks pretty cute right now, but come out anytime," she conceded. "The roads are pretty decent now."

Esther and I got in line to join the others. When we were seated, Anna said a prayer. She was so at ease with things like that and likely made a great tour guide at the Saxon Village.

"How are you, Emma?" I asked looking at her across the table.

"I'm fine, but each year Christmas just gets to be a little too much work for me and I cut back some," she complained. "I almost didn't put up a tree this year, but I knew my grandkids would be disappointed."

"I'm glad you did, because a tree can certainly lighten a person's mood!"

"I almost didn't do this project, Kate," Emma admitted. "I wasn't quite sure where to begin."

"You should have let me know and I would have helped you," I offered. "What ages did you have?"

"Well, there's a mom, dad, a couple of teenage sons, and a daughter around twelve, I think," she revealed. "That adds up financially, of course, so I mostly got gift cards. I got some gifts from Harold's Hardware, since some members of the family were male. I did feel the mother deserved something special, so I gave her one of my quilts. I certainly have plenty."

"Oh, my goodness, Emma. That is wonderful and very generous!" I praised her as I kept eating. It made me think of the quilt I gave Susan.

"It was said that they live in a trailer and don't have much space, so they'd better make room for the quilt," she said with a chuckle.

"Yes, Sharla Lee said quite a few on that list live in trailers," I added. It sounded like my coal dumper's family could be one of them. "You did great. Thanks so much!"

CHAPTER 72

When it was time for the wrapping to begin, there was total bedlam! It was too bad a video of all the excitement couldn't be captured. I stayed to the very end in case anyone needed help with their packages. Discovering generous gifts like Emma's quilt was surprising to me. The Friendship Circle came through with flying colors!

"Wow, it's so quiet," Ruth Ann exclaimed as the last person went out the door.

I laughed because she was so right. "It was a party with a great cause," I bragged. "It couldn't have happened without your being generous and allowing us to use the venue," I said to Ruth Ann.

"Well, most of the day is shot," Ruth Ann said, exhausted. "Did you bring Jack's quilt top along for me to quilt?"

"Sorry, I did not, but just give me another day or so and I'll get it to you," I assured her as I put on my coat to leave. I moved closer to her. "Ruth Ann, I'm sorry I didn't share anything with you concerning Clark. We are both enjoying a simple friendship. That's all. If there's anything between you and Clark, I'm totally unaware of it."

She laughed. "Oh! Did I give you that impression?" she asked, chuckling. "If you picked up on my jealousy, you were correct! He's an incredible catch, but I knew I wasn't getting anywhere with him when he worked here, and now I know why! You two make a perfect couple."

I was blown away by her honesty. "Thank you for being open about this," I said. "I'll be honest with you, Ruth Ann. I have a neighbor in South Haven that is also pulling my chain."

She looked surprised.

"I want some balance in my life again. I married Clay at such an early age, and it became a rather sheltered life. For the first time, I found myself when I moved to Borna. I also want you to know that I cherish our friendship and would never do anything to harm that."

"Oh, Kate," she said, giving me a hug, "you're the best! This party was a wonderful example of your love for the community. Together, you and I can accomplish a lot."

I left Ruth Ann's house feeling blessed by having her as a good friend. I also felt I could cross the charity event off of my list of things to do. Now, I had to finish Jack's quilt! Deciding to reward myself after all the hard work today, I stopped at Imy's Antique shop to check out her Santa's Workshop in a nearby shed. It looked so inviting with all the greenery and red bows! I headed straight to the front door and noticed a rustic room chock-full of Christmas goodies.

"Hey, Kate," Imy greeted me as she came out of her shop. "What do you think?"

"I'm in heaven, Imy!" I responded, my excitement showing. "I don't know how you do all of this. The sled is adorable and looks quite old. You take the simplest things and turn them into charm. I think I'll buy this for my front porch. These ornaments are precious and so personal."

"My sister, Pearlene, brings me a lot of her hand-painted things and clever antiques she finds in the city where she lives," Imy explained.

"Her painting is wonderful. Have I met her?"

"Probably not. She's very talented and prefers to be in her workshop creating, whereas I like to be the retailer in my shop. We both get a little crazy with our ideas sometimes!"

We laughed.

I stepped inside Imy's shop and spotted a painting that Imy said Pearlene had just brought in. I recognized the scene right away. It was a snowy, winter view of the road leading down to the Saxon Village showing Concordia Church in the background. The prominent steeple drew your eye to it. Pearlene obviously had an eye for beauty and design. I knew I had to have it.

"Pearlene did this from a photo," she revealed. "It's quite good, and I probably have a frame somewhere around here that would fit it, if you're interested."

"Indeed," I said, holding it close to me. "I love local scenes like this. I definitely want this, with or without the frame."

Imy had that look of accomplishment as I added to my purchases. Her Santa's Workshop was proving to be a big hit as she helped the locals with their Christmas lists. I had overheard some of the Friendship Circle ladies talking earlier today about how handy it was to stop there for unique gifts.

I came home and immediately placed the sled by my front door. It looked great with the large evergreen wreath I had purchased from Harold's. When I went inside, I danced around the house with my new painting. Imy had found the perfect frame for it. Now it just needed a home in a prominent place for everyone to see. Merry Christmas to me!

I made some hot tea and built a fire for the evening. It turned out to be a perfect day with good friends and Christmas treats. I got comfy in my rocking chair and pulled Jack's quilt top out of my basket. This was certainly a painful labor of love for my wonderful son. I hoped he would appreciate it in years to come.

CHAPTER 73

The next day, I called Esther to see if she could fit me in for a haircut. She happily agreed to see me in the afternoon. Also, Cotton knocked at the back door after he had replenished the wood in the wrought iron holder sitting on the deck. "You must be burning up the place!" Cotton teased when he came in the door.

"I know, but it's kept my sanity through this winter," I confessed.

"I'll chop some more this afternoon. You won't have a problem running out of wood with the woods behind you."

"Do you have a minute to talk?" I knew I had to update him about the encounter Clark and I had with my Peeping Tom. I started to describe the evening. I watched Cotton's face turn to anger once again.

He shook his head. "Clark has a way of showing up and saving your behind more than once, doesn't he?" he joked.

"You've got that right!" I smiled. "I couldn't believe it when I saw him wrestle the guy to the ground, just like he did Blade."

"So, are going to report this nonsense?" Cotton asked more seriously. "These are bad people, Kate."

I nodded in agreement. "You know, Cotton, I was with my Friendship Circle yesterday and we wrapped presents to give to the needy here in the county," I began. "Sharla Lee said a lot of these poor people live in trailers. I thought about this Mosely family in particular when one of our members described she had chosen a mom, a dad, and three older children. It may not be them, but I got to thinking that perhaps killing this family with kindness instead of jail time might be a better answer. What if I took them a ham and some special food that they wouldn't normally be able to afford? After all, it's Christmas."

"Are you out of your ever-lovin' mind?" Cotton asked. "They will laugh you out of town, Miss Kate!"

"Well, maybe so, but that's better than them continuing to harass me. Don't you see, Cotton? They realize by now that I didn't report them. They think they got by with something, so they are already laughing and they will likely keep playing with me. In other words, they think I'm too chicken to report them. I also keep thinking of Mrs. Mosely and what she might be going through. God bless her. I'll score more points by putting food on her table than putting her family in jail for the holidays."

"You're something, Miss Kate," Cotton said, shaking his head. "I can tell your mind is made up. Are you gonna do this by yourself?"

"I don't see why not, if I'm sincere about this," I responded. "I think I remember exactly where they live."

"I don't think I'd advise going alone. Folks like this don't take well to charity, especially the head of the house. He may chase you away with a rifle in his hand!"

"I know, but I think it is best," I decided. "I appreciate your concern. It would be wonderful if I could come when it's just Mrs. Mosley at home."

"All right, boss lady," Cotton conceded. "I have to get going before I get fired. I hope my truck starts. It was giving me a rough time when I left this morning." Out the door he went.

Suggesting my plan to Cotton made it more of a reality to me. I felt my plan was worth the risk, and I didn't think I would share it with Clark. He would not like the idea one bit!

Off to Esther's I went. I waved good-bye to Cotton who was back by the barn chopping wood. Listening to Cotton lament about his unreliable truck saddened me, and it was now going to be addressed. I was going to give him the money to buy a new truck. That would be my Christmas present to him. It affected his livelihood, which affected me as well. I believe that giving him a check written with the truck in mind would be the best thing I could do for them.

As I traveled the on the country roads, I started to look for Esther's yellow mailbox. My Mercedes was not the most appropriate vehicle for these roads. Perhaps my Christmas present should be to get rid of it after the holidays and look for something more practical!

CHAPTER 74

Esther happened to be retrieving her mail from her yellow mailbox when I arrived. "Come on in," Esther motioned with her hands.

As I parked my car, I remembered there were chickens roaming the farm, so I had to be careful where I walked. Esther offered me tea or coffee when I entered her sunporch where she cut people's hair.

"That was quite a party yesterday!" Esther recalled as she secured the cape snugly around my neck. "I would give anything to see everyone's faces when they get these gifts, but maybe it is better that we are anonymous."

"I think so," I said as I adjusted myself.

"Don't forget, next week we go caroling," she reminded me as she began washing my hair. "I saw your name on the signup sheet."

"I'm looking forward to it," I said as my head was getting scrubbed. "Where do you think we'll go?"

"There's a list of shut-ins who are mostly elderly," she explained as she began the rinse. "We won't know until that evening."

"Do you by chance know a Mosely family that lives out this way in a trailer?"

"There are several trailers out this way," she remarked. "Some are inhabited by the farm owner's extended family that also helps on the farm. Why do you ask?"

"I'm thinking of a particular family that someone had on our charity list," I informed her as she began trimming my hair.

"The only thing I know is that the neighbors have been complaining lately about some theft and vandalism from some boys who supposedly live in a trailer, but that is really all I know." She paused and stood back and looked at me. "Do you think this is short enough?" she asked, swinging me toward the mirror. "Do you think Mr. McFadden would approve?"

"Why would you ask such a thing?" I asked, surprised.

"Betsy said the two of you were at Trout's birthday party together the other night, that's all," she confessed. "I think it's just wonderful!"

"Oh, for heaven's sake. It was just a casual date. We are not an item, if that's what you think."

"I wouldn't let him get away, if I were you," Esther cautioned.

"I don't know how to answer that. But yes, I think this is short enough," I stated. "It looks great! I'd better be on my way. Ruth Ann is waiting for me to bring her Jack's quilt top to quilt and I'm not quite finished with it."

"Before you go, I want to give you a little holiday gift of some of my peach and strawberry preserves," she said as she gave me a little brown bag.

"Oh, Esther, how sweet," I said, accepting the package. "I am so negligent. I didn't bring you anything."

"That's not the point," she blushed. "You give the community so much, and that party yesterday will be one of my Christmas highlights."

"Thanks. How nice of you to say," I said, giving her a gentle hug. "Thanks for taking me on such short notice.

Merry Christmas to all of your family!" I drove away, feeling blessed to have such nice friends. I guessed that's why they called these ladies the Friendship Circle.

On the way home, I decided to stop in Dresden for some groceries. My main goal was to buy a nice ham and some delicacies for my charity basket to the Moselys. I wanted to give it to them before Christmas so they could enjoy it. Right before I planned to deliver it, I wanted to add some blueberry muffins. Perhaps the muffins could work miracles on them like they had with so many other folks.

It didn't take me long to fill my grocery cart as I thought about the holidays. I hoped to do a lot of extra baking, especially with Jack visiting. As I loaded the many bags into my car, Clark drove into the parking lot and spotted me. It was a fun surprise.

"Hey, good lookin'," Clark called as he rolled down the window. "Can I give you a hand?"

"Too late now, but thanks!" I called back. "Where are you headed?"

"Right here," he said, getting out of the car. "I needed to pick up some things. I don't suppose you'd be up for supper at my house tonight?"

"It sounds tempting, but I'd better not," I excused myself. "I need to finish Jack's quilt today. I will take a rain check, however."

He nodded with a smile. "Well, how's tomorrow night?" he asked, not giving up.

"That sounds better," I grinned, approving the plan. "What can I bring?"

"If you recall, I have a tendency to cook quite a bit, but you can come out early and help me pick out a Christmas tree to cut," he divulged. "After seeing yours, I kind of think I'd like to bring one into the house this year. I don't have a lot of room, as you know."

"So, we'll be going into the woods?" I asked.

"That's the idea," he grinned. "Better dress accordingly! I'll pick you up around one if that's okay. With some luck, we might get snowed in like last time!" He laughed.

"No we won't!" I said, raising my voice. "Should I just drive out on my own?"

He looked at me strangely. "Are you afraid it's going to look like another date?" he teased.

"Okay, okay," I agreed as I rolled up my window. Why was it getting harder and harder to say no to this guy?

As I drove toward Borna, I wondered what I may have gotten myself into. The tree was a clever idea, but was he just taking it for granted that I would spend the night? That was not good, so I'd better have Plan B ready to go.

CHAPTER 75

I settled in for the rest of the day, content to work on Jack's quilt top. Once I focused, I made good progress. I had saved the most difficult lighthouse for the end, but today, it would be done. I was pleased to get a text from John harassing me about not meeting him in Charleston. Did he really think I would take him up on his offer? I texted back and encouraged him to have fun and told him that I was pleased to know he was thinking of me.

At nine, I finished pressing Jack's adorable quilt top and felt a great sense of accomplishment as I examined my handwork. When I finished, I took a photo to send to Maggie. She would be proud of me. If Jack and Jill did indeed get engaged, I could start thinking about making a wedding quilt. I hoped I wasn't getting ahead of myself. Jill would likely have to move to New York, and I could see that as a potential stumbling block.

I was yawning my way up the stairs when the landline rang. I turned too quickly and nearly stumbled down the last steps to answer it before it stopped ringing. "Josephine's Guest House. Kate speaking," I answered.

Silence. Then, "Kate, this is Susan." Her voice was soft.

"Oh my goodness, Susan, how are you? Where are you, for heaven's sake?"

"I'm okay, but I can't tell you where I am."

"Your husband's been here asking about you more than once," I revealed. "Are you safe?"

She broke down, absolutely sobbing. "I don't know how much longer I can stay away from my son," she confessed between her tears. "What should I do? If he finds me now, he'll kill me for sure. If I continue to stay away, this beast is raising my son and who knows what they have told him about me? Am I being selfish? Should I go back? What must my son think about a mother who left him?"

"Oh, Susan, please calm down," I comforted her. "I don't know what to tell you, but if you don't think of yourself, you won't ever be around for that son of yours."

"I've thought of that, but I feel like I am also living a lie where I am," she said between sniffles. "I can't keep that up for very long. I'm calling because you are the only one I have told my story to. Thank you so much for keeping my husband at bay and not telling my secret."

"Of course, Susan," I said, feeling so sad for her. "How far away are you from here?"

"I can't tell you, Kate. I'm sorry," she said with a big sigh. "The thought of being away from my son at Christmas is really daunting for me."

"Do you think he expects you to return for the holidays?" I asked, knowing the answer. "Why don't you go directly to the police and tell your story?" I suggested. "I would think they would give you some protection with a restraining order."

"That's not going to stop him. It's going to be payback time for me. I know him too well. He'll claim that I'm an unfit mother who ran away from her responsibilities. I'm so sorry to cry on your shoulder once again, but I just had to talk to someone."

"You can call me anytime," I assured her. "If I can do anything to help, I will."

"You already have," she stated. "I hug your quilt every night, telling myself that someday I will be like you, starting over in some charming little town like Borna."

"Susan, I will pray for you to make the right decision."

"If I don't talk to you again, please have a wonderful Christmas," she said, her voice sounding happier. "Maybe next year it will be one for me."

She said good-bye and I broke down in tears. No one should ever have to hide from someone who threatens their life. My hands were tied, but I was pleased that she felt close enough to me to give me a call. I lowered my head in prayer and asked God for Susan to remain safe and get to be with her son again.

CHAPTER 76

It was very hard to sleep. I kept thinking of Susan. My little problems in life were nothing compared to hers. By five in the morning, I had given up any hope of getting any sleep at all. As I rested in bed, I missed Maggie, Carla, and Jack. They would never understand the kind of life I was leading here in Borna. I certainly didn't want to worry any of them, so it meant keeping some secrets. Mailing Carla and Maggie's Christmas presents made me sad, knowing I would not see them. Thank goodness Jack would be here with me.

I decided to make blueberry muffins this morning. Perhaps I could entice Ellie to come over for coffee. Every time I put them in the oven, I just felt the day would be good. As the muffins were baking, I started the daily fire in the living room. I was getting to be a master at this! At six-thirty, I called Ellie, hoping she would be awake. "I just took muffins out of the oven, Ellie," I announced when I heard her voice.

"I just crawled out of bed, so that sounds pretty good," she said with a yawn. "Give me about twenty minutes."

I went upstairs to shower and dress before she knocked at the door. Perhaps she could give me a little advice about my recent experience. Half an hour later, Ellie came to the back door with her own cup of coffee in hand.

"Come on in," I said, feeling the bitterly cold air. "Do you need your coffee warmed up?"

"Sure, but I thought this would save you a cup. That was

some wrapping party we had, wasn't it?"

"It really was, and it was very productive as well," I added as I served each of us a muffin.

"Oh, this fire feels so good," Ellie said, rubbing her hands together briskly.

"Have you been by to see Imy's Santa's Workshop yet?" I said as I took a bite of muffin.

"No, but driving by, it looks adorable! I'm sure you have. Am I right?"

"I stopped after our party," I stated with a grin. "You'll have to peek at my newly purchased sled on the front porch. I also purchased the neatest picture that Imy's sister, Pearlene, painted." I picked it up to show her.

"It looks like someone captured this from the upstairs at Ruth Ann's place," Ellie decided. "This is so good! I purchased some hand-painted wine bottles from Pearlene when I opened the winery. That whole family seems to be very artistic. Oh, these muffins are so good! So, do you want to tell me how your real date turned out?"

"It was a fun party and Clark was very much a gentleman," I reported.

"Girl, he's all about you!" Ellie teased. "He didn't take his eyes off of you all evening."

"When we got back to my house, we had an unexpected visitor, I'm afraid," I said, watching her face change expression from lighthearted to serious. When I described our encounter with one of the Mosely boys, she was horrified. She couldn't believe the hatred that had accumulated since they barged into my house. She remembered me telling her all about it like it was yesterday.

"You reported it, right?" Ellie asked, concerned.

I shook my head.

"I think I have another plan," I divulged.

She nearly choked on her coffee when I told her what I had in mind about presenting them a Christmas basket. I told her I would be doing it soon, and she thought I was crazy. "So, you think you're lucky enough to achieve this without an incident?" she asked, sarcastically. "You have on rose-colored glasses, my dear. I have a feeling this will not go well."

"Thanks for your concern, but I think it's worth the risk," I said, feeling even more determined. "Say, I've wanted to ask if you have heard from Carson."

"Why do you ask?" She looked like I hit a nerve. "Have you seen him?"

"No, and he hasn't called to book a room. I thought perhaps he would sometime again, since he now comes to call on Ruth Ann."

Ellie put down her coffee cup and took a deep breath. "He stopped by last week and we went to dinner in Perry," she confessed. "He said we needed to get out of Borna and talk."

"Why?" I asked impatiently.

"He told me he has moved out of the house and has asked for a divorce," she stated nervously. "She is fighting him tooth and nail, but it's a big step."

"Does it still matter, Ellie? Do you still care?"

She nodded. "I know it's crazy," she admitted. "We had such a wonderful evening and it was so nice being away from the winery. I hate having to keep our relationship a secret."

"Okay, then," I said with a sigh. "I'm the last one to judge, but if you feel he has earned your trust, I'm happy for you."

"Really, Kate?" she asked in disbelief. "I'm glad you feel that way."

When Ellie left, she was so happy. It seemed as if a big rock had been lifted off of her. How could I be hard on her? She was smart, independent, attractive, and old enough to know her own mind. I had to support her.

CHAPTER 77

It was nearly one and I was still prepping my face and outfit as if I were going to a party instead of an adventure in the woods. After my date with Clark, I seemed to know more about what pleased him. I purposely did not pack an overnight bag. Clark had asked me to dinner, not a sleepover. I still was cautious about this relationship. I didn't want things to go too far. Once that happened, I could never go back.

Before Clark arrived, I checked the mail for Christmas cards. To my surprise, there was a copy of *Scenic America* magazine which contained the article John had written following his visit to Borna. I sat down and quickly ran through the pages, looking for his article on East Perry. "A Gift in the Rolling Hills of Missouri," was printed on a scenic background. It looked to be photographed from the top of Red Creek Winery. It was gorgeous! I flipped to the next page and there was a small picture of my guest house and a log cabin seen from Saxon Village. I couldn't wait to read each word, but Clark was knocking at my back door. I quickly put the magazine in the basket of goodies that was going to Clark's house. I had his favorite wine, some cheese, and blueberry muffins.

"Hey, are you ready to go?" Clark asked with excitement. "Make sure you dress warmly! You have gloves, right?"

"Yes, Dad, I do," I joked. "Will you take this basket for me?"

"You got your hair cut!" Clark exclaimed as I pulled a sock cap over my head.

"I did! Thanks for noticing," I quipped. "Where do you go to get your hair cut?"

"There's a barber I've been going to in Dresden for some time," he informed me. "It's where I get the entire scuttle around town." We left, enjoying absolutely perfect, sunny, winter weather in Clark's pick-up truck that he called Black Beauty.

"I found this great patch of woods on my neighbor's property," he began to explain. "I told him I might swipe one of his trees and he gave me his blessing. I've helped him mend a fence or two and he's a really good guy. He's getting older and I suspect he'll be putting his property up for sale in the near future. He said his sons have no interest in the place."

"That is so sad," I responded. "It's nice of you to help him out, like a good neighbor!"

"I like the fact that he doesn't let hunters on his place," Clark added. "I don't like the thought of a bullet passing my way, plus I'm pretty fond of the critters that live in the woods, as you may know."

"Oh, you mean like the four-legged friends that you feed every night?" I teased. It was a precious memory that I had been lucky enough to witness.

We drove on gravel roads for about fifteen minutes into beautiful wooded hills. Clark seemed to know where he was going. He slowed down as if he were looking for a certain spot. "Oh, here we go," he announced as he pulled to the side of the road. "Isn't this a sight for sore eyes?"

"It's beautiful," I marveled. "One could visualize being almost anywhere with these gorgeous evergreens. I hope

East Perry Lumber doesn't find this spot. Where do they get all of their trees for lumbering, by the way?"

"They're pretty aggressive in their planning," Clark explained. "They have acreage where they grow their own trees from the ground up, you might say. You should know these answers, Miss Meyr Lumber!" We laughed.

"What size tree are you looking for?" I asked as we got out of the car and started walking.

Clark had grabbed his chain saw from the back of the truck. "Something like this little beauty, right here," Clark said as he pointed to a tall, slender pine tree. It still had a little snow on its branches.

"I like it," I agreed. "It's so straight. So, this is the one?"

"I think so," he nodded as he walked around it. "You stand back while I take it down. If you want to wait in the truck where it's warm, go ahead."

"Not on your life!" I protested. "I'm not a wimp. Let me help."

"You can help by doing what I just told you to do."

I could tell that Clark was in his element. He seemed to know what he was doing. It didn't take him long to get the tree to fall to the side. I was freezing, but was glad Clark was not by himself on what could be a dangerous mission.

"Good job." I cheered and clapped while wearing my heavy gloves, which made a thudding sound.

Clark held up his hands as the tree lay helpless. I grabbed the light end of the tree and helped him carry it to his truck. "You're a pretty strong woman," Clark teased after we got it in the truck and situated it for him to tie it down.

CHAPTER 78

Icouldn't stop shivering from the cold. I supposed it was because I'd never spent a really long period of time in the elements. It reminded me of when I nearly had frostbitten fingers as a child. I still remembered the pain from just playing outside too long.

"Let's go in and warm up before we bring the tree in," Clark suggested. "I'll bet hot chocolate sounds good right now."

We both happily embraced the warmth, and while Clark made a fire, I prepared hot chocolate. As I looked around the room, I told Clark I thought the tree would be too tall for his ceilings.

"I'm thinking the same thing, so I'd better cut some of the trunk off before we drag it in here," he suggested. "Whose crazy idea was it to get a Christmas tree, anyway?"

We chuckled.

While Clark went out to play lumberman, I pulled the magazine out of my basket to read the East Perry article. I took my hot chocolate and magazine over by the fire. I quickly centered in on the paragraph about my guest house. "A gem on Main Street, right in the heart of Borna, is Josephine's Guest House. The stately restored 1915 home is occupied by its attractive and gracious owner, Kate Meyr. It was the former home of Dr. Paulson and his wife, Josephine, for whom the house is named. Miss Meyr's hospitable personality and blueberry muffins are big attractions, not to mention her attention to the house's décor." It then gave my contact information. It was definitely a glowing account of my guest house! The article went on to tell about the Saxon Memorial, Red Creek Winery, and others. I grinned when he mentioned Harold's Hardware store where you can find everything, including a kitchen sink. Harold will be so pleased.

Clark came in to interrupt my pleasurable moment by telling me he was ready to bring in the Christmas tree.

"Look at this," I said as I pointed out the article. "John Baker, my South Haven neighbor, wrote this article after he visited here.

Clark got comfortable on the couch and read the article. Was I too presumptuous to think he would like it? Clark's name was mentioned as the local celebrity in town. However, he wasn't smiling. "Its fine, but I don't like to promote the fact that I live here," he said calmly. "He sure was impressed with the lady running the guest house, wasn't he?"

I smiled, but I wasn't sure how he really meant the comment. "I'm just grateful for the publicity," I said, getting up to put my coat back on.

Clark put the magazine aside without further comment. "Well, we've got a tree waiting for us, so grab your gloves," he instructed.

Back in the cold, we struggled to bring the tree inside. We placed it exactly where Clark had planned.

"Oh, Clark, it looks great there!" I said as I stood back to admire its beauty. "Where are the lights?"

"Right here," he said, pointing to a collection. "I have no ornaments. It's not my style."

I nodded and smiled. "You could always use natural ornaments from the woods like pinecones and such," I suggested. It fell on deaf ears.

"I'd better get dinner started," he said, leaving me to fool with the lights.

When I went into the kitchen to join him, I opened the wine and laid out some cheese. It was when I pulled out the muffins that I finally got a smile out of him. However, it became very clear that there was nothing I could do in the kitchen but get in the way. I knew from my previous visit that he didn't like me snooping around in his studio. He truly was living in a man cave. There wasn't much room for a guest, much less a partner in life. Was I creating a cave in my house?

I sat down and picked up my magazine again. Clark brought me a glass of wine.

"It smells divine," I said. "What are we having?"

"Beef stroganoff because it makes a lot for the whole week," he quipped. "I've made a salad and some corn bread."

"It sounds wonderful," I said, helping myself to a piece of cheese. "The tree made quite a mess, so why don't I clean this up for you?"

"No way. You just relax," he insisted. "You're my guest. All I have to do is set our table and we'll be ready to eat."

When I sat down at the table, I almost felt uncomfortable. The magic we shared while looking for the tree had somehow disappeared. He wanted to be in control. That was certain. Who did that remind me of?

"When do you go out of town again?" I asked, trying to make casual conversation.

He paused and swallowed. "I'm going for a check-up, so I'll be gone a few days," he said in a soft voice.

It was so easy for me to forget that Clark had battled cancer not too long ago. "Are you worried about anything?"

"What do you think?" His answer was curt.

I needed to change the subject. "I plan on caroling this week and maybe take in the church tour on the weekend," I reported. "Since Jack is coming for Christmas, I also want to do a lot of baking for him."

"He arrives on Christmas Eve?"

I nodded. "It would be really nice if you could join us for Christmas dinner, Clark."

He smiled. "How will Jack respond if I'm there?" he asked, resting his fork on the side of his plate.

"Well, Jack knows I have a lot of friends here," I replied. "I'm hoping he will give Jill an engagement ring when he's in South Haven."

"Anxious to have some grandchildren, are you?" Clark teased.

Odd question, I thought. "I suppose that would be a bonus at some point," I responded. "I just want Jack to be happy."

The meal was delicious and I told him so. Once again, he insisted that I not help him with the cleanup. At times we would touch, and it felt awkward instead of romantic. He wasn't his flirtatious self, for sure.

When I looked outside, the sky was clear and the stars were shining brightly. "Are you up for a walk?"

He looked at me strangely. "It's very, very dark out there," he observed. "It's probably not a good idea."

"Well then, let's finish up the lights on the tree," I said, picking up the last strand. We did just that and the results were stunning. Clark tuned off the other lights as we admired its beauty. I walked over and put my arms around him.

"Merry Christmas, Clark McFadden," I said, looking up at him.

He returned the greeting with a gentle kiss on my lips. "It is beautiful, Miss Myer, and you really helped," he said, returning my hug.

"Mission accomplished, and now you need to take me home," I instructed in a light tone.

He looked at me as if he hadn't heard me correctly. "Are you sure?" he asked with uncertainty.

I nodded.

"Okay, let me go out and warm up the car."

CHAPTER 79

Icouldn't help but wonder what was really on Clark's mind. We drove home, engaging in little conversation. When we got to my house, he gave me a wonderful hug and kiss when he walked me to the door. There was something about our chemistry that seemed to give us a mutual understanding regarding our relationship. I was actually pleased with the way the evening ended.

Before I went up to bed, I listened to the phone messages on my guest house phone. It was no surprise that Carson left a message wanting to book a room between Christmas and the beginning of the New Year. I wondered if Ellie had shared our conversation about him. I decided to return his call in the morning.

I turned off the tree lights and set the alarm. Thoughts of going to the Mosely house tomorrow after the muffins were done remained on my mind. It's a good thing I didn't share my plans with Clark.

After I got in bed, I remained awake for some time. I wasn't quite sure, but thought I heard a strange noise outdoors. It's funny how you get used to the normal sounds of your house and neighborhood. When it's not a normal sound, it gets your attention. I got out of bed in the dark to look out my front window. I couldn't see anything, but I thought I heard voices. I put on my robe and quietly went down the stairs. Horrible thoughts of Blade entered my mind from when he broke into my house and attacked me.

When I got to the bottom of the stairs, I stumbled around, trying not to bump into anything. When I got near the light coming in from the sunporch, I still couldn't see anything, but I sensed I was being watched. My dawn-to-dusk light would have come on if anyone was in the backyard. I remained quiet for at least ten minutes. I then gave up my suspicions and decided to blame it on my imagination. Having a house on Main Street placed me in a vulnerable location for activity.

When I settled back in bed, the warm light of love and comfort appeared. It was perfectly timed. It was morning in the middle of the night, somehow. I knew now that the light from Josephine was keeping me safe and loved. When morning came, I was totally rested. As I stretched, I actually looked forward to my visit to the Mosely's. I eagerly went down the stairs to get started on those blueberry muffins. As I closed the oven door on the muffins and they began to bake, my cell phone went off. I figured it had to be Maggie or Ellie at this early hour. To my delight, it was Aunt Mandy!

"How nice to hear from you, Auntie," I happily greeted her. "How are you?"

"I'm just fine," she said. "How's everything in that gorgeous house of yours?"

"We are looking a lot like Christmas!" I said with excitement. "I have a big, beautifully lit tree in my front window!"

"Well, honey, I hope I won't be imposing, but I'd like to come and have Christmas with you," she announced.

"Seriously?" I asked with a raised voice. "That would be fantastic!" I paused. "I just hope you'll fly in like Jack will be doing. Having you both here will be the best Christmas ever!"

"So, when is Jack coming?" she asked, concerned. "I don't want you to have to come to the airport twice."

"He is coming Christmas Eve. He may rent a car, or I'll have Cotton pick him up. So, when do you plan to arrive?"

"Christmas Eve as well, if that's okay with you," she added. "I'm very happy to take a cab."

"Aunt Mandy, I know you have a few pennies to your name, but I couldn't let you do that," I stated firmly. "I think this will work out nicely once we have both of your schedules." We talked for another ten minutes before hanging up. She was so amazing for her age. She probably realized that while she was healthy enough to travel, we needed to be together. This was such good news!

I finished up the muffins, wrapping them carefully. I was nearly dancing around the house, I was so happy. Let's hope the Moselys will be just as happy.

CHAPTER 80

I waited until the afternoon to drive to the Mosely's. Perhaps the men would be working. I was hoping I would catch Mrs. Mosley there by herself. My basket was bulging with the good-sized ham I had purchased. It took me a while to find the right road. I saw the neighbor's house Cotton had told me about, but I didn't see any sign of a pick-up truck. I pulled in near the trailer and got out of the car, taking my basket with me.

I walked around the yard cluttered with junk and suddenly a barking dog flew around the trailer and scared me to death! I shielded myself as much as I could with my large basket and tried to talk to him in a sweet voice. That was probably a stupid move since he probably was never spoken to in that manner. He was ready to bite!

"Rex, Rex!" a loud voice yelled from the trailer. "Get down! Get over here!" Mrs. Mosely came out of the trailer door.

"Thanks so much," I said in a shaky voice. "Is this your dog?"

"He belongs to the boys," she said, shaking her head.

"I'm Kate Meyr, Mrs. Mosely," I said as I walked closer to her. "I brought you a gift basket for the holidays." She looked at me, obviously confused, and placed her hands firmly on her hips. "You must have the wrong place," she responded in a gruff voice. "Our family doesn't accept charity. We take care of ourselves."

"Do you remember me?" I asked softly.

She nodded hesitantly.

"Look, I just wanted to extend a peace offering to your family. Obviously, I must have offended you and I'm sorry. It's Christmas, and since I like to bake, I just thought it would be nice to share some of my blueberry muffins. I'm sure you have many hungry mouths to feed."

She looked as if she didn't know how to respond, when just at that moment Mr. Mosely pulled in the yard in his pick-up truck. He looked very angry. "Is that bitch causing you trouble, Mom?" he yelled.

I guessed he never called her by her given name. "I'm not here to cause trouble," I assured him. "I just thought your family would enjoy some extra food for the holidays."

"We don't need a damn thing from the likes of you, and you'd better tell that boyfriend of yours that if he ever lays a hand on one of my boys again, I'll kill him," he warned. "You got that? Now get off my property!"

"I'll go, I'll go, but I'm leaving this here," I said as I placed the basket on the ground. "You need to think of your family. Despite your hatred for me, I'm going to wish you a very Merry Christmas." As I quickly got in the car, I saw him coming toward me. I slammed the door, backed out of the yard, and got on the road, not looking back. Was he going to hit me or throw my basket at me? I would never know. I knew this whole adventure had been a risky move, but my mission was successfully accomplished.

I was driving near the Heritage Museum when I decided to turn in. I needed a distraction, and I was anxious to hear from Sharla Lee about the charity gift delivery and I could certainly visit my cookie tree.

Sharla Lee was off for the day, but Gerard happily greeted me in the fairly crowded room.

"Say, Miss Kate, you're getting a lot of swell comments about your cookie tree," he boasted. "I think all of the cookies are even still there!" He burst into laughter, as he so frequently did.

"That's good," I said, grinning. "Can you tell me if all the charity gifts have been delivered?"

"Oh my, yes," he said, more seriously. "They picked up those bags shortly after we got them back here. You all were mighty generous, I'll say that."

"That's good," I responded. I felt a lot of personal satisfaction just knowing that.

CHAPTER 81

"Hi, Kate," a voice called from behind me. It was Anna. "I really like your tree."

"Thanks," I said, blushing. "I did my best."

"Kate, have you heard about Emma?" she asked with a serious expression on her face.

"No. Why?" I asked, concerned.

"They took her to the hospital yesterday," she stated, shaking her head. "They think she had a heart attack."

"Oh! Is she okay now?"

"Peggy should have called you. Emma's at the Perry Memorial Hospital in critical condition."

"Anna, how did this happen?" I asked, feeling like I might burst into tears. "I didn't realize she had a heart condition."

"Well, when I think back, she's not been in good health for some time. She's been more tired lately."

"We just saw her at the wrapping party and she seemed fine. I was so taken by the fact that she was giving one of her quilts to a charity family."

Anna nodded, giving a faint smile. "I know. That's just her," she said, tearing up. "Peggy is close to some of her children, so she'll be the one to keep us posted on her condition."

"Is she conscious? Do you think we can see her?" I asked, feeling anxious.

Anna shook her head. "She's in critical condition, so only family is allowed to see her."

"We've got to do something," I stated, considering the possibilities.

"We can send flowers as soon as she is conscious, I suppose," Anna suggested. "I need to go, Kate. Just keep her in your prayers."

I followed Anna out the door and got to my car as fast as I could. When the door closed, tears poured down my cheeks. I begged God to save her. She was one of my favorites in our Friendship Circle. When I felt more composed, I called Ellie. "Ellie, did you hear about Emma?"

"Yes, Peggy called," she said in a sad voice. "Have you heard anything new?"

"No, I just saw Anna and she told me," I reported. "I just can't believe it. I love her. She was so endearing when I was introduced to your group."

"Yes, she is quite the mother of our group," Ellie confirmed. "I know they can do so much medically these days, so perhaps she'll come around."

I felt a tad bit better after talking to Ellie. I was mentally drained from the Mosely encounter and news of Emma's heart attack. I just wanted to be alone. Just a short time ago, I had left the house so happy after I had heard from Aunt Mandy, and now all of this had come about. The day sure had gone down from there.

When I got home, I didn't have the energy to make a fire, despite the chill in the house from a cold front approaching. I went straight up the stairs and threw myself across my bed. I wondered if Emma was still clinging to life and at the same time wondered what happened to my gift basket at the Mosely's. I was about to fall asleep when my cell phone rang.

"Kate, it's Peggy," she announced.

"Oh, Peggy, I'm sorry I didn't get your earlier voice message, but I was running errands," I explained. "Anna told me what happened. Is there anything new with Emma?"

"That's why I'm calling," she began. "I just got word from her son that she passed away a few hours ago."

I couldn't believe what she had just said.

"She had a couple more heart attacks and the last one took her."

A great silence hovered between us.

"Peggy, Peggy, this is horrible," I responded. "This is so hard to believe after just seeing her."

"It's the pits, for sure," she said, clearly distressed. "No plans have been made, of course. She has one son here and one out of town. I will let you know immediately when I know something. I'm at such a loss."

"Peggy, the Friendship Circle needs to meet," I said without thinking. "She is one our sisters and we need to decide what to do for the funeral."

"I know," she agreed. "It's our first loss and there will be a void in the group, that's certain. I'm so sorry to bring you this news."

When we hung up, I thought of Emma's poor family. Emma had been a widow for some time, but she was a mother that truly would be missed. I went downstairs to make myself a cup of calming tea. I wished for a fire to comfort me, but it was too late in the evening to start one.

CHAPTER 82

The next morning, I did make a fire and sat down in front of it to savor my coffee. I was supposed to go Christmas caroling tonight. How could I possibly sing about Christmas cheer when I felt so sad? Cotton and Susie pulled in the driveway. I had forgotten it was the day for Susie to clean. I answered the door, still in my bathrobe.

"Good morning, Miss Kate," Susie greeted me happily.

"Is everything okay here?" Cotton asked, looking concerned when he saw my face. I'm sure it was quite puffy from all the crying I had done.

"Sure, come on in," I answered.

"Have you by chance seen what's on your back steps?" Cotton pointed in that direction.

I stepped onto the deck and saw the Mosley's ham. I couldn't believe it! "That's the ham I delivered to the Mosely family yesterday," I explained, shaking my head. "I left it inside a whole basket of food."

Cotton and Susie stared at me in disbelief.

"Well, the good news is that they decided to eat or keep the blueberry muffins."

"You're something else," Cotton said in disbelief. "Those low-life people ought to be in jail."

"The really sad thing here is that the father is so full of hate. He's denied his family food they would have enjoyed," I said, frustrated. "Well, I did my good deed, so let's hope I don't continue to have problems with them."

I poured Cotton and Susie cups of coffee. We sat in the sunroom as I told them about the passing of Emma. The nuisance and the anger the Mosleys had caused just didn't seem as important as it had been previously. They both listened as I shared my sorrow. "I'm supposed to go caroling tonight with the Friendship Circle, but I just don't see how that can happen."

"Miss Kate, it's none of my business, but I'm sure Emma wouldn't want you to miss this event because of her," Susie said sympathetically. "And, I wouldn't let the bullies of the Mosely family dictate my Christmas activities. They got the pleasure of having the last word by leaving you this ham, so let them be."

I was shocked at Susie's outspoken response.

"Susie's right, Miss Kate," Cotton stated, backing Susie up.

"Well, I guess I'm outnumbered here," I said with a smile.

"I'll take that ham off your hands," Cotton offered. "It should still be perfectly good by the way it's all wrapped up. Our dog, Jumper, would enjoy that bone!"

"Well, you are welcome to it," I responded, glad for the opportunity for Cotton and Susie to take the ham. "Jumper. What a cute name for a dog."

After Cotton left, I felt so much better. I gave Susie her instructions and started to rethink my day. I called Ruth Ann and asked if she would like me to pick her up for the caroling. I knew Ellie had to work at the winery.

"Oh, Kate, I'm so glad you called," Ruth Ann answered. "I am so depressed about Emma."

"I know. So am I," I replied, wanting to tear up again. "I

QUILT THE TOWN CHRISTMAS

am certainly not in the mood to go Christmas caroling, but I think we should go ahead and do this for Emma."

"I was thinking the same thing," she added. "I need to be with somebody. I have been working on getting things ready for the big East Perry Christmas party, and I need a break."

"I'll pick you up about six, okay?" I suggested. "We'll see how it goes. I need to have something positive happen, and I'd like to support Esther with all the work she has done to organize this event."

"Indeed," she agreed. "Dress warmly. They are predicting snow showers. By the way, come inside when you arrive. I have a surprise for you!"

"Really?" I asked, hoping it would be Jack's quilt. "I'll look forward to it." When I hung up, I felt like I had to bake something. I decided it would be cookies, starting with chocolate chip. I could send some home with Susie and bring a plateful to Ruth Ann. If I had known where Emma's son lived, I would have taken him some, too. With Christmas at our doorstep, I decided to make a double batch.

Susie was delighted as she smelled the fruits of my labor. "No one bakes like you do, Miss Kate."

As I fixed her cookies to go, I told her about Jack and Aunt Mandy arriving on Christmas Eve. She offered to help in any way she could. As soon as Cotton picked up Susie, I went upstairs to get ready for the evening. Coming out of the shower, my phone rang. It was John. I should have let it go to voice mail, but I answered, hoping he couldn't see me with just my bath towel. "Hi neighbor," I answered.

"How's my favorite neighbor?" he asked in return.

"Promise to close your eyes," I teased. "I just got out of the shower."

251

"Hmmm," he murmured.

"I've had a rough day," I began to explain. "We lost the oldest member of our Friendship Circle to a heart attack."

"I'm sorry to hear that. Tell me about her."

I did just that, which was comforting in some way. He was always such a good listener. John knew how important these friends had become to me when I moved to Borna. When I told him I was committed to going caroling, he thought I was doing the right thing.

"I miss you. Do you realize that?" he said when I gave him a chance to talk.

"You are always very sweet to say that, John," I said, feeling embarrassed. I knew he wanted me to say the same.

"Are you still planning to come here after the holidays?" he asked.

"Yes, but the weather will tell the story," I reminded him. "By the way, I loved your article. I meant to text you right away when I read it. Thanks for sending it to me."

"It was my pleasure, and I hope it brings you a little business," he added.

We talked a little bit longer before hanging up. The attention I was getting from this younger man never ceased to amaze me.

CHAPTER 83

When I arrived at Ruth Ann's, she couldn't wait to show me the results of Jack's lighthouse quilt. Knowing how good she was at quilting, I knew I would not be disappointed. It took my breath away when she opened it up for me to see. She had used all nautical quilting designs to bring it alive. I couldn't thank her enough for her creativity, and I knew Jack would be thrilled.

We hurried to Concordia Lutheran Church to join the others for the caroling. When we walked in, we saw Ellen, Anna, Betsy, Mary Catherine, and Esther. When we saw their faces, we all broke into tears and did a group hug. We hadn't planned this moment together, but it was the perfect occasion to grieve our missing sister.

"Where is Charlene?" I asked when I realized she was the only one missing except Ellie.

"She has a terrible cold and didn't want to get out in this weather," Esther explained.

"Now, ladies, we have to get our act together and do this tonight for Emma," Esther said as she had her arms around Peggy. "Emma loved to go caroling and had signed up to go with us this evening. I think we can all fit into my big van. There will be another car following us as well.

"How long will we be gone?" asked Anna. "I can't be gone too long."

"Under the circumstances, we don't have to visit as many

places as I had originally planned," Esther explained. "There are snow flurries now and then, so we'll have to watch those curvy roads."

I was so glad I didn't have to drive any farther than the church.

"There are refreshments afterwards here at the church for those who can stay," Esther said.

We drove a good distance, talking mostly in whispers. Esther told us that our first stop would be an elderly couple who was pretty much homebound. The man was in a wheelchair and his wife was his caregiver. Their home was a lovely well-kept farmhouse. They left a porch light on for us.

"They expect us every year," Esther informed us. "This really makes their Christmas!" Esther explained that we would sing two or three carols and finish with "We Wish You a Merry Christmas." Esther concluded, "I have song sheets here if you need them."

We jumped out of the van, securing our coats and scarves to protect us against the cold. Esther did her best to get us energized in spite of our weak voices. When we started singing "O Come, All Ye Faithful," the couple came to the front porch. I couldn't remember the last time, other than church, when I had sung a Christmas carol. The next was "Silent Night." The emotion that hymn evoked made it hard for all of us to get through. I kept going as tears rolled down my cheeks. So far, this was not bringing joyful energy to our Christmas caroling.

"Okay, let's give them a good sendoff, ladies," Esther encouraged us. In cheerful loud voices, we sang "We Wish You a Merry Christmas."

We agreed that we needed to leave our tears behind

at the next stop, which was at a small, rundown house in Dresden. A young mother came to the door with five or six children clinging to her clothing, as if they were afraid. In her arms was a child under the age of one. Esther said we should start with "Here Comes Santa Claus" for the children. It did put smiles on all of their faces, and, as I observed their environment, I hoped they had been one of the families on our charity list.

We went to a few more places, which actually took us by the Mosley's trailer. I almost told Esther to stop her van, but I wasn't sure if I should drag everyone into my horrid situation. When we got back to the church where everyone's cars were parked, we agreed to go inside and help ourselves to hot cider and cookies. It was Christmas, after all, and it was good being together.

I walked into the church, and to my surprise, there stood Ellie.

"I couldn't stay away completely, knowing you were here," Ellie said, giving me a hug. Everyone was so glad to see her. We started sharing our night's experiences with her so she would feel included.

"Being together tonight really helped all of us," I told Ellie. "I'm glad I came, or I would have moped around the house all night. Emma would be pleased that we were all together, thinking of her."

We stayed there at least another hour. As we filled our cups with cider, Peggy made a toast to our friend, Emma. This evening was a better tribute to her than standing in line at a funeral parlor.

It was late when I finally got home. Seeing my lit tree when I walked in the door reminded me of the real meaning of Christmas, despite life's disappointments. As I undressed for bed, I thought about Clark and whether he knew Emma. It seemed that in East Perry County everyone knew everyone, and so if there was sorrow or joy, everyone felt it. Before I crawled into bed, I peeked out of my front window to see the falling snow. I was glad I was home, safe and sound. I wanted to share my night with Maggie, but I knew it was too late to call. I went ahead and sent a text to her that she could read in the morning. I really did miss Maggie and Carla. Jack should be arriving in South Haven by now, so I hoped I would hear from him soon. I went to sleep thinking of Emma and how she was now joined with her dear husband.

CHAPTER 84

The next day, I turned down an unusual request to have a whole family stay at my guest house through the holidays. I hated turning down business, but this was not possible since I only accepted adult guests. When I began to feel bad about my restrictions, I remembered Clark telling me early on that I was in control of my business.

I used the morning to finish wrapping Christmas gifts. My list had grown since I had moved to Borna. The last gift I needed to get was from Ellie. I had asked her to order me the best single malt scotch she could find. I knew that would be a big treat for Clark.

Clark had been gone for several days. For some reason, he kept his medical treatment location a secret. I assumed it was in St. Louis. He said he would contact me when he returned, but I wasn't counting on it. I couldn't let myself think about Clark's serious health challenges. I just had to assume he would be okay.

It continued to snow as the day progressed. The wonderful fireplace kept me company. I wondered how the weather would affect Emma's memorial service tomorrow. I tried not to think about her not being at the next Friendship Circle meeting when we met in January. Our December meeting was our wrapping party, and it was good to remember the fun and success of that last meeting with all of us together.

I was polishing some silver for the Christmas dinner when Aunt Mandy called to give me an update about her travel plans. She said Jack was nice enough to call her and tell her he would be renting a car to drive from the St. Louis airport to Borna. She was delighted and it was sweet to think of them spending some time together.

Ellie called at five to say she had closed the winery for the evening because of the weather. She said she was unthawing a couple of her homemade chicken pot pies if I'd like to join her for dinner. I was delighted and perfectly willing to don boots and tromp over to her house. What would I do without my sweet Ellie?

When the grandfather clock struck six, I wrapped up some of my cookies for Ellie and headed over to her house. I told Ellie when I arrived that we needed to put in a sidewalk between our houses instead of walking on the busy road or trudging through our yards. I took off my boots and relished the warmth of Ellie's kitchen.

"I haven't had chicken pot pie in years." I admired Ellie's work as I watched her pull them out of the oven.

"I make six at a time and freeze them. I also made a spinach salad. I brought home a bag from the winery so it wouldn't spoil."

"Nice combo. Do you want me to pour the wine?"

"Sure. The glasses are up there," she pointed to a cabinet. "Are you going to the church tour, Kate? I think this weather is going to really impact the attendance. They have never cancelled before, and they have no other optional date."

"I would like to go. I just love it. If someone else would drive, I would go."

When we sat down to the hot, savory pie, Ellie asked

about Clark. "You haven't seen him for a while, have you?" she asked, sounding concerned.

"Well, as you know, when he goes out of town to work, he can be gone any length of time." I decided to try to dodge the question.

"So, he doesn't call you or say when he's going to return?" Ellie asked as she sipped her wine. "I thought you two were an item these days." She grinned, knowing I didn't like to be teased about Clark.

"Oh, Ellie, stop," I said, putting down my fork. "I'm tired of explaining our relationship. I did, however, help him cut down a Christmas tree last week. He hasn't had a tree for a long time. I will tell you that this guy is very happy being in control of his man cave out there. I did ask him to come to Christmas dinner. Does that make you happy?"

"Good girl!" Ellie replied between bites.

"He's worried, of course, of what Jack might think," I sighed. My cell phone rang and it was Jack. "Oh, do you mind?"

Ellie shook her head.

"Hey, Mom," Jack began. "I'm here at Jill's house with her mom and dad. We just finished a wonderful dinner that Maggie made for us. We're on speaker phone so we can share our news with you."

I took a deep breath.

"I have asked Jill to marry me and we have received her parents' blessing."

"My goodness!" I screamed. "Congratulations, you two! Thank you, Jill, for accepting!"

They laughed.

"I wish I were there with you! Jill, are you sure you can't make it to Borna with Jack?"

"Thanks, Kate, but I need to get back to work the day after Christmas," she confirmed. "I'm glad you're happy about our news, and of course, my mother is dying to talk to you."

Having figured out the content of the conversation, Ellie glowed as she listened to me.

"Kate, can you believe it?" Maggie giggled. "Our dream is coming true!"

"Hug them both for me, will you?"

"I'll be happy to."

"Is there a date set?" I asked to no one in particular.

"They said they don't have a date right now, so we'll keep pushing that, won't we?" Maggie teased.

CHAPTER 85

After lots of love was expressed over the phone, I hung up in total delight. Ellie came over to give me a hug. "This is really awesome, Kate. Let's make a toast to Jill and Jack."

My eyes were filled with tears. "Oh, Ellie, I wish Clay could be here to celebrate this news," I said without thinking.

"Of course you do, but let's just wish Jill and Jack all the best," Ellie said, raising her glass.

As we continued our visit at Ellie's kitchen table, I was on cloud nine. "I meant to tell you that Carson did book a room for after Christmas."

Ellie smiled like she already knew. "He insisted on being here for my New Year's Eve party, so what can I say?"

"I have to ask. Do you believe him when he says he is getting a divorce, or do you think the two of them may just be separated?"

She sighed. "Look, I'm not going anywhere and I have to take him at his word. I don't like having feelings for a married man. That, I can tell you, is the truth, my friend. Time will tell."

"Does he mention wanting to move here after the divorce?"

"Heavens, no!" she answered quickly. "He would want to live in the city where the headquarters is located for his work. He would go crazy living in a small town like Borna."

"So, would you ever consider moving so you could be with him?"

"You think I'm bad when I ask about Clark," she teased. "Do you really think I could do that? I am married to Red Creek Winery. I do like having a man care for me, I'll admit, but I am very limited about what I can give in return. I think you know that. You are more suited to having a man in your life than I am."

"Really?" I had to think about that.

"Yes. You're a nurturing person. You nurture people with your homemade food, for starters. You nurture your home with lovely touches like only you can do. You love nurturing your guests too, which is a fine quality. I am driven by the bottom line in business, I'm afraid. I'll be growing grapes, come spring, which is going to demand even more of my attention."

"That is so wonderful to know about the grapes. It's good to hear that is all about to happen."

"Trout has really pushed me about that," she revealed. "He will play a major role in the expansion because of all of his knowledge. I'll lose a good bartender in time, but it'll be worth it. I know he's been sticking around to see this happen. You know, the hills here in East Perry are perfect for grapes."

"How wonderful," I said as I took my last swallow of wine. "It's so exciting that you have such a vision for your future. I'm not sure I can see past the holidays."

We laughed.

"Does Carson know your plans?"

She nodded as she looked out the window. "Boy, oh boy, this looks like a major snowstorm!" Ellie sighed. "That means we'll have to close tomorrow, most likely."

"I can't believe how the weather seems to shut things down here in the country, unlike in South Haven. Hey, Ellie, I was wondering if you remembered to order Clark's scotch."

"Well, Trout and I met with the rep and he narrowed it down to several of his top sellers," she reported. "I hope you're ready to pay some big bucks!"

I laughed and nodded.

"Glenfiddich is the largest selling malt worldwide. It's light and fruity. Macallan is also a favorite. A Macallan still is even printed on the back of a Scotland's ten-pound note."

"Whatever you decide will be fine," I reassured her. "I don't know how anyone can drink the stuff, but I do know that Clark will enjoy it. I'd better get on home."

"I'll watch until you get there," Ellie said, smiling. "Be careful!"

"Thanks so much for a delicious dinner," I said, getting on my sock cap and coat.

"I'll continue to enjoy the cookies," Ellie added.

We hugged before she opened the door to the North Pole of Borna.

CHAPTER 86

An early phone call from Ellen woke me the next morning. "Sorry to have awakened you, Kate," Ellen began. "I am desperately calling to staff people at Concordia tonight for the church tour. My scheduled ladies are either sick or refuse to go out in this weather. We certainly do not want to cancel. Since you live close to the church, I wanted to know if you could greet folks for a couple of hours this evening. Oh, and by the way, they postponed the memorial service for Emma. They think it will be next week."

"Oh, Ellen, I don't know what to say," I murmured, still feeling half asleep. "I'm a big chicken when it comes to driving in this weather. What is today's forecast?"

"Not good, but they are wrong many times, as you know. I'm sure they will plow the road sometime today, so you should be fine. Could you cover between seven and nine? Please?"

"Okay, I'll try," I answered reluctantly.

I slowly got out of bed and looked out the window. The wind was howling and the snow was blowing. What had I just agreed to do? I was just like everyone else in that you couldn't say no to Ellen. Was South Haven this bad in the winter or did they just handle the snow better?

Still in my robe, I went downstairs to make a fire. This is where I really wanted to stay today. My phone rang and I saw it was Cotton. We chatted and he told me he would be by later in the day to shovel. I told him not to come until the snow let up. I sat by the fire with my coffee thinking about all of Emma's relatives who had to change their plans. As I sat there, I wondered if I should invite Ruth Ann and Ellie to lunch since they were within walking distance. I looked in my freezer and saw some shrimp, which told me shrimp scampi would be a good option. If I had the time, I could make a quick loaf of bread. Yum!

The first call was to Ellie, since I knew she was an early riser. She jumped at the offer. After Ellie accepted, I called Ruth Ann. She had a list of reasons why she should not come.

"Tomorrow night is the big East Perry Lumber Christmas party and I still have some things to do," she complained. "I hate missing any kind of party, so perhaps I could just take a break and come for a short time."

I smiled at my success. Before I got dressed, I started preparing the bread as the shrimp was unthawing. When I placed the bread in the oven, I set the dining room table as if the queen was arriving for lunch. I clipped some pine sprigs from my large Christmas tree and made a holiday arrangement. I put on Christmas music and kept trying to think happy thoughts, like Jack and Jill's marriage, instead of my dreaded trip for the evening. Now, I was ready to go upstairs to make myself presentable.

Ellie was early. When I opened the back door to let her in, she challenged me to come out and make a snow angel with her. I laughed at her suggestion, but told her I was a kid from up north and I could challenge her to a good snowball fight. She decided to come in and get warm instead.

"I brought wine," she said, lifting up her prize. "I'm always good for that."

We laughed.

"Put it in your wine rack if no one wants any."

"We're having shrimp scampi, so that wine might taste pretty darn good!"

Ellie sliced the hot bread while I put another log on the fire and poured some wine, just in case it was well received. She was surprised to see such a holiday setting for our lunch. I then heard a pounding at the back door, which was likely Ruth Ann. She looked like someone from the North Pole! Her face was beet red and she was shivering. She had undoubtedly decided to walk from her house to mine. Her feet and legs were snow covered, so she peeled off layers of outerwear before she came into the sunporch.

"Women will go to such extremes to go out for lunch!" Ruth Ann exclaimed, making us laugh.

"This is sure better than eating a hamburger in Marv's smoky bar," Ellie added.

"There is a part of me that's been lonelier since Emma passed," Ruth Ann shared as she sat down. We both nodded. We understood what she meant.

"So, are you excited about your first really big party?" I asked Ruth Ann. "Do you think the weather will affect the attendance?"

She shook her head. "Ellen told me they will shuttle employees from various locations," Ruth Ann revealed. "This is a huge deal for the company. Wives certainly look forward to this fancy occasion and the menu is nothing but the very best in seafood, pork, and beef. The guys, of course, love the open bar. The wine and beer will be flowing!"

"I'm staying off the roads that night," teased Ellie. We all had another laugh.

"I guess Carson will enjoy the wine sales," Ellie said.

"I'm sure he will," Ruth Ann nodded. "I've got a new rep starting in January, though."

Ellie looked shocked.

"I think he is way too high, and frankly, I don't like his chauvinistic attitudes toward women. Of course, he's not the first vender to be that way. Women aren't supposed to have a business head on their shoulders." The last comment was laden with sarcasm.

Ellie's mouth and eyes were big, and it was clear that she did not know what to say. It was definitely time to change the subject!

CHAPTER 87

"Time to eat," I interrupted. "Doesn't this smell divine?"
"It really does," agreed Ruth Ann. "I might have to hire you at the banquet hall."

"Well, at some point, Ruth Ann, you may need a desssert chef to be at your disposal," I grinned. "I might be able to do that for you. My bread and muffins would still be hot on delivery!"

That's a deal," Ruth Ann cheered, holding her hand up to join mine.

"Wonderful idea!" Ellie said. It was clear that she was still processing Ruth's description of Carson.

"Hey, tell me what you know about Wittenville," I asked. "I still haven't been able to check it out, but it seems like many folks are from there."

"Sure. In 1839, it was settled at about the same time as Borna and a few other villages," Ellie said as she put her wine glass on the table. "It's on the river, so some refer to it as one of the 'drowned towns.'"

"What does that mean, exactly?" I asked, thinking I may have heard her wrong.

"Well, it never came back after the floods of 1973 and 1993," she stated. "There are many towns like that. In other words, they drowned completely. It was a pretty thriving town at one time. We'll drive down there sometime. There's nothing left now but some foundations, steps, and a monument where the church was."

"Oh, how sad." I pictured the scene in my mind.

"My mom said Wittenville was where the last train robbery in Missouri took place," Ruth Ann reported. "They got around $100,000 and the robber used to be with the original Jesse James gang years ago."

"Well, you two are just full of good information. I think Sharla Lee should have tours available for that county."

"Speaking of Sharla Lee, they have the altar and pulpit from St. Paul's church that was in Wittenville. Do you remember seeing that in the museum?"

"Of course," I responded. "I just didn't make the connection." I passed around a platter of cookies.

"These aren't some leftovers from your Christmas tree, are they?" teased Ellie. "I just had some dental work done."

We chuckled.

"On a serious note, ladies, Ellen called early this morning to ask me to greet people tonight at Concordia during the church tour," I stated, shaking my head. "I'm a really big chicken when it comes to driving in this weather. Would one of you or both consider going with me?" They looked at me like I had asked them to walk across burning coals.

"Not I," exclaimed Ruth Ann. "I shouldn't even be here now with all the work I have to do."

"They need to cancel, for heaven's sake," Ellie added. "No one's going to come out tonight. She called me, too. I told her no. I can't believe you agreed to do that."

"They never cancel, Ellen said," I said sadly. "I just can't say no to her. I know I live fairly close to the church, but I have a Mercedes, not a pick-up truck like everyone else has around here. I can't believe how they don't take care of the roads any better than they do. I'm not used to that."

"Well, good luck," said Ruth Ann as she helped herself to another cookie. "Where's that good lookin' man I see you with lately? Maybe he can take you."

"Oh, stop," I said, taking one of my cookies. "He's out of town and why would I want him to get out in this mess?"

"Call her back and cancel," Ellie instructed me as she got her coat. "I'm sorry, but she's asking a lot from you."

They both got ready to leave soon after my unpopular invitation. The lunch and visit were a nice break on a winter's day. When they went out the door, I finished my glass of wine by the fire. The plans for the evening weighed heavily on my mind. I decided to call Cotton to see if his arrival would fit in with him taking me to the church. If I could get there, someone would surely take me home.

Cotton answered the phone, which surprised me. "I was about to call you, Miss Kate. I won't be coming by after all. My truck won't start and Susie and Amy Sue are down with fevers."

"Oh, I'm sorry to hear that," I said, feeling sorry for them, "You don't need to get out in this weather anyway. Give them my best and take good care of them. You come over when you can."

"Are you okay?" Cotton asked thoughtfully.

"I'm fine," I said, feeling I was telling him a half truth. "You all take care."

"Sure will, and I'll see you soon," Cotton said in closing.

I took a deep breath and started cleaning up my luncheon table. I concentrated on some laundry and looked out the window every fifteen minutes, as if the snow would somehow go away. I still had every intention of making the trip as the day went along. My Mercedes was nice and dry in the garage, so that was a pleasant thought. If folks thought enough of the church tour to attend, I surely could get there to greet them.

CHAPTER 88

A few hours later, I put the fire out and began to bundle up for my short trip to the North Pole. I prepared a plate of cookies to offer any guests that might arrive at the church. I told myself to be brave and prayed for a safe journey as I went out the door. I proceeded to the garage, my feet making deep impressions in the snow. When I made it to the garage, I said hello to Mirty, which was my nickname for my Mercedes. She started like a dream, as always.

Strapped safely in my seatbelt, I backed out of the garage very slowly. There wasn't any traffic on Main Street, so no one cared that I barely moved along. I tried to follow in the tracks where someone else had driven, but it was causing my car to slip and slide. I was driving toward Ruth Ann's place and knew I'd have to turn left at a nearby road that would take me to the church. As I began to make the turn, I was headed down a long hill without much traction. One or two cars passed me by, making me very nervous. My northern driving experiences reminded me to turn into the slide instead of the reverse. A pick-up truck was on my tail. I stayed focused, but I could feel every muscle in my body tightening up.

All of a sudden, the driver of the truck made a move to go around me, nearly taking my car along with him. My reflexes caused me to swerve away from his vehicle so we wouldn't collide. That was a huge mistake because it caused me to travel uncontrollably down the hill. Mirty had a mind of her own and took me straight into a ditch! It felt like I watched it all in slow motion until I felt the impact. My worst nightmare had just happened! I opened my eyes and looked at my windshield which was covered in snow. The pick-up truck was long gone and I sat there in silence.

Mirty had died. She was not making a sound. Now what? I looked out of the snowy windows to see if I could see anyone or any car around me. I was perched in a car with its nose in the ditch. The closest house was up a steep hill, so that wasn't going to be an option. Who could I possibly call to come out and help me now? I knew I was on my own. The snow kept coming down. I realized that I would never get to the church. My only option was to walk back up this horrid hill and hope someone would come along. Before I removed my keys from the ignition, I tried to start the car, but to no avail. Backing out of this big ditch would be impossible anyway, so what was the point? Mirty was just going to have to stay here until I could call someone to rescue her in the morning. If I stayed with her, I would freeze to death.

Dressed for warmth and wearing big, tall boots, I could barely squeeze out of my car door. I stepped even deeper into the ditch which was covered with snow at least a foot high. I locked my car and got myself out on the road. The wind blew sharply in my face, making it hard for me to see where I was going. I couldn't see where the road started and ended. I thought of Ellen's disappointment as I put one foot in front of the other. I should have tried calling her before I left my car. Not meeting any cars told me there couldn't be very many attendees on the tour.

When an older car came toward me, I waved my hands for them to stop. It was a couple of teenagers who assumed

I was being friendly or cute and they drove on past me at a good speed. Now and then I stopped to get my breath. It reminded me of how out of shape I was getting. The hill seemed to get higher and higher instead of disappearing. My feet were so cold that they became numb. If I could make it as far as Ruth Ann's place, I could collapse there for the evening or at least warm up.

Another car came down the hill very slowly. I thought I surely had a chance to get them to stop. They kept on going, looking at me strangely like I was the crazy one on the road. Surely someone would connect the dots when they saw my car in the ditch. So much for Borna's hospitality!

I got to the top of the hill with a great sense of accomplishment. Now, I could see Ruth Ann's house. I had to focus on her place, picturing a warm, cozy shelter where I could unthaw. I walked faster as I got close enough to see her front door. I found myself silently praying that she would be home. To get to her house, I first had to make it to Main Street. When I got to Main Street, it still hadn't been plowed. Why did this entire town have to shut down? What if there was an emergency? I was an emergency, for heaven's sake.

When I got to Ruth Ann's large front porch, I just had to sit and rest. I knew now that I was close enough to get some help. When I got to her front door, it was unlocked, as always. Now I just had to get in her elevator to get to her private quarters. It was warm, so very wonderfully warm and dry. I could have crashed on the floor of her lobby and been perfectly comfortable for some time. I pulled out my phone to call her and let her know I was on her doorstep. My fingers were completely numb. This was not going to work.

CHAPTER 89

Forgetting any advance notice, I got to her elevator which took me to the hallway of Ruth Ann's living quarters. It didn't matter now if she happened to be home or not. I had shelter and I wasn't going anywhere. I rang the doorbell. It seemed like an eternity before she opened the door. When she saw me, she didn't know whether to laugh or cry.

"I landed in a ditch and walked here," I blurted out at once. I wanted to start crying. Someone had to feel sorry for me!

"Well, for heaven's sake, get in here," she said, clearly alarmed at my appearance. "Sit on this chair and let's get those boots off."

I could tell she was sincerely concerned for me. "Thanks. I just couldn't make it all the way home," I said, feeling the exhaustion. "I'm frozen!"

"Where is your car?" she asked as she removed my scarf and gloves.

"At the bottom of the hill, going toward the church," I explained as I waved my hand in what I thought was the right direction. "It was so slick and I couldn't see where the road started and ended. Some idiot passed me and ran me off the road. I have got to call Ellen and explain why I didn't show up."

"You just sit here and warm up," Ruth Ann instructed. "I'll give her a call. Ellen is the least of your concerns. I'll get the tea kettle going for some hot tea and turn on the gas fireplace for you."

I did as she said. As I began to get warm, the parts of my body that had felt frozen quickly began to ache. I remembered this pain from my childhood. When Ellen returned to check on me, she told me she had reached Ellen.

"She feels really badly that she encouraged you to come out tonight," Ruth Ann explained.

"Not half as bad as I do," I said in disgust.

"Is your car locked?" Ruth Ann wondered.

I nodded. "I'll call a wrecker in the morning. I cancelled my road service when I left South Haven since East Perry County was not on their radar screen." Occasions like this made me feel like I had moved to another planet.

"Can I just rest here for a minute?" I asked, glancing at her nearby couch.

"Yes, of course," she immediately responded. "Here, put this afghan around you."

Within minutes, I was asleep. I woke up fifteen minutes later, feeling embarrassed. "Oh, Ruth Ann, I'm so sorry," I said as I sat up. "I need to get on home."

"No, you don't," Ruth Ann said sternly. "We are both staying put. It's very late and very gruesome out there. I'll get you a robe to change into for the night. In the morning, I'll drive you home."

"Oh, I feel so stupid," I admitted.

"You are just a crazy lady that doesn't know how to say no," Ruth Ann countered. "You could have really been hurt if you had hit another car. How about we have some wine and a few calories to make us both feel better?"

"Oh, that sounds wonderful," I said, grinning. "I really appreciate this." I changed into her comfy terrycloth robe, feeling better already. I insisted her large leather couch was perfectly comfortable for me instead of staying in her guest room. By around ten that night, we both were relaxed from the wine and ready to call it a night.

My cell rang around midnight, scaring me when I woke to unfamiliar surroundings. It took a bit for me to find my purse and grab my phone.

"Kate, it's Clark," he said in concerned tone. "Are you okay?"

I tried to gather my thoughts.

"I was on my way home tonight and passed a car in the ditch that looked like yours."

"It's mine," I whispered, trying to be quiet after the scurry for the purse and the phone. "I was on my way to Concordia Church to help with the tour but didn't quite make it. I had to leave my car and walk back up the hill to Ruth Ann's place. I was nearly frozen. That's as far as I got, so I'm spending the night here. I'll call someone in the morning to get my car. Hopefully, there won't be any or much damage to it."

"I can't believe you went out in this weather. It's not like you," he complained.

"Kate? Is that you talking?" Ruth Ann said, coming into the living room in her pajamas.

"Yes, I'm sorry," I answered. "I didn't mean to wake you."

"Oh, no problem, it just had me concerned," Ruth Ann said, turning to go back to her bedroom. "Good night."

I didn't want to tell her it was Clark checking on me.

"Are you in trouble?" Clark asked humorously.

"Yes, I need to hang up," I said in a whisper. "Is everything okay with you?"

"I'm still alive," he joked. "I did get some good news today. My brother, Rock, is coming to visit for Christmas.

It's been over a year since I've seen him."

"That's great," I said too loudly. "You must bring him with you to Christmas dinner."

"We'll see," he answered, but there was hesitancy in his voice. "I'd better let you go. Can you handle your car situation?"

"Sure. It'll be fine, but thanks," I said with confidence. "Thanks so much for calling."

Off he went, in Clark fashion. At least he was back in Borna, which was comforting. His call had been the best part of my day.

CHAPTER 90

The next morning, I woke up to the wonderful aroma of bacon. Ruth Ann was busy cooking up a storm. I couldn't believe how well I slept. After I folded up my bedding, I joined her at the breakfast bar, looking for my first cup of coffee.

"It looks like driving you home won't be a problem," Ruth Ann observed. "They plowed the road early this morning. I'm surprised it didn't wake you. Here is the number of someone who can help you with your car. I used them once before when I had some car problems."

"Thanks," I said, giving her a warm smile of appreciation. "I should probably call them before I leave here this morning."

"Not before you have some of my mean pancakes and crispy, fried bacon!" Ruth Ann tempted.

"You got me there," I happily answered. "I'm starved!"

After a scrumptious breakfast, Ruth Ann drove me down the road to my house. I was so glad to be home. I promised myself to trust my gut feelings about things the next time. I knew the trip was going to be risky. Ellen's call on my cell came in as I took off my coat.

"Oh, Kate, I am so sorry about last night!" she cried. "I should not have asked you to come out in that terrible weather. Are you okay?"

"Yes," I assured her. "It was smart of me to spend the night at Ruth Ann's place instead of trying to get all the way home. They'll have my car back here sometime this morning."

"I just hope you don't have any damage. Thank you again for being such a trooper. I told Oscar that he needs to help you find suitable transportation here. You can keep your Mercedes in the garage for when you go to church!"

I had to laugh. "I totally agree," I reassured her. "I would truly welcome his help."

"I'll tell him to get right on it," she said, laughing. I knew Ellen meant every word of it. Hopefully, Oscar wouldn't mind.

While I waited for my car to be returned, I wanted to warm the house up with a fire and do some baking. It would calm my nerves and Christmas Eve was now at my doorstep. The thought of Aunt Mandy and Jack arriving soon was terribly exciting. Their rooms were waiting, beds were made, and their presents were wrapped and placed under the tree. Now, I could make some meals ahead of time that I knew Jack would enjoy. He loved my chili and manicotti. Those would be nice to have on hand.

It was early afternoon when the car finally arrived. I felt sorry for poor Mirty who couldn't handle the countryside. I put on my coat to greet the two men and give them the payment. Before they left, I wanted to see if the car would start. To my surprise, it purred like a kitten. I was sure Mirty was happy to see me once again. I drove the car into the garage and wiped off all the dirty snow. So far, I couldn't see any significant damage. I would have Cotton get it washed and have him take a look at it, too.

Before I went into the house, I checked the mail. I had six more Christmas cards. I quickly went into the house and opened the one from Maggie. It was strange hearing from her on paper. I hadn't bothered calling this week, knowing they were all busy with Jack's visit and the announcement of the engagement. I couldn't help but feel neglected and envious about the joy taking place in South Haven.

CHAPTER 91

Emma's service was held at Trinity Church in Dresden. The attendance was small, but all of us from Friendship Circle sat in the same pew as we listened to her homily. We tried to stay strong and hold in our emotions, but it was difficult. Emma's sons seemed very nice and invited us to join them for lunch at the church hall afterwards. Ellie said this was a typical practice in country funerals. The food was prepared by the Trinity Ladies' Aid, a group to which Emma had previously belonged. The variety of food was amazing and all homemade. The ladies that served the tables wore fancy aprons which were totally charming.

Ellie dropped me off after the service. At last, the snow was starting to melt. That was good to see as I thought of Jack driving on these roads. Jack was used to winter snow, but not these hills and curves. O'Brazo's Christmas Walk was tonight, but I was feeling too melancholy to enjoy such celebration. It sounded so wonderful. I was certainly impressed with all the holiday festivities this county had to offer.

That evening, I sat in front of the fire in a rather somber mood, thinking of Emma. I enjoyed the peace and quiet, knowing the days ahead would be hectic. I reflected on many unanswered questions. Would Clark come for Christmas dinner and bring his brother, Rock? Where was poor Susan with the holidays at hand? Would she go home to be with her son? What if she were hurt or killed? What was going on in the Mosely household? Would Mr. Mosely allow the family to have any kind of Christmas? Would the family cause me more problems in the near future? Why did I let myself even think about these things?

Tomorrow, I planned to have a Christmas breakfast with Cotton and Susie before they took care of some chores for me. Their presents were under the tree, which included a nice check for Cotton to use for a new or used truck. Their loyalty was worthy of rewarding.

After Christmas, I would have to get serious about advertising this guest house. Carson would be one of my first guests, but I had no one registered after that. Ruth Ann and I decided we could do some creative advertising that would benefit both of us. Ellie warned me that this was going to be a destination business that would have to be advertised. Admittedly, I had done very little advertising so far. Ruth Ann was energized after hosting a successful East Perry Lumber Christmas party. Her bookings for weddings were also going to begin picking up. That would help my business as well.

Now, I felt I could start planning my next trip back to South Haven. All I needed was a block of days where the weather would be clear enough to drive. Part of me hoped I could see more of John. Why I enjoyed his company so much was a bit of a mystery to me. He was so energetic, smart, and interesting. Why did he have to be so young? I hoped by now he had received the framed print of the Saxon Village that I had sent him for Christmas. I felt like going up to bed, but thought I should give Maggie a call to thank her for the nice Christmas card.

"Hey, girlfriend," she answered happily. "We just got home from the country club Christmas party."

"Oh, how was it?" I asked, sincerely interested. "I could use a little gossip."

She laughed. "Well, you'd be interested to know that James turned up with a date," Maggie shared. "Can you believe it?"

I snickered. Another womanizer, I thought. "Yes, somehow I can," I said, remembering poor Sandra's suicide. "Did you recognize her?"

"No, but the word on the street is that she is a rich socialite from Grand Rapids," she added.

"That should help his pocketbook," I snipped. "I wonder what his children think about him dating."

"From the way the two were acting, they must have been a couple for some time," Maggie guessed.

"Well, like his brother, they loved their women!" I stated, feeling a familiar resentment.

"Oh, Kate, I'm sorry," Maggie immediately cut in. "I shouldn't have brought any of that up."

"Was there any talk about how the lumber company is doing?" I asked, curious to know.

"They are still in business," she said sarcastically. "It's a shame that Jack has to separate himself from the family. He feels really badly about how they treated you. Do you realize that?"

"You didn't tell him about Clay's affair, did you?" I asked, concerned. "I don't want him to think about his father in that way. He really looked up to him."

"Heavens, no," she claimed.

We talked about a few more things, like Carla enjoying her work at John's condo. Carla had bragged to Maggie about how much she liked him. That didn't surprise me. Maggie tried to get more information about the relationship between me and John, but I wouldn't go there. She was very pleased that my aunt would be joining me for Christmas, especially since she had just been here for Thanksgiving. We ended the conversation by talking about Jill and Jack. She said they refused to be pushed for a wedding date at this time. The talk with Maggie certainly helped my mood. I smiled and was glad that I still had a home in South Haven.

CHAPTER 92

Cotton, Susie, and Amy Sue arrived early the next morning for our Christmas breakfast. I knew Susie was particularly fond of my French toast casserole, so while that baked in the oven, I made some omelets. Cotton was perfectly content with blueberry muffins, but I wanted to go all out for them today.

Amy Sue immediately ran to the Christmas tree, eyeing the many presents. It reminded me that Christmas was really for children. I convinced Susie to let her go ahead and open a couple of gifts to occupy her.

"Susie, you can open a couple of gifts that I have for you as well," I said as I picked them up to show her.

"Miss Kate, you shouldn't have," Susie said, blushing. "You do way too much for us as it is." She looked like a little girl as she discovered what was inside each of them. She couldn't believe the assortment of luxury bath items that were in one gift box. I knew that was something Susie would never allow herself to buy. When she saw the aqua crocheted shawl, she beamed and quickly wrapped it around her. Cotton was the first to tell her how beautiful she looked.

When the food was ready, we gathered at the table, including Amy Sue, who was delighted to have her very own muffin. I then asked to say grace, thanking our Maker for such good friends.

"Oh, Kate, you made my favorite dish," Susie exclaimed,

helping herself to a serving.

"Do you make these omelets often?" Cotton asked as his eyes admired his serving. "I can't say I ever tasted one of these fancy things, Miss Kate."

We laughed.

"It's got everything in here but the kitchen sink! I never thought of having mushrooms and the like at breakfast time!" He laughed as he bragged again about how delicious it tasted.

"I'm glad you like it," I said, enjoying the results of my cooking and baking.

"I have a little surprise for the two of you," I teased as I reached for an envelope I had place nearby. They stopped eating and looked at me with curiosity. I handed the envelope to Cotton since he had not received any presents.

He opened the envelope and pulled out the contents. The look on his face said it all. "Oh, Miss Kate, this can't be right!" he responded, utterly astonished.

"What? What?" Susie asked.

Cotton handed the check and note for her to see. The note expressed my thanks for their service and loyalty. I also stipulated that this money was for a new truck which was an investment in my future as well as theirs. Susie broke into tears. She was speechless as she got out of her chair to give me a hug.

"I hope this is enough to get you something reliable to drive for a while," I said as I, too, felt tears springing to my eyes.

"We'll be forever be grateful, Miss Kate," Cotton finally said. I could tell he was at a loss for words.

"Well now, I feel really silly giving you this little gift," Susie said, suddenly embarrassed. She reached into her purse and pulled out a small, wrapped package.

I unwrapped the paper and inside was a nicely framed photo of the three of them. It was darling and so meaningful to me. "I love this more than you know," I said, holding it close to me. "You are all dear to me, like family, really. This will make me smile every time I look at it. Thank you so very much." They seemed to be relieved with my response.

"Well, this breakfast was pretty special, so I'd better start earning my keep around here," Cotton said after he wiped his mouth with his napkin. "I'll go take care of your car while Susie and Amy Sue help you around here."

"I hope we get to meet your son while he's here," voiced Susie.

"I'm sure you will," I said, beginning to clear the table.

"It'll be nice to see your Aunt Mandy again," Susie noted. "I really liked her. She must think a lot of you to make that trip again."

"I agree and I'm very pleased," I said, grinning. "She's the family member that reminds me to think of my roots."

"Every Christmas, I really miss my Granny May," Susie reflected as she cleared our plates. "I loved her stories and she was really more of a mom to me than my real mom." I smiled, but did not respond. I was sure there was a leading story that we did not have time for at this moment. Amy Sue was totally absorbed with her new toys while Susie and I looked over the list of things to do today.

CHAPTER 93

I was ready! I had prepared all I could, physically and mentally, for this Christmas Eve. I hit the ground running, knowing this was the day my son would come through the door with Aunt Mandy. It was a cold, cloudy day, but the sun was shining bright in Josephine's Guest House.

Before I went downstairs for coffee, I took Jack's Christmas stocking out of the drawer to fill it as I had for over thirty years now. It was showing some wear, but it made me giggle with joy as I packed it full of Jack's favorite things. It was a lot easier when he was very young and happily amused with any toy.

I spread the goodies on the bed, ready to start fitting them into the long, narrow stocking. Jack would know and expect a pair of socks to be put into the toe because that was what I had done for so many years. He would complain, of course, but the other items made up for the practical socks. Besides money and gift cards, he knew there would be his favorite black licorice. We would always tease him about his black teeth after eating it on Christmas Day. It occurred to me that I would need to start planning a stocking for Jill as well for future Christmases.

I couldn't help but think of Clay, since he shared many of those memories with me. I'll never forget the year he put a set of car keys in Jack's stocking after he turned sixteen. It belonged to a used car that he had fallen in love with, but we had acted as though we were not supportive of the purchase. I don't think I ever saw Jack happier. I only hoped that Clay was watching our family continue in the best way we could in his absence.

My cell phone rang and it was Jack! "I'm waiting for Aunt Mandy's plane to arrive in the next couple of hours," he reported. "How is the weather in Borna today?"

"It's just fine. I'm antsy waiting for you!" I said happily. "Are you sure you know how to get here?"

Jack snickered. "Between the rental car's GPS and Aunt Mandy's recollection, we should be fine," he assured me.

I hung up feeling so happy that he was just hours away. I dressed and got ready to carry the stocking downstairs to put it on the fireplace mantle. I wished now that I had prepared a stocking for Aunt Mandy. When I got to the bottom of the stairs, I looked out my front door oval glass window, just as I had every morning since I moved to 6229 Main Street. There were a couple of packages sitting on the front porch. One looked like it had been left from FedEx and the other one was a shirt-sized box wrapped in Christmas paper.

I quickly opened the door and brought them in. I put the FedEx box aside, seeing that it was from John. The other intrigued me as I pulled the twine bow and noticed that the paper looked old and crinkled. Inside the box was tissue paper that contained a beautifully crocheted doily! Looking closer, I could also identify a row of what I recognized to be hand tatting on the lovely handmade piece. I saw an enclosed note. It must be from one of my Friendship Circle friends. I pulled the note out of the envelope and read: *Miss Meyr, Thank you for your kindness. I am sorry for any hurt my family may have caused you. This was made by my grandmother and I thought it belonged in a fine house such as yours. Please enjoy it and have a Merry Christmas. Agnes Mosley.*

I couldn't believe my eyes! She chose one of her few prized possessions to give to me. How sad for her to have to be the one to apologize when she did nothing wrong. I wanted to cry. You just don't realize what goes on behind closed doors and what people might be feeling. I would make sure to find a special place for this. There was no doubt that this was going to be my most cherished Christmas present.

CHAPTER 94

After reflecting on the beauty of Mrs. Mosely's gift for a few moments, I decided to open John's package. It was beautifully wrapped from a department store or specialty shop. I opened a card that read: *Holiday wishes, my dear friend. This looked like you. Enjoy! John.*

I unsealed the gold adhesive label that held the tissue layers together and found a white bathrobe that was amazingly soft. I noticed my initials monogrammed in gold thread. Underneath the robe was a pair of matching slippers fit for a queen. It was a yummy gift, but a bit too personal, really. It was very beautiful, but it wasn't going under my Christmas tree for any show and tell!

I got some coffee and stared at the two contrasting gifts before me. Christmas sure had a way of providing surprises. I had a quick bite of coffee cake before I prepared the ham for tonight's dinner.

I took the two gifts upstairs to find a place for them. My Victorian dresser had a spot where I kept a few favorite perfume bottles. The doily would fit perfectly there and I would be sure to see it every day.

I heard the doorbell ring. Could there be more presents? I was surprised to see Ellie standing there. She usually came to the back door. "Merry Christmas," I greeted.

She gave me a big smile. "I have something for you in the trunk of my car, but I need you to help me bring it into the house," she explained.

I looked outside and saw her car parked out front. Her trunk was open. "Ellie, what have you done now?" I walked out with her to the car. "I can tell you right now, you shouldn't have done this!"

She laughed.

"Let me help you."

It was a sizable, heavy, awkward box, wrapped in brown paper and tied with a red bow. Together, we managed to get it into the entryway.

"Okay, just go ahead and tear in," Ellie instructed me.

I pulled off the bow and made the first rip, still not recognizing what it was.

"It's a wine cooler that you can keep in your kitchen," Ellie explained. "I ordered one wholesale for my house and thought you could use one, too."

I couldn't believe it! "Are you serious?" I asked in amazement. "This is way too generous, Ellie. It's a luxury I would never have bought for myself, so thank you!" I gave her a big hug. "Please come in and sit down."

"I was thinking it could go right about here, under this cabinet," Ellie suggested as she pointed to a possible home for the gift.

"It's perfect, but why do you always have to outdo me with gifts?" I complained, embarrassed. I went to the Christmas tree and pulled out her gift. I really was embarrassed. She smiled as she tore into the box.

"This looks like a much more personal gift," she surmised. She pulled out the cream-colored shawl I had purchased at the museum, and her face seemed to light up. She then spotted the Heritage cookbook and really got excited.

"Do you like it?"

"Oh my, the shawl is beautiful, but I've wanted this cookbook," she admitted. "I have a couple of recipes in here from my family." She immediately started flipping through the pages. The first one she found right away was on page thirty-three which had her ice box rolls recipe.

"I must try that," I said when I realized it was hers. "I bought one for myself as well. I'm so glad you like it."

"Thank you so much, Kate," she said sincerely. "You always pick out such personal gifts. I also came by to share some good news that I heard yesterday."

"What? What?" I asked, helping her clear away the wrapping paper.

"Well, Charlene is quitting her job at the bank and plans to open a coffee shop in Dresden," Ellie announced.

"After all these years of working at the bank? Where is the shop going to be?"

"You know that cute little old bank on the corner when you come around the curve? You have asked me about that building, remember?"

I nodded, remembering. "Oh, that would be perfect, and I think there is space for parking."

"You know, her mom makes that delicious coffee cake we all enjoy, so she'll be selling it at her coffee shop," Ellie added. "She's already gutted the place and her dad has all the construction connections, so she's well on her way. It will need a lot of work, but it will be as cute as all get out when it's done."

"Oh, it will," I agreed. "Do you know what she'll call it?" I couldn't wait to hear.

"She said either Cashier Coffee or The Coffee Haus. They

are of German heritage, so I encouraged her to name it the Coffee Haus."

"That would be my pick as well. This is so exciting and it'll be a big change for her. We need more folks to make this kind of investment. We still have a lot of vacant buildings that need attention. The place won't hold very many customers, will it?"

Ellie shook her head.

When I followed Ellie out the front door to her car, I told her about the two Christmas presents I found on my front porch this morning. She was speechless on both accounts, not knowing what to think or say.

CHAPTER 95

It was hard to imagine my Christmas Eve getting any better. So far, it was nearly perfect. I figured that Aunt Mandy and Jack would arrive around four if everything went as planned. That would give me a good hour to set the dinner table and prepare the food. My cell was ringing on the kitchen counter and it displayed Clark's name. Did he decide to start using his cell phone?

"Merry Christmas," I answered.

"Aren't you a bit early?" Clark teased.

"It's been such a good day so far, and Jack hasn't even arrived yet," I proclaimed. "So, are you and Rock going to join us for dinner tomorrow?"

"If you'll have us," he said begrudgingly. "I think Rock just wants to come see what you look like."

I laughed. "Well, he can look all he wants," I teased back.

"What can I bring?" he offered politely.

"Not a thing," I responded. "I have so much food that you can't believe it. How about coming here around five? Will that work for the two of you?"

"We'll be there with bells on!"

I turned up the Christmas music, wanting to dance all around the house. When I breezed by the dining room table, I decided I would make place cards for the Christmas dinner tomorrow night. I didn't want Jack sitting next to Clark. I would put him next to Aunt Mandy. With the candles lit, this would be a festive table throughout the holidays.

I got the ham ready for the oven and began preparing my scalloped sweet potato casserole that Jack dearly loved. I was starting to feel nervous, hoping nothing would go wrong. I wanted them to arrive while it was still daylight so they could enjoy the beautiful drive. I also felt a bit guilty about not going to Concordia's Christmas Eve service. Ellen would be looking for me. She had bragged about the parts her grandchildren would be playing in the service. It would have been very nice, but the timing was not going to work with Jack and Aunt Mandy's arrival. Anxiously, I checked both my cell and landline for any missed messages.

Suddenly, a car horn honked in the driveway. It must be them! I ran out the back door without a coat to see my handsome son in person. I couldn't believe how much he looked like Clay. We hugged and hugged. He was really here in Borna and in my arms. I finally let go to hug the best aunt in the whole wide world.

"Mom, this is beautiful," Jack said, looking at the house and yard. "Aunt Mandy was really a big help getting us here. She remembered a lot."

Aunt Mandy grinned. I could tell right away that they had bonded.

"Come in, come in!" I said, linking their arms in mine and leading them up to the deck and onto the sunporch.

"It smells like Christmas Eve dinner," Jack said kindly. "Let me guess. We're going have country ham, scalloped sweet potatoes, and asparagus." I had to laugh and Aunt Mandy shook her head in disbelief.

"It's all for you," I said, looking him over once again.

"I feel so special to be a part of your Christmas," Aunt Mandy admitted as she gave me a little hug. "I told Jack right before we got here that I was ready for that special wine you called Merry Merlot!"

We laughed.

"Well, that's a perfect name for it today," Jack agreed. "Do you have any beer, Mom?"

"Of course," I nodded. "Bring your things in while it's still light and then we can relax with a drink by the fire. It will be just the three of us tonight."

"Great. Just tell me where you want our things," Jack obliged.

With the luggage inside, I showed him around the house. When we got upstairs to his room, he commented about how strange it was to see his furniture from home in a new setting. "Wow, this is so fancy that I'm going to feel like I'm one of your guests," he confessed. "I hope I don't mess anything up too much!"

"Don't be silly," I joked. "There is a nice private bath off of this room and you'll be right across from my bedroom and next door to Aunt Mandy's room."

"This is pretty awesome," he said as he walked around, taking in the details of the guest house.

"Come see the attic suite," I said. "This is a special place for those who want some privacy and a more unique atmosphere."

"This view is amazing from up here," Jack added.

We finally came down the stairs to join Aunt Mandy. Jack told her how impressed he was and how surprised he was to see so many antiques. It was good to know that he approved. We continued with our drinks as we enjoyed the delicious aromas wafting from the kitchen.

CHAPTER 96

"I almost forgot, Mom, I brought you something from Maggie," Jack said, picking up a bakery box that looked like it was from the Golden Bakery.

"Oh, my goodness," I responded when I opened the box to see the scrumptious blueberry scones. "This is perfect for tomorrow's breakfast."

"That's what she thought," Jack confirmed, grinning big and proud. "They should still be pretty fresh. She said it's the first thing you head for when you come home."

He was still calling South Haven home, I noticed. "Aunt Mandy, I don't know if you've ever had these, but you're in for a real treat," I promised.

"I took a peek on the way here and you're lucky there's still some in that box," Aunt Mandy kidded.

"I'd better refrigerate them right away," I said, heading to the kitchen.

When I returned, Aunt Mandy and Jack had poured a glass of wine for me and were ready to make a toast. "On behalf of Josephine's Guest House and being your closest relative, I'd like to welcome you both to my home," I toasted. "Thank you so much for making this trip." We lifted our glasses and cheered.

"Hear, hear!" they both said in unison.

"Now, let's get down to catching up," I said, getting more comfortable. "How is Jill?"

"Well, she's fine but kind of bummed out because she has to be at work so soon after Christmas," Jack answered, shaking his head.

"It would have been so perfect to have had her with us," Aunt Mandy lamented.

"Oh, I agree," I added.

"She said to thank you for your present," Jack remembered. Then, his eyes spied something fun across the room. "Hey, is that my old stocking hanging there on the mantel?"

"Of course, but you know the rules. You can't peek until Christmas morning," I said with a chuckle.

"Oh, Mom, you're something!" He had already sprinted to the stocking and was feeling the shapes inside.

"I'm sorry that you and I don't have a stocking, Aunt Mandy," I teased.

"I would have just gotten a lump of coal," she responded as she took a sip of her Merry Merlot.

"You know, I'm pretty hungry," Jack said as he was checking his cell phone. "Is anyone else ready to eat?" I had to snicker as I watched him trying to juggle many things at once, just like his father.

"Sure, just give me a few minutes," I answered as I went to the kitchen. The hot rolls were just nice and brown, so it was good timing as I took them out of the oven and put them in my antique silver bread basket.

When they saw the rolls, they gathered at the table. I managed to say a short prayer, which took Jack by surprise. He hadn't seen us pray at the table since he was very young. Clay was gone for so many meals that we got away from the habit. Jack dug in immediately after his quick amen. The chatter started between bites. When I told them that Clark and his brother would be joining us tomorrow, Jack looked bit taken aback.

"Oh, I'm so glad," Aunt Mandy responded. "Clark is such a fine gentleman."

Jack continued to look puzzled as we went on talking, but to his credit, he didn't jump in and ask more about this guy named Clark.

It made my heart swell to watch Jack eat so heartily. It brought back so many memories. The conversation was mostly between Jack and me, but Aunt Mandy understood why. I had to take advantage of my son being with me for this short span of time. When we finished, Jack put more logs on the fire while Aunt Mandy helped me clear the table. I knew she was exhausted from her day, so when she turned in early, I totally understood. It left Jack and me alone in the living room to talk, which was very pleasant.

"You have created a special place here, Mom," he commented as he stretched out on the couch. "You seem happy."

I nodded.

"Oh, before I forget, John Baker said to wish you a Merry Christmas."

"Oh? When did you see him? When you were at the condo?"

"Yes, a few days ago," Jack nodded. "We were walking together from the parking lot to our condo. "He's really a nice guy, but I get the impression he's hardly ever there."

"Did he tell you that he's been to Borna?" I asked, taking Jack by surprise. "He came here to write a story about East Perry County for the magazine he writes for." I lifted it off the side table to show Jack and extended it to him so he could take a look. "He's a travel writer, so this area was intriguing to him."

"I can't believe he actually drove here," Jack said as he began flipping through the pages. "Did he stay here?"

I nodded. "He was just here a couple of days while he traveled around the county," I added. "He's a great writer and has written a few books, too."

"Well, this is sure good publicity for you and the Red Creek Winery," Jack noticed as he was reading. "Your friend, Ellie, owns the winery, right?"

"Yes, and I hope we can get by there. I know she really wants to meet you. There are so many places I would like to take you."

Jack smiled as if he understood my enthusiasm.

"Well, I think I'm going to call Jill and then turn in, too," Jack said, getting up from the couch. "I have an early appointment with Santa in the morning."

I laughed. "Tell her hello for me, and if you need anything, just holler," I said, like he was a guest of mine.

When we got to the entryway, Jack paused in front of Josephine's wall quilt. "Hey, this quilt is pretty cool. What's the deal with the names written on it?" Jack inquired as he touched it. "Whose names are they?"

"They are folks who have stayed here at the guest house," I explained. "Will you sign it?" I handed him the pen.

"Sure, but Mom, there aren't very many names on it," he observed as he looked it over.

"Well, I haven't had very many guests. I'm pretty new at this, and the winter has been brutal. They aren't very good about clearing the roads, so it's mostly locals that pass through here."

Jack signed the quilt and gave me a kiss before he went upstairs. I put the fire out and prepared some things in the kitchen for my first Christmas morning in Borna.

CHAPTER 97

As I remained for a few moments in bed, I had to pinch myself. It was Christmas morning. My dearest family was actually sleeping under my roof. It was my first Christmas in the guest house. Last year, I was in South Haven, packing up to go to Borna. I was so excited about the coming events of this day.

I knew it was very early in the morning, but I wanted to have everything ready for a special breakfast. As I got dressed, I glanced at the doily from Agnes Moseley on my dresser. It made me smile and feel like everything was well with the world. Today, we would be celebrating the birth of Jesus. I wanted to look a little more festive, so I chose to wear a red sweater with some dark-washed jeans.

Jack was most certainly asleep when I came into the hallway. So much for getting up at the crack of dawn like he did when he was little! I tiptoed quietly down the stairs and turned on the Christmas tree lights. It was still dark outside, but my heart was glowing bright inside the house.

After I got the coffee going, I started making the same strata I had made on Christmas morning for as long as I could remember. When I got it in the oven, I started cutting up some fresh fruit. I was anxiously awaiting my first bite of the blueberry scones from the Golden Bakery. I reset the table, leaving the greenery and candles. I changed up the china and brought out some solid red napkins. I was getting this breakfast ritual down pretty well. It seemed to be my calling since I had opened up the guest house.

I was filling the glasses with orange juice when I heard Jack coming down the stairs. "Merry Christmas, Jack. How did you sleep?" I asked as he stretched.

"Pretty good, but the weirdest thing happened last night," he mentioned as he filled a cup with coffee. "I woke up in the middle of the night thinking it was morning because it was light. I thought I had overslept, but then I looked at the clock and it was only two in the morning. It was totally dark outside."

Where had I heard this before?

"I thought I must have been dreaming, so I just tried to go back to sleep. Do you have an electrical problem with the house or anything?"

"No, I don't," I replied. "So, did you go back to sleep okay?" Of course, I knew the answer.

"Oh yeah," he bragged. "I slept like a baby. I really didn't want to get up. It felt so good sleeping in my bed again!"

"Oh, I can imagine," I replied with a big smile. I guess Josephine had welcomed him with her warm light. No need to explain, I thought. "Go ahead and open your stocking, if you like."

He grinned like a little boy. "I'll get a fire started for you first. It's a bit chilly in here. It's so weird to have a real Christmas tree, Mom. It's so big!"

I went into the living room to join him. "It's what most folks around here have," I added. "You should see the wonderful live trees they have in the churches. They have a Christmas church tour that is really something to see. Your dad, of course, would have never allowed me to bring anything live like that into the house of ours."

"Yeah, I could see Dad really being a downer about things like that," he agreed. "He was such a perfectionist, when I recall his behavior. I'm afraid I did pick up some of his habits."

I was shocked to hear him admit that. "There are a lot of your traits that are like him, but they're not bad. You are looking more and more like him. You know how I thought he was very handsome."

Jack blushed, but pressed on. "I know the Meyrs have been bitter and rude to you since they did not inherit this property, so is that the real reason you were in such a hurry to sell the house and move to Missouri?"

His question caught me off guard.

"A lot of people were really shocked by your actions, Mom."

"Really?" I said lightly. "I needed a change, Jack, as I've told you before. Initially, I didn't come here with the intention of staying, but it didn't turn out that way. I finally found a place I could make my own."

"I can see that now, "Jack said, nodding in agreement. "It just seemed to me that you were running away from something. All your friends are in South Haven, and then you left Lake Michigan to come to a small town. It was odd."

I wasn't sure how much to explain. "You're pretty observant, Jack," I said, sitting down next to him.

"It was Dad, wasn't it?" he suddenly blurted out.

"What do you mean by that?" I asked softly.

"Dad's drinking had to be difficult for you, Mom," he began. "I know it was a heavy wedge between the two of you, no matter how you tried to disguise it."

I took a deep breath and nodded. "I was very angry," I said, looking down. "I felt he cheated both of us by his drinking. After a while of watching that behavior, your feelings and respect for a person change. When you see they don't attempt to get help or accept it when it's offered, it's hard to watch."

He nodded, his sadness evident.

Why did this have to come up now? I decided to continue. "I've had to let go of that resentment. Your father paid a great price for his bad habits."

"There was more to it than his drinking though, right?" The question seemed to tumble from Jack.

Thankfully, Aunt Mandy entered the room.

CHAPTER 98

"Good morning and Merry Christmas, you two," Aunt Mandy greeted us cheerfully when she arrived at the bottom of the stairs. She always looked so perfectly groomed.

"Merry Christmas to you, too," I said, standing to give her a peck on the cheek. "I'll get you some coffee. Jack is about to look in his stocking to see what Santa brought him."

He laughed, looking a bit self-conscious. "Aunt Mandy, Mom thinks I'm really surprised when I reach in for all her goodies," Jack teased. "I can predict each and every thing I'm about to pull out!"

"I think you should act surprised, Jack," advised Aunt Mandy. "I wonder what smells so good."

"That would be the black licorice I get every year!" he joked.

Aunt Mandy laughed. "How fun is that?" She giggled once again. "I used to love it myself."

Jack pulled out each item, making a cute remark about each and expressing a little thank you to Santa.

"This really big box is from me, Jack," I said, handing him the wrapped quilt. He looked stunned.

"For me?" he grinned. His reaction when he opened the box was priceless. Once the paper was off, he quickly unfolded it to be able to see the complete top. Aunt Mandy was equally surprised, judging from her reaction. I had my cell phone ready to capture the moment.

"Mom, did you make this?" he asked in disbelief.

I nodded, smiling.

"This is so awesome!"

"I really did!" I boasted. "I was so tickled when you said you would love to have a quilt from me for your room in the condo. It took me forever, it seemed!"

"Well, I certainly recognize the big red lighthouse in South Haven," Aunt Mandy commented.

Jack came over and enveloped me in a big hug. "I can't thank you enough, but I was at a loss as to what to get you," Jack said, handing me a wrapped box. "This can't compare to what you just gave me."

I opened the box to find a lovely framed photo of Jill and Jack.

"Maggie insisted we have this made to announce our engagement," Jack explained. "Do you like it?"

"It is just adorable and I will treasure this," I said as I stared at it. I had to remember that Maggie and Mark were still in South Haven's social scene and that she would want the media exposure for her daughter. Clay would have wanted it as well. I had left that scene, but this was a good reminder.

"It is really a good photo," chimed in Aunt Mandy.

Jack pulled out another box for me to unwrap, saying that this one required some explanation. "We did some work for the Food Network a while back, which was quite exciting," Jack began. "I kept thinking of you and how much you like to bake, so I bought some autographed cookbooks from some of their famous chefs."

I was surprised, to say the least, as I pulled them out of the box. I couldn't wait to look through each one of them. I jumped up with excitement and told Jack he was the best son in the whole wide world. These were precious gifts, mostly because he really gave it some thought and was inspired to give me something he knew I would love.

When it was Aunt Mandy's turn to open the white shawl I gave her, it was almost embarrassing. She seemed to love it and then presented me with her gift.

"Oh, my goodness," I said, pulling out a good-sized framed collage of family photos. Some showed me as a young girl. It was so personal! I couldn't hug her enough for her thoughtfulness.

"Aunt Mandy, I asked Jill what she thought I should get you," Jack said, handing her a gift. "She said no matter a woman's age, she still likes to smell nice and feel good. She picked this out for you." It was a beautiful gift box of lotion and body products. "She said it's her favorite, and she hopes it will be yours as well."

"That is so sweet, and if Jill loves it, it must be good," Aunt Mandy responded with delight. "I will write her a note to thank her."

"I'll call her after dinner so you can tell her yourself," he suggested. "She always smells like soap, which I prefer instead of perfume."

I had to grin at their exchange. "I think breakfast is calling if we want it to be nice and warm," I interjected.

"I'll pour us more coffee," Aunt Mandy offered.

"What can I do, Mom?" Jack followed me into the kitchen.

"You can bring your appetite and that strata to the table," I instructed him.

After I said a quick prayer of thanks, we dug in like we hadn't eaten in days!

CHAPTER 99

"I was thinking that after breakfast, you could show me around the town," Jack suggested between bites.

"That's a great idea," Aunt Mandy agreed. "I'll clean up here. I imagine that most places will be closed. What is your dear friend Ellie, doing today?"

"She was going to see her aunt," I recalled. "I'm hoping she'll stop by later tonight for a drink. I want Jack to meet her."

"That would be great," Jack agreed.

"These small towns have such possibilities, but unfortunately, some are vacant and run down," I said, enjoying another bite of my scone. "I have to admit, however, that since I have restored the doctor's house, my friend Ruth Ann has renovated the large building down the street and turned it into a banquet center. Ellie just told me recently that another friend of ours is opening a coffee shop in the old bank building in Dresden."

"It stimulates positive energy," Jack said, sincerely interested. "Remember how we saw some of that take place in South Haven?"

I nodded.

"I imagine that real estate is still pretty affordable around here."

"Compared to the prices in South Haven, it is," I agreed. "The county is generating a fair amount of tourism here. The

East Perry Alliance organization and the Heritage Museum do a great job of promoting the area. The real obstacle in getting folks to invest is that there are no regulations in place. No one wants to take a risk and invest in something that may get a trailer parked next door. There are no protections in place for these old buildings either, so someone can tear them down without anyone doing anything about it. Thank goodness that didn't happen to this house."

"Oh, you are so right!" voiced Aunt Mandy, shaking her head. "Sometimes it takes fresh eyes like yours to see the possibilities as well as the dangers. Some may not realize what they have."

"That's for sure," I said, pouring myself more coffee. "Once those buildings are gone, you have eaten away at your town's history. Ellie often tells me about what neat, historic buildings were here and there before they were torn down."

"Sounds like you may have a new calling here, Mom," Jack teased. "Maybe you need to educate them."

"I'm not a native to the area, and I think that makes a difference," I explained. "Who wants an outsider coming into town telling them what to do with their properties?"

"I think it would be a plus," Jack argued. "You have put your money where your mouth is showing them what can be done. You could get some of your Friendship Circle friends to form a committee to get a study done of what buildings are worth saving and which ones are not."

"You are such a smart young man," Aunt Mandy stated. "Too bad you aren't here to help with the idea. You have a talent like your mom to envision things. That's how it starts!"

"Not as good as Mom," Jack said. "We have to think outside the box all the time at work. I can see what she has accomplished here. I'm sure you had plenty of critics telling you that you were crazy to put your money into this place."

I laughed and nodded. "Yeah, the realtor was the first one, and then your Uncle James thought I was crazy," I said, shaking my head. "He had a personal reason, however."

"That still burns me to this day!" stated Jack. "Maggie said he already has a girlfriend. Can you believe that?"

"Maggie told me, too. But that's no longer my business. I do hate when I hear that he is running the business into the ground, though."

"Me too," Jack concurred. "However, we can't worry about that."

"My goodness, no," Aunt Mandy agreed. "You have plenty to think about right here in Borna."

CHAPTER 100

It was a long Christmas breakfast with excellent conversation. I was so pleased that Jack had an interest in my life here in Borna and welcomed his observations about the town.

"You kids get on your way," encouraged my aunt.

Jack and I dressed warmly, and when we got out to the garage, I told him about my adventure with Mirty that landed me in the ditch. There was some slight paint damage, but thankfully no dents. Jack inspected it carefully and said I should do something soon about getting a different vehicle.

Since we were closest to Saxon Village, I turned on the road that could just give him a glimpse of the log cabins. I shared my experience of judging a chili cook-off contest there. He seemed to be impressed with both. As we drove along, he couldn't believe how many churches there were, considering the populations of the villages.

I had made the same observation when I arrived. "They are very proud of their churches and seem to support them well financially," I added. "It drives a lot of the social happenings around here."

When we arrived at the First Lutheran College in Dresden, Jack had to get out of the car and walk around the log structure. He also admired the museum, which was closed for the holiday. I told him I had decorated a cookie tree inside of the museum for the tree contest. He thought it was a rather cute idea, but when I told him I won, he bent over in laughter, giving me a congratulatory pat on the back.

"So, will your picture be in the local paper?" he asked teasingly.

"Are you making fun of me?" I asked when we got back in the car.

We passed Harold's Hardware store, which made me recall my appreciation for all Harold had helped me with when I arrived here. "He's the one who gave me Clark's name to help me with my custom woodwork," I added. I probably shouldn't have said that.

"Oh, yeah?" Jack responded. "Is this guy, this Clark, pretty important to you? I assume he must be since he's invited to dinner."

I paused and knew enough to know to be careful regarding my response. "He is a good friend, but we're not an item, as your age group would say," I explained. "He's really famous for his woodcarvings, so I was lucky to get him to agree to do my cabinetry work. He was at my house a lot, so we became friends. He happened to always arrive when my muffins came out of the oven!"

Jack laughed. "Ah, the power of those muffins," he teased. "So, I gather that he's single. Has he ever asked you out?"

I had to think about how much I wanted to tell him. "Once," I answered. "There was a birthday party at the winery for someone we both knew. It was no big deal. He is a dedicated bachelor and that is perfect for me."

"Well, I'll check him out," Jack said with a grin.

"Oh, please don't," I said, getting serious. "It's nice to talk to a man once in a while because I'm surrounded by women a lot. Does that make sense?"

"I think it's great," Jack said as I turned to go up the hill to the winery. "Is this where the winery is?"

"Yes, I hope this road is okay from all the snow we've had," I said, concerned. "Oh, Trout is here!"

"Trout?" Jack repeated.

"Trout's the bartender here," I explained quickly.

"Hey, Kate!" Trout called from his vehicle across the parking lot. "You know we're closed."

I nodded.

"Merry Christmas!"

"Merry Christmas to you, too," I responded.

Trout headed back down the hill and I followed.

"Wow, you know the bartender here," Jack joked. "Do you hang out at the winery a lot? It's beautiful up here with the view and all."

"I know. Ellie has a great spot, and no, I don't hang out here," I explained. "Sometimes I come out to eat and then leave. Trout is Ellie's right-hand man and the nicest guy ever."

We drove around for another half hour, going slower in front of Ruth Ann's banquet center. Then he got a look at Imy's workshop and couldn't believe she did business in the little buildings. I told him it was where I had made many a purchase and how she was such a gem to the community.

"I'd bet you'd like to stop for a cold beer right now," I suggested boldly. "I see Marv's is open. How about that?" The parking lot was nearly filled.

"Are you a regular here, too?" Jack teased with a wink.

"Marv and his employees have been very good to me," I explained. "Everyone is very friendly and it's where I hired my plumber, heating and cooling guy, and my contractor."

Jack was getting to see and hear a new side of his mom.

"Hey, Kate," Marv said as we approached the bar. "Merry Christmas!"

"You too," I responded. "Marv, I'd like you to meet my son, Jack, who is visiting here for the holiday.

"Well, it's mighty nice to meet you, son," Marv said, extending his hand to Jack.

"This is quite a place you have here," Jack said, looking around.

"Yup, it's been in the family a long, long time," Marv bragged. "We have a pretty good cook here, don't we Kate?"

I nodded in agreement. "He makes the best chili, hamburgers, and friend chicken you've ever had!"

Marv blushed.

"Well, I hope to try some before I go home," Jack responded graciously.

We each ordered a beer and I thought Jack was going to faint when he heard my order. He had never witnessed me drinking anything but red wine.

CHAPTER 101

It was a wonderful day with my son. He just got a good dose of what his mother's life was like in East Perry. Aunt Mandy was taking a nap when we returned, so Jack decided to do the same. As much as I wanted to take a break, I had too much to do before dinner.

After I got the pork roast in the oven, I went upstairs to shower and change. The one beer I had caused me to want to take a nap. As I showered, I had to chuckle about the day's conversation and events. I wondered what Jack was really thinking about Clark and me. It made me nervous to think what it might be like tonight at dinner. Clark was probably concerned as well. Having Rock join us should minimize the potential for things feeling awkward.

My cell phone rang as I was getting dressed. It was Maggie calling to wish me a Merry Christmas. They were going to Mark's parents' house for dinner. I excitedly told her about what a great day I had with Jack. "Thank you for the scones! We devoured them at breakfast this morning."

"Great," she replied. "Have you talked to Carla today, by chance?"

"No, why, is she okay? I planned to do that yet today."

"She's pretty down, and I wondered if she was feeling okay," Maggie informed me.

"I don't think it could be money. I am still paying her," I said.

"Maybe you should ask her more questions when you call," Maggie suggested. "She knows you better."

Now my concern was about Carla, despite the rest of our conversation. Maggie said Jill had left and I should pump Jack for any further information regarding any wedding plans. We ended with words of love and hopes of seeing each other very soon in South Haven.

I came downstairs looking festive in winter white. I wore a gold watch necklace that Jack had given me for Christmas many years ago. I loved it and wanted him to see me wearing it. Jack and Mandy were still in their rooms, so I got busy preparing appetizers for the cocktail hour. As I was arranging some on a platter, the doorbell rang. Who would be arriving this early? When I got to the door, I didn't see anyone. A green Volkswagen was pulling out of my drive. It had to be Susan! I then noticed a gift basket that had been left on the step. I went out to pick it up and saw a fresh pineapple surrounded by tangerines. It had a note attached. It read: *"Merry Christmas, Kate. I'm on my way to see my son for Christmas. I'll be filing for divorce and moving to Dresden. I owe all my strength and encouragement to you. Love, Susan. P.S. The pineapple represents your generous hospitality."*

I smiled to myself. Another great Christmas surprise! I couldn't believe what I saw and read! I was so happy she was going back to her son, but was also worried for her safety. Had she been in Dresden this whole time? Was that why her husband kept snooping in this area? I could only hope and pray that all would go well for her.

I was icing the champagne when Aunt Mandy joined me in the kitchen. She looked festive in a red pantsuit, which was a striking contrast with her gray hair. She saw the basket of fruit sitting on the counter, so I told her to read the note. She was as delighted as well.

"Now, put me to work!" she insisted.

"You can fill the water glasses but I'm not serving dinner until seven," I informed her. "We are in great shape and the day has been marvelous so far."

"Indeed, honey," Aunt Mandy said with a big smile. "I think Jack is really enjoying his visit, don't you?"

"Yes, I do, and I'm so glad we had some one-on-one time together," I added. "He did ask me about Clark. I just told him we had only gone out one time and that we were just good friends."

"And he went for that?" Aunt Mandy winked and smiled at me.

"He did, because that's all it is!" I confirmed, just in time for Jack to enter the room.

"I just hate the thought of the two of you leaving," I said, swiftly changing the subject.

"Hey, Mom, should I start a fire?" Jack offered.

"That would be wonderful. Did you get a nap?"

"Yeah, it must have been the couple of beers I had," he joked. "No wonder Mom likes it here so much, Aunt Mandy. She's got a tavern next door and hangs out at a winery!"

Aunt Mandy roared with laughter.

"Jack!" I protested, as he left to get more firewood.

"It beats a stuffy country club, doesn't it honey?" Aunt Mandy said in my defense.

"These sausages are really good," Jack said, helping himself to the appetizers. "You used to make these all the time."

I nodded and smiled at his good memory. "Don't eat too many now or you'll spoil your dinner," I warned, suddenly aware I was speaking to him like he was a child.

"Right, Mom," he said with a laugh. "I don't think I ever spoiled my dinner in my entire life!"

We had a chuckle and nodded in agreement.

"I think your guests have arrived," announced Aunt Mandy as she looked out the window.

"Where did the time go?" I questioned as I hastily removed my apron. "Jack, will you open another bottle of Merry Merlot?"

CHAPTER 102

"Merry Christmas! Come on in," I said to Clark and Rock. They grinned.

"Rock, this is Kate," Clark said with a suggestive smile. "Kate, this is my brother, Rock."

"Pleased to finally meet you, Kate," Rock said politely. "I've heard a lot about you and I'm very pleased that you were willing to feed two hungry bachelors."

"My pleasure," I said, looking at another handsome version of Clark. "Meet my son, Jack, from New York and my Aunt Mandy from Florida."

Everyone shook hands and Rock handed me a bottle of wine as a hospitality gift. Clark gave Aunt Mandy a hug and kiss like they were long-time friends. I got the feeling that Jack was taking note of all the relationships in the room. While everyone chatted, I got Clark and Rock bottles of beer. Like all men, they spotted the appetizers and quickly helped themselves.

Clark approached me. "I have something for you in the car," he announced in a soft voice. "It's in the back of my truck and I need to bring it in the back door, okay?"

"Really?" I agreed, but could not hide my surprise.

Jack watched as Rock and Clark went to the back door. I shrugged my shoulders, displaying my innocence. Jack and I stood on the deck and watched them unload a good-sized butcher's block. I was surprised that it was for me!

"Oh, my!" I exclaimed, holding the door open for them.

"This was custom made, Miss Meyr, so you cannot return the merchandise," Rock kidded.

"It's beautiful," I responded. I looked at Clark who wore a modest grin.

"Wow, Clark, this is pretty awesome," Jack said slowly.

"Your mother bakes a lot, as you well know, so this way, she doesn't have to flour up her entire breakfast counter."

I wondered why I hadn't thought of that! "I don't know what to say, but you know I will certainly use it." My words seemed to be coming out clumsily. Aunt Mandy observed the activity and stood shaking her head as they placed it next to my counter. Everyone went back into the living room except for Clark and me. I looked into his eyes and said a quiet thank you as I watched him blush.

"I have something for you, but certainly nothing like this," I said, suddenly feeling shy. We left the kitchen and moved toward the tree.

"Well, what are you waiting for?" Clark joked.

I handed Clark his wrapped gift as I watched Jack and the others wonder what might be exchanged next.

When Clark pulled out the expensive, rare bottle of scotch, he yelped with pleasure. "Mighty nice, Miss Meyr," he said, eyeing the bottle with delight. "Check this out, brother!" He held up the bottle like it was a grand prize.

"Well, I'm not a malted scotch drinker, but this must be mighty special," Jack ventured. "I think you hit the jackpot, Mom!"

Everyone laughed.

"Well, let's have a taste!" Rock challenged. "After all, it's Christmas! You aren't going to keep this for yourself!"

"Are you sure, Clark?' I asked, not knowing what to do. He nodded and grinned, so I got some crystal glasses from the dining room cabinet.

"I'm game!" Jack joined in. "I won't be able to ever afford a drink of this stuff on my own."

I had to laugh to myself at how silly the men had become.

Aunt Mandy just smiled and shook her head. "I'll stick to my Merry Merlot," Aunt Mandy stated.

"I'll have to at least take a sip," I said, deciding not to be a party pooper. "Ellie went to a lot of trouble to special order this for me. Be sure to thank her, Clark."

"I will," Clark said as he filled the glasses. "Now, let's make a toast!" Everyone became silent. "Here's to the perfect hostess and to the best drink known to man!" Laughter broke out, along with the clinking of glasses.

I took a tiny sip and my face crinkled in response to the horrid taste.

"Here, Mom, don't waste that drink just trying to be cool," Jack teased. "I'll help you out. This is pretty good!"

I reminded myself that I had a dinner to get ready. I left the merry group and started putting food on the table. When they noticed the delicious aromas, everyone gathered at the table and noticed I had made place cards. Without a word, they took their assigned seats.

I took advantage of the rare moment of silence. "This Christmas is extra special to me," I began. "I am so grateful to have Jack and Aunt Mandy with me. Clark and Rock, I am honored that you could join us as well. Please join me in prayer." After everyone echoed the amen, Jack looked at me, wondering what would come next. I think he wondered what else he had been missing.

"Everything looks so delicious," voiced Rock as he lifted his wine glass. "I would like to make a toast to my brother, Clark, for finding Kate Meyr. He continues to surprise me." There was another clinking of glasses as I blushed. I didn't look at Jack.

The pork loin roast, dressing, and side dishes were a big hit. The homemade bread seemed to win the prize, however. Rock was eating like it was going to be his last meal. Jack began asking more and more questions.

"How long have you been carving wood?" Jack asked Clark. "I'm really impressed with that tree you carved for Mom."

Clark smiled. "I carved that tree long before I met your mom," Clark explained. "I liked its shape and it was a real challenge. I felt guilty about having it. It only seemed fitting that it be kept in this house."

"Clark lives in a pretty remote cabin in the woods along Indian Creek," I added to the conversation.

"Yeah, he's a lone wolf out there doing his handiwork," Rock teased.

"I'd like to see it sometime, Clark," Aunt Mandy requested. "Kate, this meal is just wonderful!"

"Thank you." I beamed. "It makes me happy to see you all enjoy it. With that, I took a sip of wine, feeling totally relieved.

CHAPTER 103

"I don't know if this is the proper time to make an announcement, but here goes," Aunt Mandy said, taking us by surprise. We all felt the suspense and stopped eating.

"Are you okay?' I asked, concerned.

She smiled. "I've never been better," she said with a nod. "It's been so wonderful sharing my time with Kate and all of you."

We waited for more.

"I'm not getting any younger and many of my friends are no longer around. This has caused me to think about how I want to spend the rest of my life. If Kate doesn't object, I'd like to find a little place and live right here in Borna so I can see more of her."

"What?" I asked, completely shocked. "This is awesome, but when did you decide this? You never once gave me a hint!"

"I've been thinking about it since Thanksgiving," she admitted. "I think I could be helpful to you and we have such fun together."

I felt goosebumps of joy.

"That is really cool," Jack added.

"I might build a new house somewhere, and I'll bet Clark could help me find just the right spot," she grinned, looking at Clark.

"I'd be happy to, but keep in mind that Borna is not the happening place that you may be accustomed to with that posh, senior community you have experienced."

"It's downright boring," Aunt Mandy claimed. "All they talk about are their latest operations."

We laughed heartily at her unexpected comment.

"I still want to be active and have some family to share life with. I can afford to live anywhere and in a style better than most, but if you don't have love around, something is missing."

How insightful, I thought.

"This lady is onto something," Rock said enthusiastically. "Don't worry, Clark, I'm not gonna move here."

We all had to chuckle.

Rock continued more seriously, "I believe that change at any age is so good for you."

"I'm still in shock," I said, hoping I could contain my tears of happiness. "I thought I was brave to move here."

"I'd say another toast is in order," Jack announced. "All those in favor of Aunt Mandy moving to Borna, raise your glass in approval!"

Everyone cheered and offered a resounding "Aye!"

"This is the best Christmas ever," I stated, still trying to hold back the tears. "I guess I can still hope that Jack will move here someday."

That got a quick reaction. "Oh boy! Oh no, Mom!" Jack said emphatically as the others laughed. "I love you, and I love Borna, but I my heart's in New York City. My challenge is to convince Jill to live there."

Somehow I knew that. "It doesn't hurt to suggest," I defended myself, smiling.

"Hey, is there any dessert coming our way?" Jack inserted, probably hoping to change the subject.

I went back to being a hostess and brought out a tray full of Christmas cookies and my German cheesecake with raspberries. They all moaned and groaned, but everyone still helped themselves.

"So, Aunt Mandy, how soon will you be able to move here?"

Jack asked as he took another cookie.

"Well, I'll put my condo at the center up for sale when I get back," she stated. "Before I leave here I want to have some direction on whether to build or not. There might be a cute little house here that is move-in ready. I'm sure I'll get plenty of advice from Clark and Kate while I'm here."

It was the first time I had heard anyone use our names together. "I can't recall anything, but I know just who to call," I offered with a smile.

"Who, Kate?" Aunt Mandy asked with interest.

"Ellen and Oscar," I said, taking the last bite of cheesecake. "They know this community like the backs of their hands. If you decide to build, Oscar will certainly have the contacts for you."

"That's wonderful," Aunt Mandy said, clearly relieved. "I remember meeting Ellen."

"I still can't believe this," I said, wanting to pinch myself. "I hope there will be enough excitement for you here."

Everyone chuckled.

"I think I could be a good house sitter for you when you travel, Kate," Aunt Mandy suggested. "You can take your time and not hurry back."

"Good thinking," added Jack. "She may even fly to New York to see her son!"

I shook my head. "Let's go into the living room to consider all of this," I suggested. "Who needs more coffee or who would like an after-dinner drink? Jack, another log on the fire would be good."

"I'll get it," offered Clark, like he had done it many times. "Jack, I hear you're leaving tomorrow."

"Yes, unfortunately," he answered, following Clark to get more wood. "I'm glad I got the lay of the land here and am able to see how happy Mom has become."

Clark nodded, as he handed Jack a couple of logs.

We had gotten comfortable around the fire when my cell phone rang. "Oh, it's John," I said, looking at my phone. I shouldn't have announced it out loud, but there it was. I did just announce it, I suppose.

"John Baker?" Jack questioned.

I nodded. I went to the kitchen to take his call.

"Merry Christmas, neighbor!" John greeted me cheerfully. "Am I interrupting anything?"

"No, we just finished dinner. How is your Christmas?"

"Well, I decided to stay here in South Haven because they want me to leave for Atlanta tomorrow morning," he explained. "It's snowing here, so I hope I can fly out in a timely fashion. How did Jack take to Borna?"

"I think he loves it," I answered as I watched him socializing in the living room. "We had an extra surprise at the dinner table with Aunt Mandy announcing that she is going to move here to Borna. How about that?"

"That's great and how nice for you," John said, registering his approval. "Tell her Merry Christmas for me."

"I will," I answered quickly. "By the way, thanks for the beautiful robe and slippers."

"I thought they were totally you and pictured you wearing them," he teased. "Then, I pictured you not wearing them."

"John!" I said, shocked. "I'm hanging up now. I have people waiting."

"Okay," he replied with a chuckle. "I'll call you on New Year's Eve."

"Merry Christmas, you naughty boy!" I said before hanging up. Why did he always have to tease me?

CHAPTER 104

"John Baker called you?" Jack asked with disbelief when I walked back into the room. Clark was looking directly at me.

"He just called to wish us a Merry Christmas and he wanted to know what you thought of Borna," I casually explained. "Aunt Mandy, this call was for you, as well. John wishes you a Merry Christmas."

"Oh, that's so nice," she responded.

"So, is he in South Haven or out of town?" Jack asked, interested.

"In town because he leaves tomorrow for Atlanta," I added in hopes of ending the conversation.

"Does my brother have some competition here?" Rock asked in a teasing tone.

Clark and I looked at each other and laughed.

"Not unless Mom wants to rob the cradle!" Jack teased back.

"Shame on you, Jack," Aunt Mandy scolded. "Your mom knows a lot of folks of all ages, as you are finding out, and I think she likes her life just the way she has it!"

I walked away from the conversation shaking my head and started clearing the dishes from the table.

"Let me do this, Mom," Jack offered. "You've worked hard enough. I can fill a mean dishwasher."

I smiled and went back into the living room. "Rock, how

long will you be in town?" I asked, sitting down next to him.

"I'll be here a couple more days. I was thinking that maybe you and your aunt would like to join us for dinner tomorrow night at Clark's cabin. When I suggested it to Clark, I told him I would do the cooking."

"So you both like to cook?" I asked, smiling at them.

"It sounds good," Aunt Mandy volunteered for the both of us. "What do you think, Kate?"

"Well, I guess," I offered, feeling awkward about my answer.

"If you think you can make it, I'd like to ask Ellie and Trout, since they will still be closed at the winery," added Clark.

"Do you have enough room?" I asked, grinning.

"The more the merrier," Rock cheered. "If the winery was going to be open, we'd have the party there."

"Well then, Rock, we'd better be on our way if we have a party to plan," Clark suggested. "Jack, I'm certainly glad I got to meet you."

"Likewise, Clark," Jack said, coming from the kitchen. "You too, Rock. Clark, keep an eye on my mom for me, will you?" Jack protectively put his arm around me.

"You don't want to put Clark in charge of her," warned Rock in a teasing manner.

"No one is allowed to do that!" I joined in.

"Kate, thanks so much for a really great meal," Rock said sincerely as he gave me a light hug. "I hope we see you tomorrow night."

"Thanks again for the butcher block, Clark," I said, giving him a safe peck on the cheek.

He blushed and I loved watching him do so. "I'm glad you like it, and the scotch was truly a great surprise," Clark beamed. "The rest of the bottle belongs to only me. Did you hear that, brother?"

The two of them went out the door, leaving us sitting by the fire. Jack went back to kitchen duty, and I was anxious to visit more with Aunt Mandy and question her about the announcement at dinner.

"I think your phone call from John got Clark's attention." Aunt Mandy brought up the subject that I had wished to avoid.

"Oh, don't be silly," I said, shaking my head.

"I know stuff, little niece," she teased. "Clark certainly gave you a nice Christmas present."

"He did, didn't he? Come to think of it, he has given me many nice gifts over time."

"He is so smitten with you and you are with him, too," Aunt Mandy teased. "You both just don't want to admit it."

"You're probably right," I smiled as I calmly agreed with her.

CHAPTER 105

I finally convinced Jack to leave the rest of the cleanup behind and join us in the living room.

"So, what did you think of Clark?" Aunt Mandy asked boldly.

Why did she have to put him on the spot?

"He's very nice," Jack nodded his approval. "He certainly is very talented."

We were all surprised when we heard a knock at the back door. I jumped, hoping nothing was wrong. When I opened the door, I saw my dear friend, Ellie. I was happy to see her for many reasons.

"Come in. Merry Christmas!" I gave her a little hug.

"The same to you," she smiled. "Am I too late to meet that son of yours?"

"Of course not," I said, taking her hand. "We're just sitting in here by the fire. Clark and Rock just left. How about a drink?"

"Coffee would be good," she suggested.

"Sure, but first meet Jack," I said, leading her to him.

"At last," Jack stood, accepting Ellie's handshake. "I've certainly heard a lot about you."

"All good, I hope," blushed Ellie. "I just got home and saw you still had the lights on, so I couldn't resist stopping."

"I'm so glad you did," I agreed, handing her the cup of coffee. "How was your dinner this evening?"

"Wonderful," she replied, sitting down. "I saw some relatives I wasn't even expecting. How was yours?"

"I can answer that. It was great and beyond expectations," Jack bragged. "Mom really outdid herself."

"I wish you were here for my New Year's Eve party, Jack. We throw quite a party at the winery."

"I'll bet you do. We drove up there to see it and we even saw Trout. It's such an awesome view from up there."

"Isn't it? Did your mom tell you I'll be planting more grapes come spring?"

"No, but that's not surprising with these beautiful hills! This area is perfect for wine country. I'd like to take home some wine, but since I'm flying, I don't want the hassle."

"I'm glad you got to see Borna and that you got to experience what a great job your mom is doing here," Ellie boasted.

"With your help at times, I understand. Thanks for being there for her."

"Aunt Mandy, do you want to share your news with Ellie?" I said, smiling at her.

"Well, Ellie, I have decided to move to Borna to be near my sweet niece," she announced with a big smile.

"Oh, how perfect," Ellie said. "Do you have a place in mind?"

"I'm leaning toward the notion of having something built for me, since I'm over the age of thirty-nine," Aunt Mandy joked.

"That's great," Ellie agreed. "I'm sure you will get lots of help and advice."

I added, "Of course, you know that I am absolutely thrilled. We are going to visit with Ellen and Oscar tomorrow to see if they are aware of anything that is available or whether she should consider building."

"You're asking the right folks," Ellie said after another sip of coffee. "You very seldom see for sale signs up around here, though."

"Unlike my niece here, I've gotten used to new and convenient surroundings," Aunt Mandy admitted. "I don't think I would have much patience for rehabbing."

"It's all very exciting to think about your moving here," voiced Ellie.

"I told Kate that I don't want to go back home until I have this all in place," Aunt Mandy informed her.

"Well, if I can do anything to help, just let me know," Ellie offered sweetly.

"We're invited to Clark's cabin tomorrow night for dinner," I divulged. "Rock has offered to cook, and he said they were going to ask you and Trout to come as well, since the winery is still closed."

"Oh, I'm not sure I should with all I need to do before the New Year's Eve party," Ellie said with a sigh.

"I can't wait to see his place," Aunt Mandy quipped.

"You'd better hang on to your hat, Kate," Ellie teased. "You're about to have a new resident in Borna that is ready to rock and roll!"

We busted into laughter.

CHAPTER 106

It was pretty late, but I decided to call Carla after Jack and Aunt Mandy went to bed. Carla's phone rang and rang before she finally picked up. "Merry Christmas," I said when she answered. "I hope I'm not calling too late, but I had a houseful of guests tonight."

"How nice," she said softly. "I'm still up and I had a pretty quiet day. I went to my niece's house last night for a Christmas Eve dinner."

"That's good. And how is Mr. Rocky, the wonder dog?" I asked, hoping to be humorous.

"Spunky as ever," she claimed.

"So, how are you doing?" I asked.

She paused before answering. "Well Kate, it's been a rough couple of weeks," she admitted.

"How so?"

"I'm joining the forces of millions of women who have gotten breast cancer," she said with a quiver in her voice.

"No, Carla. Not you! I am so, so, sorry!"

"I'm scheduled for surgery in a couple of weeks," she said with a deep sigh. "It's my left breast and I'm afraid I ignored the symptoms way too long." There was silence as she gathered her emotions. "I'm so scared!" She broke into tears.

"Of course you are," I said, hoping to console her. "I would be, too. Don't worry, because women are surviving this at a greater rate than ever before. You will be fine. I will be there for you. Please do not worry." I wanted to break down and cry, too. "Let me know when you get the details, okay?"

"Oh, Kate, I can't put you through this," she said.

"Well, then think about me coming to take care of Rocky while this is happening," I joked.

She did laugh at that.

"So, are you feeling okay otherwise? Have you been able to work?" I worried about her income through all this.

"Physically, I'm good, but mentally, I'm a wreck," she admitted.

We talked another ten minutes before I reminded her that God would see her through this. I couldn't remember Carla going to church, so I hoped she had a spiritual faith of some kind. I hung up feeling drained and so frightened for her. Having something like this to go through during the holidays, when everyone else is happy, must be the pits.

I put out the fire and went on up to bed. I had many prayers to say. I had so much to be thankful for. Saying good-bye to Jack in the morning would be tough, but I was so blessed to have him and Aunt Mandy here with me right now. I had my good health and many friends that I didn't want to take for granted. Until Carla's news, this had been an awesome Christmas.

Now, I would have to seriously plan my trip home and be there for Carla just as she had been there for me many times. I had to look for a window of good weather so I could drive there safely. Seeing Maggie and my quilter friends would be good for me, and seeing John again would lighten my days.

Tomorrow, we would start planning Aunt Mandy's move. I couldn't believe how Borna became my home and now it would be home to a family member as well.

I kept looking at the clock as I watched the hours go by. Why couldn't I sleep? All of a sudden, a warm, bright light came over me like it was the crack of dawn. I knew right away what was happening and I embraced the comfort it offered. I felt love and peace and knew everything would be okay. How Josephine and my Maker knew I was struggling was beyond me, but I had unquestionable faith in both of them. In no time, I faded into a blessed sleep.

Fully rested, I was up and going the next morning, hoping to convince Jack to eat breakfast before he left. I tried not to think of what I might feel like after he went out the door. It wasn't much longer and Jack came down the steps carrying his luggage. After a nice morning hug, I felt I had to share my news about Carla. I knew Jack thought a lot of her. "I want to make sure I am with her when she has to go into surgery. I wish she would have shared this information with me earlier. Maggie sensed something was going on with her."

"That is such awful news for her," Jack said, worry in his expression. "I hope you can be there for her as well, Mom. Keep me informed, okay? Right now, I need to be on my way, so coffee is just fine."

"Don't you want to say good-bye to Aunt Mandy?"

"I don't want to wake her," Jack said kindly. "I am so glad she is going to live near you."

I smiled and nodded. "It was a special Christmas gift, for sure," I confirmed.

"You're not going to sneak out of town without giving your favorite aunt a hug, are you?" Aunt Mandy said, joining us in the kitchen.

"Hey, good morning," Jack responded by giving her a big hug. "I'm sorry I have to run, but you two behave yourselves, okay?"

"We'll try," Aunt Mandy assured him. "Tell that fiancé of yours Happy New Year, and that I don't want to wait too long for a wedding invitation."

Jack laughed. "I will, but I think she will be the driver when it comes to setting a date," Jack admitted.

So, holding back my motherly tears, we both saw Jack to the back door where I received my last hug before watching him drive away.

"Now, honey, I know how you must feel right now, but you have so very much to be thankful for," Aunt Mandy reminded me. "What a fine young man he has turned out to be!"

With my eyes brimming with tears, I agreed and poured her a cup of coffee.

"I'm glad you both didn't leave at the same time," I mentioned, feeling sorry for myself.

"We've got to think seriously about our dinner invitation tonight as well as that visit with Ellen," Aunt Mandy reminded me, letting me know she was completely serious about securing a home here in Borna.

"If the weather holds off, I suppose I'm game to venture out there," I said without much enthusiasm. "How about you?"

"I'm game!" she said with excitement. "I'm eager to see what Ellen and Oscar have to say, and those boys are quite fun! It will be a great day!"

I had to snicker. "You are something else!" I teased. "You'd better watch out or those brothers are liable to fix you up with some country gentleman!"

She almost choked on her sip of coffee.

I called Ellen and asked if she minded if we stopped by for a short visit. She took the opportunity to invite us for lunch. There was no way to say no, nor did I try. As I finished a bite to eat, Clark called and was pleased to hear that we would be coming for dinner. I asked him to make it at an early hour and he agreed.

We both were upstairs dressing for the day when I saw Cotton pull into my driveway. I rushed down to let him in. "How was your Christmas, Cotton?"

He gave me a big grin. "Thanks to you, it was much more generous than some," he joked. "Amy Sue was a hoot to watch, but she sure didn't like that visit to see Santa Claus!"

"So, did you start looking for a truck?"

He nodded. "I can't afford to waste time when it comes to that," he assured me. "I've got some buddies keeping an eye out for me, too."

"Good," I replied. "I want to go to Perry when I get back from South Haven and look for something different for me as well. I don't have a date to leave for South Haven yet, but I hope you'll keep an eye on things while I am gone."

"No problem," he assured me.

"Good morning, Cotton," greeted Aunt Mandy.

"Good morning, Miss Mandy," he responded.

"My dear aunt has decided to permanently live here in Borna," I announced with pride.

Cotton looked surprised. "Well, we make you kindly welcome," he bowed, having fun. "When will that happen?"

"As soon as we can find something appropriate for her," I answered. "How about some coffee?"

"Not this morning, Miss Kate," he said, shaking his head. "I just dropped by to see if you need any help from Susie and me. I see you still have plenty of wood."

"Tell Susie to come in a couple of days," I said after giving it some thought.

"Tell her to bring along that sweet child of yours," Aunt Mandy requested sweetly.

"I'll tell her," he said before leaving.

As he went out the door, I commented to my aunt how helpful Cotton would be when it came time to get her settled into her new home. "It's a village here where everyone helps everyone," I bragged to Aunt Mandy.

She grinned in approval.

CHAPTER 107

Just I expected, Ellen prepared a delightful lunch for us and served it on her dining room table. Aunt Mandy marveled at her lovely home and Ellen was happy to show it off. Ellen immediately responded to the good news of Aunt Mandy moving to Borna. Of course, Ellen had many questions and was genuinely excited about the prospect of Aunt Mandy moving to the area.

We had just finished our first course of cucumber soup when Oscar came in from outdoors. His gentlemanly manner flattered my aunt as I made the introductions. She hung onto every word Oscar had to say when he responded as to why we were there.

"I doubt if you'll find anything to your satisfaction right now," Oscar explained as he poured himself a glass of iced tea. "You'd do well to consider building something new if you're not in a big hurry. We certainly have resources to help you with that option."

"Well, Oscar, first she has to find the land if she chooses to build," Ellen corrected him, sounding a little curt. Oscar paused as he sipped his tea. "I don't want to interrupt your lunch, ladies, but I'll just drop a notion that you might discuss."

There was silence as we waited.

"I think you have the answer right under your noses."

"Really?" I asked. "What are we missing?"

"Haven't you thought about that lovely acreage you own right behind your property? To my way of thinking, you don't have any plans for it, do you Kate?"

I shook my head.

"I'll bet there would be a nice acre that would face the road which could accommodate a nice little house."

Aunt Mandy's face immediately lit up. I was really caught off guard. It was a creative idea. "Oh, Oscar, I never even thought of that," I admitted. "That would be just perfect, wouldn't it, Aunt Mandy? Would you want to be that close to my house?"

"Well, yes," she said, catching her breath.

"Does it have access to electric, water, and sewer?" I asked, trying to think of what would be needed to build a new structure there.

"Why, sure. The Miesner farm is just a mile or so down the road," he noted. "That should be no problem."

"Of course, Kate, I would pay you well for such a spot," Aunt Mandy added with excitement.

"No, you won't," I objected. "I wouldn't think of it. What a grand idea! I can't believe none of us at the Christmas dinner table thought of that!"

"I'll get a surveyor to check it all out for you, if you like," Oscar offered. "There's a pretty good retired architect that just moved here to be with his daughter in Dresden. I'll bet he'd love to take on a project like this. His name is Wilson Schumacher. I met him at church last week. You remember him, don't you Ellen? Seemed like a nice fellow that had a pretty good career before he retired."

Ellen paused and then nodded in agreement. "I do remember that name," Ellen recalled. "He seemed to be a very nice gentleman."

"I would love to have his information," Aunt Mandy requested. "Kate, you may want to take some time to think this through, though."

"Honestly, it's perfect," I responded happily. I knew this was meant to be. "I knew we would find some answers here!"

We laughed together.

"Well, now that I have stirred the pot, I'll leave you ladies alone," Oscar said as he was leaving the room. "Just let me know how I can help."

"This was such a delicious lunch, Ellen," Aunt Mandy complimented her. "Everyone here in Borna has been so hospitable and generous."

As we continued to finish our dessert of carrot cake, I could see Ellen's mind was on a mission to welcome a new member to the Borna community. Ellen also encouraged her to become a member of our Friendship Circle. I agreed that it would be a nice gesture to make my aunt feel like she belonged.

After we left Ellen's, we went to the Heritage Museum to take down the cookies on my Christmas tree. It was Aunt Mandy's first visit to the museum, so Gerard was happy to give her a tour while I disassembled my tree. I could tell she got a kick out of Sharla Lee, who looked especially embellished with the many beads she had chosen to wear today.

We both admitted that going to Clark's for dinner was stretching our energy for the day, but we didn't want to be rude and back out. Aunt Mandy rested for a short time while I put together a tray of fresh shrimp cocktail to take to dinner. I had to admit that I was curious about what the "boys," as Aunt Mandy called them, would have prepared for us.

CHAPTER 108

Somewhat refreshed, we ventured off toward Indian Creek to Clark's cabin. Aunt Mandy marveled once again about the scenic countryside.

"Come on in, ladies," Clark greeted us as we came in from the bitter cold.

"Oh, it feels so good in here and it smells wonderful," Aunt Mandy commented. "This is quite a remote and charming place you have here, Mr. McFadden."

Clark chuckled and nodded. He eagerly took the tray of shrimp and gave me an approving wink.

"What smells so good over here?" Aunt Mandy said, approaching Rock, who was stationed by the kitchen stove.

"Have you ever had pheasant?" Rock directed the question to both of us.

"I sure haven't, but I'm game," I said in jest. "No pun intended."

They laughed as Clark took our coats and requested our drink orders. A fire was crackling and we both gravitated toward the warmth. Aunt Mandy's eyes were roaming the place, just as mine had when I visited for the first time. I surmised that Clark and Rock had enjoyed a few too many beverages before we arrived, judging by the way they were joking around.

Ellie and Trout arrived together, making the chatter crazy and even more deafening.

"You didn't think this would be a nice cozy dinner like you had here once before, did you?" Clark teased.

I grinned, watching Trout become the center of attention with his dry sense of humor.

We finally sat down to an amazing display of food featuring pheasant with dressing, roasted brussels sprouts, sweet potatoes, and a garden salad. After a toast to our chefs, we shared silly New Year's Eve resolutions. To my surprise, Aunt Mandy shared her plans to build on my property, which brought applause from the dinner guests. Ellie then proceeded to remind everyone to come to her New Year's Eve party.

"Now, I can't speak for Kate, but you young folks will have to do without me on New Year's Eve," Aunt Mandy announced. "I know everyone will have a great time at your party, Ellie, but with some luck, I may be on my way home. Or I'll be perched in front of Kate's fireplace where it will be quiet and peaceful."

"What about you, Kate?" Rock asked, putting me on the spot.

I started to respond but Clark interrupted saying, "I'll see to it that she gets there." I felt embarrassed and caught off guard.

"That would be called a date, brother," Rock teased. "I'll hold you to it."

Clark's eyes remained on me for a reaction. I wondered if the others were trying to read my mind.

Dessert was crème brûlée, which Rock said was one of his signature dishes. I hadn't eaten that delicacy since my luncheons at the South Haven County Club. I was feeling a bit drained and tired from the loud commotion. Aunt

Mandy seemed to be handling it better than me, but she didn't hesitate when I suggested that we leave.

"I'll call you on a time," Clark said as we were putting on our coats.

I nodded. I wasn't in the mood to debate whether I really wanted to go in the first place.

Our drive home was mostly somber with a chuckle or two about Trout and Rock. When we arrived at home, I saw I had missed a text message from Jack. He said he had made it home safely and mentioned again about what a grand time he'd had in Borna.

Aunt Mandy went to bed while I responded to some Internet guest requests. I also received an email from Carson, who cancelled his room reservation. I had a feeling he would be staying at Ellie's house now that he had declared he was getting a divorce. I was not looking forward to seeing him at the party.

As I walked up to bed, I remembered how uncomfortable I was at last year's New Year's Eve party. Being with Clark had its benefits, but if I had my choice, I wouldn't mind spending a night alone in front of the fire, just as Aunt Mandy had described.

CHAPTER 109

The next day, we were busy with various folks stopping by to visit with Aunt Mandy and talk about her plans. Oscar certainly got the ball rolling. Oscar himself came with a contractor friend of his who could intelligently advise her on the best piece of land for her house.

We got in my car and followed Oscar down the road very slowly until we got to a curve. He pulled to the side of the road. Oscar claimed he knew this property pretty well, which made sense since he had offered to buy it from James. We got out of the car and Oscar explained how the placement of the existing trees played a role in the location of the house and how the curve in the road would provide good access for getting in and out of the property. Everything he suggested made good sense. Aunt Mandy was in agreement. Thank goodness for Oscar.

Oscar's contractor said he would stake out the appropriate acre to work with for the architect, whom Aunt Mandy was meeting with tomorrow. Things were moving fast, which pleased her. I had to admit that it was very exciting.

We had left Susie and Cotton working back at the house. When we returned, Susie and I took off the cookie decorations so Cotton could remove the Christmas tree. I had wanted to keep it up until New Year's Eve, just as I did last year, but it was much too dry and was becoming a big mess.

My thoughts went to Carla and I called to check on her. She sounded in better spirits than during our previous conversation. I asked if she wouldn't feel better staying with me at the condo while she recovered from her surgery. She quickly made it clear that she wanted to be in her own home. She said her cleaning clients all understood, including John who was still out of town. I could tell it gave her a sense of relief knowing that I would be there for her.

It had been a long day and it felt nice to have my living room back, minus the Christmas tree. Aunt Mandy and I sat there mulling over the decisions of the day. I assured her that I would supervise it all until she returned. To her credit, she was taking lots of notes and considering special requirements she wanted to present to the architect. She told me about an octagon structure she had seen and she hoped he could design it for her. Not having money issues certainly made the project easier. I pictured it in my own mind and thought about how clever it could look nestled in the wooded area.

While we shared an after-dinner drink of amaretto on the rocks, Maggie called in a panic after hearing about Carla's breast cancer. She wondered if I knew and I told her about my plans to be with her. That made Maggie feel better and she, too, wanted to do anything she could to help.

Aunt Mandy asked if I had heard from Susan. It was a concerning question, because her life could be in danger going back home. She may not have been able to be with her son like she had envisioned. Who knew when and if she'd return to Dresden, as she had written in her note to me. It made us both sad to think about it.

We turned in for the evening but my mind had not. I was thinking about Clark when a text came from John. It was like he knew the late hour would be a good time to get my attention. He wanted to know what my plans were for New Year's Eve. I was too tired to respond. And yes, the longer I rested there, the more South Haven tugged at my heart. I missed Maggie and my Beach Quilter friends. Seeing John was always a bonus, but Carla made me feel needed. I couldn't forget those who had been there for me for a very long time.

CHAPTER 110

The next morning, I once again checked the long-range weather forecast. The weather had to break fairly soon, I hoped. Aunt Mandy and I finished our breakfasts in prompt fashion because Mr. Schumacher, the architect, was scheduled to meet with us this morning. If we could settle on a plan today or tomorrow, Aunt Mandy would likely leave to settle her matters in Florida. She would then return to stay with me until her house was finished.

I was scrolling through the emails on my office laptop when I saw a gentleman approach the front door. I assumed it was Mr. Schumacher, so I went to open the door. "Good morning," the handsome gentleman greeted. "You must be Kate Meyr. I'm Wilson Schumacher. I'm here to see Mrs. Malone."

I liked his perfectly groomed gray mustache. "Sure, it's nice to meet you," I responded, giving him my hand. "Please come in."

He stepped inside the entry hall and immediately looked around the open rooms. "This is quite a lovely guest house you have here," he complimented me.

"Thank you," I said, feeling proud. "It keeps me busy. Come in the dining room and meet my aunt, Mandy Malone."

"It's so nice to meet you, Mr. Schumacher," Aunt Mandy said, shaking his hand. "You are so kind to make a house call."

He smiled. "That's no problem because I no longer have an office since I retired," he explained. "I'm flattered that Oscar asked me to do this project."

"Why don't the two of you sit here at the dining room table where you can spread things out?" I suggested. "May I get you some coffee or tea?"

"Tea, if you would be so kind," he answered, giving me a gentle smile.

The two quickly started their conversation by Aunt Mandy explaining why she had decided to move to Borna. He seemed to understand, since he had moved here to live with his daughter. When she explained her vision of the octagon-shaped house, he was aware that there were existing models of just such plans, with the exception of an added-on screened in porch. Aunt Mandy said the screened porch was something she was accustomed to having, and it would allow her to enjoy the view behind her house.

Their chemistry was refreshing. They were two sophisticated adults who could converse and understand each other. It became obvious they both had lived comfortably during their lifetimes and were near the same ages.

"How have you adjusted to living in East Perry County?" I interrupted.

He grinned. "Well, it's a much slower pace than I was used to," he said with a chuckle. "It's so nice to be near my daughter, Barbara, and those grandchildren of mine."

"How nice," commented Aunt Mandy. "That's how I feel about being close to my dear niece. I envy you with those grandchildren."

"It took a bit to get used to, but I have a good section of the house to myself in case it gets to be too much," he explained. "I'm impressed, Mrs. Malone, that you want to take on a project of this magnitude."

"Please call me Mandy, like everyone else," Aunt Mandy corrected.

"Then you must call me Wilson," he insisted. "I frankly find this project pretty exciting, not to mention the bonus of getting to meet a fine lady like you."

Aunt Mandy blushed. This was definitely an interesting match!

Two cups of coffee later, he said he would mail the plans and other paperwork to her for approval. He assured her he would see her through the whole process, which gave my aunt instant gratification. When he said his good-byes, I was hardly acknowledged. Their eyes were for one another only!

"What a nice fellow," Aunt Mandy gushed after he went out the door. "I think he really understands my needs."

I couldn't agree more, with what I had witnessed. "Yes, and I hear he's a good architect, too," I teased. "You were flirting with him, dear auntie!"

She was taken by surprise. "I was?" she questioned, wearing a wry smile. "I'm not sure I remember how to do that!"

"I think it comes back like riding a bike," I teased. "I certainly don't blame you. He's quite handsome and very charming. I think Oscar steered us in the right direction."

"I do feel so at ease with all of this," Aunt Mandy admitted. "It's pretty exciting now that we've started the process, don't you think?"

"Oh, yes," I said, picturing the entire plan.

CHAPTER 111

It was New Year's Eve day when Cotton arrived at the back door to take Aunt Mandy to the airport. I had mixed feelings about her leaving, but it was comforting to know she would return. "I'll be back as soon as I can," Aunt Mandy promised. She seemed excited to get on with her long-range plans. "I think this was all meant to be, and I cannot thank you enough, Kate." She gave me a big hug.

"I'm so glad that the next time you come you won't be leaving me again," I said, returning her hug.

"I'm pretty excited for you, Mrs. Malone," voiced Cotton. "Susie and I will be glad to help you in any way we can."

"I'm counting on that," Aunt Mandy replied. "Kate, you and Clark have a wonderful evening. Remember, it's the start of a whole new year. You both need to realize that life is so short."

That was pretty heavy advice, I thought. I didn't comment, but instead gave her a nod and another squeeze before she got in Cotton's truck. As they drove off, my eyes glazed over with tears. I truly felt we both shared a genuine family love for one another. How nice that we could share the rest of our lives together in this little community.

I went back into the house feeling the comfort and quiet of just me and Josephine. That was what it was like the first day I moved into this house. Many people come and go here, but it was just nice to sit alone and reflect in silence.

I would have been perfectly happy to bring in the year alone and just call Maggie and Carla with a New Year's greeting, but it wasn't going to be that simple. A flurry of snowflakes came in the afternoon, but nothing stuck to the ground. I hoped the roads would remain clear, but knew bad weather would not stop Ellie's big party.

As I was surveying my wardrobe to see what I might wear tonight, Ellie called to make sure I was still coming. She said Carson had arrived and that I should not freak out if I saw Carson's car at her place overnight. I could tell from her voice that this was an exciting time for her. She was a mature woman who knew her relationship was risky. I guess there are times in our lives when our hearts take over our good common sense.

Instead of choosing jeans like I knew everyone else in town would wear, I went for black slacks and a black heavy sweater. It would be warm and I would look a little more festive since it was New Year's Eve.

Why wasn't I looking forward to this party? The whole town seemed to have party plans somewhere. Was I turning into a recluse that just wanted to nest in her guest house? I kept rechecking the weather. Was I hoping for it to turn worse so I wouldn't have to go? Getting dressed, I thought of Maggie getting dressed for the annual party at the country club. Carla would no doubt be home alone and would be worried about what was looming ahead of her.

Waiting for Clark to arrive, I called Jack to wish him a happy New Year. He was still at work and was about to leave and planned to hang out with work friends at a nearby pub for the evening.

"Be careful tonight, and when you talk to Jill, please wish

her a happy New Year for me," I instructed him, sounding just like a mother.

"I will," he said with confidence. "Are you going to Ellie's party with Clark?"

I didn't know what to say. "Yes, for a little while," I said calmly.

"Tell him hello for me and try to have a good time."

"Thanks, and I'll call you next year," I joked. "I love you, Jack."

After him wishing me the same, we hung up. My son was a real gem!

CHAPTER 112

Clark arrived right on time and I asked him to come in. "You look great," Clark said immediately.

I smiled. "I know I'm not wearing jeans, but it is New Year's Eve," I explained. "Besides church, no one here seems to get dressed up."

He nodded in agreement.

"Do you want to have a drink before we leave?" I asked, hoping to prolong leaving for the party.

"Sure," he nodded, smiling.

I fixed Clark a glass of scotch and water and I poured myself the usual glass of red wine. We sat down and engaged in small talk about Aunt Mandy's progress. "I'm very certain that Aunt Mandy will return since she hit it off with Wilson Schumacher, the architect," I joked. "It was so interesting to see how their relationship clicked. They hardly acknowledged that I was in the room."

"That would be great for both of them," Clark replied after he took a sip of his drink. "She is a good-looking lady for her age."

"Like me?" I teased.

"Like you, by golly," he said, grinning. "Rock thinks you're the cat's meow. He cares a little too much about my personal life, if you ask me."

"That's pretty sweet, I think. I always wished that I had a brother."

"I wanted to tell you sometime this evening that I'll be leaving town again for a couple of weeks," he shared.

I sensed some hesitation as he told me. I immediately thought about his health. "Is it work or is it time for another checkup?"

"Actually, both," he said, getting up to take his glass to the kitchen. "We'd better be on our way or before you know it, we'll miss ringing in the New Year!"

Yup, that was all the explanation I was going to get from him. "Oh yes, and all the fireworks I remember from last year," I said sarcastically.

We got on our way as the snowflakes landed on our heads and shoulders. When we finally got to the winery, it was so crowded that there were cars parked along the road. I wanted to suggest turning around, but I knew we were committed to making an appearance, at least. We also had to park at the bottom of the hill. We slowly walked up, hand in hand, as we followed the sounds of the loud country western music.

When we got inside the crowed winery, the first people I spotted were Ellie and Carson, locked in an embrace on the dance floor. Trout was tending the busy bar, so we decided that was the best place to perch ourselves, rather than to look for a table. I was just going to suggest that we leave, but before you knew it, Trout served each of us a drink. We laughed and clinked our glasses, giving into the madness.

Carson and Ellie approached us with merriment written across their faces. I knew Ellie could read my mind about the party commotion. "You may enjoy the fire pit we have going out back," Ellie suggested. "It's a little quieter out there and it's comfortably warm."

"Great. I could use some fresh air," I said, looking into Clark's eyes.

"You heard the lady," Carson said, jumping into the conversation.

"Oh, sorry Carson, I don't think you've met Clark McFadden." I gave a warm smile as I introduced the two men.

"I've heard a lot about you, sir," Carson said, shaking his hand. With that exchange, I drew us toward the back door.

The fire felt good and the crowd wasn't as rowdy. There seemed to be mostly romantic couples and a few young people hanging out together.

"So that was Ellie's heartthrob I just met?" Clark asked, his voice laced with sarcasm.

I nodded. "For better or worse, I'm afraid," I said with hesitation. "Ellie said he's in the process of a divorce, but we'll see. I think he has really taken advantage of her, but that's just me sounding off as a friend."

"She is a good friend to both of us, so we definitely don't want her getting hurt," Clark added. "I know Trout doesn't like him, so that says a lot."

"You're right," I said, nodding. "Carson had reservations at my guest house for the weekend but he cancelled to stay at Ellie's."

Clark grinned. "So you have an unexpected vacancy, do you?" Clark teased.

I wasn't going there.

Clark continued, "I'll have to admit, I was surprised that you agreed to go to this party."

"I am, too," I chuckled.

Clark put his arm around me as we leaned closer to the fire. "Are you getting warmer?" he asked sweetly.

"Now I am," I said, accepting his embrace. It did feel good.

"So, it appears we both will be going in different directions next week," Clark mused. "How long will you be in South Haven?"

"I'm not sure because I want to be of help to Carla and I don't know what will happen with her surgery," I explained. It made me wonder what she was doing right now. "I owe her that."

"I'm glad we've had this time together," Clark said before he kissed me on the cheek.

I had to admit it was nice for both of us to have each other. I snuggled up to him.

"I don't think I have told you that I love you, Kate Meyr," Clark whispered in my ear.

Did I hear him correctly? I wasn't expecting him to say this! What do I say? How should I respond? Help! Now what?

Cozy up with more quilting mysteries from Ann Hazelwood...

Wine Country Quilt Series

After quitting her boring editing job, aspiring writer Lily Rosenthal isn't sure what to do next. Her two biggest joys in life are collecting antique quilts and frequenting the area's beautiful wine country. The murder of a friend results in Lily acquiring the inventory of a local antique store. Murder, quilts, and vineyards serve as the inspiration as Lily embarks on a journey filled with laughs, loss, and red-and-white quilts.

The Door County Quilt Series

Meet Claire Stewart, a new resident of Door County, Wisconsin. Claire is a watercolor quilt artist and joins a prestigious small quilting club when her best friend moves away. As she grows more comfortable after escaping a bad relationship, new ideas and surprises abound as friendships, quilting, and her love life all change for the better.